Death
by Chocolate
Raspberry
Scone

Kensington books by Sarah Graves

Death by Chocolate Cherry Cheesecake

Death by Chocolate Malted Milkshake

Death by Chocolate Frosted Doughnut

Death by Chocolate Snickerdoodle

Death by Chocolate Chip Cupcake

Death by Chocolate Marshmallow Pie

Death by Chocolate Raspberry Scone

Death by Chocolate Raspberry Scone

SARAH GRAVES

Kensington Publishing Corp.
www.kensingtonbooks.com

KENSINGTON BOOKS are published by

Kensington Publishing Corp.
900 Third Ave.
New York, NY 10022

All Kensington Titles, Imprints, and Distributed Lines are available at special quantity discounts for bulk purchases for sales promotions, premiums, fund-raising, and educational or institutional use. Special book excerpts or customized printings can also be created to fit specific needs. For details, write or phone the office of the Kensington special sales manager: Kensington Publishing Corp., 900 Third Ave., New York, NY 10022, attn: Special Sales Department, Phone: 1-800-221-2647.

Library of Congress Control Number: 2023951844

KENSINGTON and the KENSINGTON COZIES teapot logo Reg. US Pat. & TM Off.

ISBN: 978-1-4967-4411-1

First Kensington Hardcover Edition: May 2024

ISBN-13: 978-1-4967-4413-5 (ebook)

10 9 8 7 6 5 4 3 2 1

Printed in the United States of America

Death
by Chocolate
Raspberry
Scone

One

"Standing in front of a hot oven during a heat wave is not what I signed up for," I complained, sliding another batch of chocolate chip cookies onto a platter.

"You could stand over there by the hot cash register," my friend, Ellie White, replied, waving the knife she'd been using to smooth frosting onto a cupcake. "Or the hot display case, or . . ."

Ellie and I owned and ran a small, chocolate-themed bakery, the Chocolate Moose, on Water Street in the island village of Eastport, Maine. Ocean breezes cooled us reliably here, or had until recently. But outside our shop window now, relentless heat shimmered under a mercilessly blue sky.

"Even the walk-in freezer is starting to look good to me," I said, spray-rinsing soapsuds off the baking sheets I'd just scrubbed. "I mean as a place to sleep."

It was August, the height of Eastport's tourist season, with a high-pressure system lodged stubbornly over us, rocketing the thermometer above ninety for five days straight. And we weren't the only ones; just two miles across Passamaquoddy

Bay the Canadian island of Campobello lay sweltering under a sun so cruelly bright, even the seagulls should've been wearing sunglasses.

Ellie finished frosting the cupcakes and offered one to me. "Chocolate cherry. Lots on top, just the way you like it."

But the only kind of cupcake I wanted was frozen and had a gin-and-tonic wrapped around it. "Thanks. Better put them in the cooler before they melt."

The little silver bell over the shop's front door jingled and a half dozen tourists came in. In their L.L. Bean summer garb they all looked adorable, but also as if they were sweating to death.

"No air-conditioning?" one of them inquired disappointedly, dragging the back of his sunburned arm across his forehead.

We did have a big AC unit in the kitchen window, but with the oven on it didn't help much. Our century-old building's vintage paddle-bladed fans turned overhead, too, and a portable electric fan in the open back door kept the air moving.

But it was still hot air. The newly arrived tourists looked around uncertainly as if they might leave, until Ellie rushed out and cajoled them to a table by the front window; iced coffees and slices of ice-cream-topped chocolate cake followed swiftly.

Past them through the window I caught sight of a blue-and-white power boat motoring into the harbor across the street. Two people stepped up onto the pier, each lugging one end of a long black bag.

The third person off the boat was a woman who even at this distance looked vaguely familiar, but I couldn't quite place her, and anyway it was the bag that interested me. While the tourists chatted happily over their refreshments, I followed Ellie back out to the kitchen.

"Hey, somebody just brought in a body bag. With, I'm pretty sure, a body in it."

Not that we hadn't been expecting this; Paul Coates's boat, *Sally Ann,* had been found by the Coast Guard running in circles way out past Cherry Island, two days earlier.

Coates hadn't been aboard, nor in the water nearby. But now he'd been found floating or washed up on shore, I supposed.

"Sally will be relieved," Ellie said.

Coates's widow, she meant. It seemed to me a strange kind of relief, although I guessed it might help to put a stop to the worst of the bereaved woman's imaginings. Still, the reality was just as bad: cold salt water, fast currents, sharp rocks . . .

"Not the cheeriest thing for a new top cop's first morning on the job," I said.

Eastport's new chief of police was supposed to start work today, and amazingly for Ellie and me, we didn't even know his name, yet. The Moose had been madly busy this summer and we'd had other things going on, too, that had kept us hopping. So all we did know was that the new chief had a strong recommendation from our previous one, Bob Arnold.

And since Bob had been caring, thoroughly competent, and a good friend, besides, we figured that was enough. Ellie rinsed and dried her mixing bowl and utensils, then turned to the big butcher-block worktable in the center of the kitchen.

"All right, now," she said determinedly, eyeing the ever-present "To Bake" list taped to the refrigerator, "what's next on the hit parade?"

But then the bell over the shop door rang energetically again, signaling the start of the midmorning rush. That was when people—even sun-hammered tourists—began feeling that they might just possibly eat a little something: a fudge-frosted brownie topped with a scoop of vanilla, say, or a chocolate cannoli stuffed full of sweetened cream and with cinnamon, cocoa powder, and powdered sugar lightly sprinkled onto the top.

You know, something light. "I'll go wait on them," said Ellie. "And how about you run up to the bank, meanwhile, and get us some change?"

I'd have hit the bank earlier, but major construction was under way at my house (see *things going on,* above) and talking to building contractors always makes me too crazy to be able to count money correctly.

"Fine," I said, grabbing the cupcake that Ellie had offered me. The mingled flavors of dark chocolate and cherries hit my brain as I stepped out into the shop area; by the time I reached the counter, my face must've looked like it belonged on a saint being drawn bodily up into heaven.

"Ellie'll be out here in just a minute," I began around a mouthful of frosting, and then I saw who the customer was.

"Hi, Jake," said the woman at the counter. "How are you?"

"Hi, Lizzie," I managed. She had short, spiky, black hair, blood-red nails that matched her vivid lipstick, and smoky-dark eye makeup applied skillfully and with a feather-light hand.

"I'm fine, how are you?" I added inanely. She was wearing dark blue tailored Bermuda shorts and a black, short-sleeved T-shirt whose fit flattered her well-toned arms and shoulders. A badge was on her belt, a holster with a .38 auto nestled in it was on her hip, and she was, I suddenly understood, Eastport's brand-new police chief.

"Congratulations," I said calmly, just as if her sudden reappearance in Eastport hadn't knocked me for a loop.

But it had.

My name is Jacobia Tiptree—Jake to my friends—and when I first came to Maine, I thought big crime only happened in big cities. Ones like New York, I mean, where back in the bad old days I'd been money manager for a crew of guys so evil that just knowing them at all was probably a felony.

Then when their criminal fortunes went south and mine were about to, I ran, leaving my husband and his many girl-friends and moving—along with my then twelve-year-old son, Sam, twelve going on twenty (by that time he'd already known so much about drugs, he could've started a pharmaceutical company)—into the two-hundred-year-old Eastport house that we still live in, today.

With thirteen rooms, eight fireplaces, three porches, an attic, and a two-story ell, the house was much larger than anything I'd lived in before; for a while Sam and I rattled around in it like marbles, unused to so much space.

But nowadays the place is so fully inhabited that people and animals are practically tumbling out the upstairs windows. Sam and his wife, Mika, and their three kids; my husband, Wade, and I; and my elderly dad and stepmother, Jacob Tiptree and Bella Diamond, all live in it. I'd put a chair outside the bath-room door recently so that the person waiting—in our old house, someone was always waiting—wouldn't have to stand.

Which brings me back around to the hot August morning when Lizzie Snow showed up at the Chocolate Moose:

"Would you like to sit down?" I invited, indicating one of our black cast-iron café chairs. It was just like the one I had outside the bathroom, part of a crateload we'd bought at a deep discount when we opened the Moose.

Lizzie shook her head. "Just came in to say hello." She looked around at the exposed redbrick walls, slate tile floor, and the whitewashed barn boards fronting the cash register.

"Nice place," she said approvingly, sniffing the coffee-and-chocolate-scented air with evident pleasure.

"Thanks, but . . . what're you doing here?" I asked. From what I knew of her, she could've worked anywhere, and East-port—two hours from Bangor and light-years, or so it often seemed, from anywhere else—wasn't exactly a step up on the career ladder.

"New chief," she confirmed without answering my question.

Two summer-garbed customers came in and approached the display case to make their selections; after that, two more couples and a trio arrived, all looking hot, tired, grouchy, hungry, and thirsty.

Ellie hurried to help relieve these difficulties while I wished Lizzie Snow good luck with her new job.

"Let's hope no more of those anytime soon," I added with a wave toward the harbor and the boat that brought the body in.

"Jake," Ellie reminded me, quick-stepping with the coffee-pot in one hand and the ice-water pitcher in the other, "if you are going to the bank at all, you might want to . . ."

Hustle it up, her tone implied, and she was right; soon it would be wall-to-wall people in here again and we'd need coins to make change.

Outside, my car sat baking at the curb: a '74 Fiat Spider with a black canvas top, five speeds forward, and the classic Pininfarina body still with most of its original apricot paint.

"Mind if I ride with you?" Lizzie got in without waiting for an answer and settled into the passenger-side bucket seat. I turned the ignition key, exhaling with relief as always when the engine rumbled to life—FIAT, in case you didn't know, stands for "Fix it again, Tony"—and we pulled out onto Water Street.

"So that was Paul Coates's body you guys brought in?" I asked, because of course it had been Lizzie I'd seen getting out of the boat.

Lizzie Snow, I marveled silently; who'd have thought we'd see her again around here? Last time, she'd been in town hunting for her dead sister's daughter. She didn't know if the child was dead or alive, and she didn't know what sort of life the child might be leading if she was alive.

She'd said then that she'd never quit until she located her

niece, and I'd thought I understood. But that was back when I didn't have grandchildren at home; now the thought of losing one of them—or any child, really—made my heart lurch painfully.

Driving slowly up Water Street between rows of sun-baked parked cars and throngs of visitors strolling in and out of shops, I wondered what sort of loss Lizzie Snow was living with, and if I dared ask her.

"Yeah, the body was probably Coates," Lizzie replied after a thoughtful silence. "It was pretty banged up," she added as we passed the Eastport breakwater.

The massive L-shaped concrete structure extending out over Passamaquoddy Bay had a paved deck so vehicles could drive out onto it; now cars and trucks crammed the parking spaces, while below, the boat basin held docks and wooden finger piers with large and small boats tied up at them.

"The medical examiner's office will let us know for sure," Lizzie said, watching the white van I'd seen earlier exit the breakwater and turn onto High Street.

"I just went out with them to start getting my sea legs," she went on. "Not many boats way up where I was."

In Maine's vast northern wilderness territory, she meant: the state's wild rooftop, where the trees outnumbered people a thousand to one and so did the bears.

"The body was otherwise okay, though?" I asked, by which I meant dead but without, for instance, a bullet in its head or a knife in its chest.

"What?" she asked distractedly. On Washington Street, a kid on a skateboard raced toward us, spinning in circles and jumping the sidewalk's cracks in high, fracture-inviting leaps.

"Yeah," she responded, still watching. "Yeah, it was fine. No foul play signs that I noticed."

Our no-skateboarding ordinance was mostly just meant for

downtown, where visitors gazing dreamily at the pristine water, picturesque fishing boats, and quaint, nostalgia-inducing old buildings were as vulnerable as bowling pins.

But the rule was enforceable anywhere in town, depending on how much of a hard-ass a police officer wanted to be. So when Lizzie flashed the kid a thumbs-up sign and a grin, it gave me some hope that her new job might actually work out; in Eastport, picking your battles is a skill worth having.

Something about her still reminded me of a fuse waiting to be lit, though. It was one of the reasons I'd been glad to see her go last time, and so flustered by her reappearance: the sense that when Lizzie Snow was around, so was trouble.

And now she was here.

"I think all the guys on the boat expected me to throw up when I saw the body," she said.

We crossed High Street between the bank, the sail-making and repair shop where long rolls of canvas were just now being delivered, and the laundromat. "You mean because it was bad?"

Lizzie made a face. "No, 'cause I'm a girrrl," she drawled exaggeratedly, and laughed.

I did, too. "Yeah, well, I know the guy whose boat you went out on," I told her.

When Frankie Munjoy wasn't ferrying cops and dead bodies, he took people out on sightseeing voyages around the bay.

"And I happen to know he gets sick at the sight of a loose egg," I finished. "You didn't, though, did you?"

"Get sick? No. But I could've. He'd washed up on a stony beach out there, tide rolled him around. Rocks'd bashed him."

Also he'd been in salt water, which wouldn't have helped. I pulled into the bank's driveway and parked.

"Want me to put the car top up?" I asked as I got out.

It was nearing noon and the sun overhead continued to be brutal; my straw sun hat was pretty much essential gear lately, and today I was tempted to tuck some ice cubes around the brim.

But sunglasses were Lizzie's only concession to the heat and brilliance. "I'll be fine, take your time."

I squinted against the glare bouncing off the Fiat's hood. "Fine," I said, "but when I come out here again I want some real answers. To why you're here, for a start."

And for how long, at whose suggestion . . . but mostly it was the *why* that I wanted, because Lizzie Snow was no more a small-town police chief by nature than I was the Queen of Sheba.

She was a murder cop. She'd been one in Boston and then in northern Maine; pretty successfully, too, from what I'd heard, so if her hunt for her niece was over, why try something here instead of going back to the city?

There had to be a reason, but ten minutes later when I came out of the bank I was no closer to knowing it. Instead, my attention was captured by a tall, dark-haired man in a yellow polo shirt and white tennis shorts who stood by the Fiat.

After an instant I recognized him as Dylan Hudson, Lizzie's old . . . what? Buddy, boyfriend, something in between?

I didn't know that, either, but I remembered him from her last visit, when he was still a Maine state cop; he'd been hanging around her then, too. Now Lizzie leaned back against the Fiat's headrest, her hands raised in a warding-off gesture.

"Okay, okay," he was saying as I approached, "I just wanted you to know I'm here, so it doesn't come as a surprise."

"Nothing can surprise me anymore where you're concerned, Dylan," she said tiredly as I got in and started the car. "You just do your thing and I'll do mine, that's all."

Dylan Hudson had dark, deep-set eyes that gleamed with intelligence, angular features that weren't handsome but instead something better, and a wolfishly mischievous grin that promised fun plus sharp teeth.

"Fine," he said, backing away undiscouraged; the smile was the kind you wanted to fall headfirst into, whether you liked him or not. "I'll see you around, then."

"Not if I see you first," she muttered as he stood watching us go, but despite her heavy sigh somehow I didn't believe her; not quite.

"So, are you and Ellie still snooping?" Lizzie changed the subject as we started back downtown. By now the Chocolate Moose would be packed full of customers; I didn't really have time to ask what Lizzie was doing here, and hear the reply.

If she gave one. I pressed the gas pedal. "Sometimes. Now and then."

Because as I'd learned nearly as soon as I'd moved here, I was the nosy type and so, as it turned out, was Ellie. Also I found out that big crimes weren't confined to big cities; not even major crimes, like murder.

"But it's been quiet for a while," I said, as we turned onto Water Street and parked.

We got out of the car and into a swirling wave of people licking ice-cream cones, kids spraying Silly String, and dogs lapping at water bowls placed outside shop doors.

Packed sidewalks, full restaurants, shops crowded with visitors searching for the perfect souvenirs . . . it all looked busy, happy, and prosperous, a real sea change from the days when tourists in Eastport were scarce as shark's teeth.

Which were visiting, too, I'd heard—the sharks, I mean, not merely their teeth—in our waters recently; there'd been articles about it in the *Quoddy Tides*, our local newspaper, and sightings by several fishermen around the bay.

Fortunately, though, the sharks weren't my problem, or so I still thought as I yanked the shop door open and shouldered my way through the small crowd of people inside the Moose.

Behind the counter, Ellie was counting out nickels and pennies with one hand while refilling a coffee cup with the other, meanwhile smilingly telling a fellow who'd just stuck his head in behind me that no, we didn't have a public restroom but the port authority building did.

"Half a block that way at the breakwater entrance," Lizzie told the man, whose expression brightened considerably once he'd gotten a good look at her.

Because sure, she was a cop: shiny badge, sensible shoes, and the gun, of course. But with her clipped-short black hair and flashing eyes, those red lips, and the snug, black T-shirt that she wore like a second skin, she was also, as my son, Sam, would've said, a complete knockout.

I tossed the bank bag at Ellie, who caught it one-handed while answering the ringing phone again. Then I nudged my way behind the counter and began slinging cake, cookies, and iced coffees, taking money, and handing back change. For a while it was quite the little whirlwind of chocolate-themed commerce, and I forgot all about Lizzie until I looked up and she was gone.

"Who was that on the phone?" I asked when the latest rush was over. Two local ladies sipped tea at a table in the corner, but otherwise the Moose was finally quiet.

Ellie put the heel of her hand tiredly to her forehead, shoving back stray blond curls. "A big catering order was on the phone, that's what." She sighed, sinking into a chair.

The tea-sipping ladies got up and paid their check, then went out to the jingle of the bell over the door.

"How big?" I asked cautiously; very cautiously, in fact.

During our first couple of years at the Moose, the money situation had been perilous in the extreme; it's why we'd added dessert catering to our repertoire. But this summer the shop had boomed, so we were already scrambling hard to keep up.

"Really big," she replied, "at least for us. Four dozen chocolate-raspberry scones with egg wash and sanding sugar."

"Oh, is that all?" I managed after a moment, then took a deep breath. We were already alternating sessions of baking late at night so that we'd be stocked and ready for the next day's clamoring hordes of . . . I mean, for our valued customers.

"When?" I asked weakly. Sanding sugar, by the way, is the glittery, large-grained kind, good for decorating and crunch.

"Saturday. Darn this hair," she added, grabbing a handful and snapping it back into a rubber band.

"But, Ellie," I said gently, "we've never made chocolate raspberry scones before."

She nodded resignedly. "I know. It's for a bunch of shark scientists coming here this weekend for a conference. They're going out on boats and doing observations and so on, and there's refreshments afterwards."

"They'd better hope they don't turn out to be refreshments, themselves," I said, hoping to make her smile.

She did. Then: "This is the kind of catering job we want," she added, heading back toward the kitchen, where I'd spied the ingredients for chocolate dream bars already set out.

"Big job, big paycheck," she said. Where she'd found the time for dream bars, I had no idea, but I wasn't shocked. With her strawberry-blond curls, pale freckles like a scattering of gold dust, and wide, long-lashed eyes the exact same color as woodland violets, she might've looked like a princess out of a storybook but she was as tough as an old boot.

"Anyway," she called from the kitchen, "we'd better put our thinking caps on, because I said yes and in four days we'll need those scones."

Great, I thought, and of course they'd feature raspberries as crimson as blood drops; just right for shark enthusiasts.

Outside, summer in Eastport continued despite the heat. On

the sidewalk across the street, an athletic-looking woman with a small dog in a backpack strode vigorously along. She'd rigged up a small blue umbrella that stuck up out of the backpack to keep the sun off the dog.

Behind her came girls in bright halter tops, sun hats, and shorts, like schools of exotic tropical fish; beyond them where the water glittered, fishing boats puttered in and out of the harbor with lobster traps stacked on their decks.

I turned back to the shop, where the paddle-bladed fans slowly stirred the heat under the pressed-tin ceilings. Scones, I thought again; lots of them, and soon.

On the plus side, however, the rest of the afternoon passed quickly and without incident. Between waiting on customers and producing more baked items to feed them, I didn't have time to wonder any further about Lizzie Snow, and Ellie didn't, either.

"Wow," was all she said when I finally got the chance to tell her Lizzie was our new police chief. As she spoke, she zipped by me carrying a tray loaded with eclairs, a brownie, three iced coffees, and a slab of chocolate cream pie.

It was the final order of the day; it was almost five o'clock, and the cooler and the glass-fronted display case were nearly empty. Once this last table had finished up and departed, we could close.

"You know what I think would be good?" Ellie mused as I wiped down the counter and the coffeemaker.

When Ellie says something would be good, I listen; she's the one who invented chocolate-covered bacon, after all.

"Fruitcake with chocolate in it," she answered herself, leaning in to clean the last cookie crumbs out of the cooler. "Good fruitcake, I mean, the homemade kind."

"Ooh," I replied; good fruitcake is the food of the gods even without chocolate. "And a thin chocolate drizzle on top," I suggested.

She looked up. "Dark chocolate," she agreed, "but not so dark that it isn't—"

Sweet, she'd have finished, but instead the bell over the shop door jingled yet again.

"I'm afraid we're closing," I began as a tall, blond woman came in.

Then I figured out who it was and put down my cleaning cloth as Ellie hurried from behind the counter.

"Sally!" she cried. "Oh, you poor thing, what're you doing here? I thought you'd be—"

"What, lying down in a dark room, sobbing?" she asked with a grimace. "I've got three kids, I don't have time for that."

Sally Coates was in her late thirties, but her face today was the lined, haggard visage of someone much older. It was probably her husband, Paul, whose body they'd brought in.

"I'm so sorry," I said uselessly as Ellie guided the new widow to a chair.

"I had hopes," Sally said shakily, "but now . . ."

Her blunt-cut, wheat-colored hair, normally smooth, was a rat's nest; her ragged denim shorts and stained, much-worn T-shirt said that the usually spiffy Sally had reached the end of her rope quite some time ago and was now barely clinging to it.

Ellie handed her a glass of ice water and she drank some; meanwhile I ran through a short mental list of reasons why she might've come here. But there was only one good one, and Ellie seemed to think the same as our eyes met over Sally's head.

I shook my own head minutely *no*. We didn't have time, not to mention extra energy, for . . .

But Ellie glanced away from me. "Sally? Is there something we can do for you?"

There was only one thing Ellie and I were known for, and it was just what Lizzie had mentioned earlier: snooping.

Into murder, mostly. Sally bit her lower lip hard enough to stop its trembling.

"Please. Please help me. I need you to find . . ."

She sucked in a shuddery breath. ". . . to find out who killed my husband!"

Two

"Paul had been fishing alone since he was twelve," Sally Coates said. "He could no more fall overboard by accident than I can fly."

From the way she said it, I thought she didn't believe Paul had gone overboard at all. And it was true that he'd been alone on the boat, no one with him to do anything to him.

Like pushing him, for instance. "But then whose body did they bring in this morning?" I asked.

We waited in the golden late-afternoon sunshine outside the Chocolate Moose while Ellie locked up. Shock and grief had sent Sally down a rabbit-hole of denial, I'd already decided. But we could listen; if nothing else, it might make her feel better.

"Fred Monk," Sally answered promptly. "Who jumped off the bridge in Lubec last week."

The Fiat was parked right in front of the store. "Poor Fred. He'd been threatening it for years," said Ellie as she climbed into the car's vestigial rear seat.

I waved Sally into the passenger seat beside me and started the car, backed out, then set off down Water Street.

"Fred Monk," I reminded Sally, "jumped when the tide was turning."

Which meant he'd have been carried under the bridge he'd jumped from and drifted southwest, out toward Grand Manan, not up into the bay's northern passage where today's body had been recovered.

I might have pressed Sally about this, but a kid on a bike suddenly shot out of Hayes Alley right in front of me, claiming all my attention.

"What makes you think Paul's been murdered?" Ellie asked from behind us.

"Or even dead at all?" I added once the kid had passed. "I mean, like you said, until they do identify him . . ."

The Fiat growled slowly along in second gear past the local crafts emporium, a vintage clothes shop, two art galleries, and Wadsworth's hardware store until we reached Key Street.

"Because this washed ashore," Sally said, shifting to pull something dark and bulky from the canvas satchel she carried.

I glanced sideways: it was a man's brown leather boot with brown leather laces and a worn wooden heel, all water-logged.

"It's Paul's," she said. "He wore those that day because his rubber ones had finally fallen to tatters. Some boys found this on the beach this morning and took it home. One of their dads knew Paul, and he brought it over to me."

At the top of the Key Street hill, my house came into view: a two-hundred-year-old white-clapboard Federal with three redbrick chimneys, forty-eight old double-hung windows, and more park-bench-green wooden shutters than you can shake a stick at.

I waited for a lumber delivery truck to back out of the driveway, then pulled in. On the lawn lay a new stack of plywood sheets and a pile of insulation rolls, also just delivered.

Beyond them loomed what there was so far of the new wing that we were adding onto the house; right now the finished parts consisted of the foundation, wiring and plumbing preparations, and some framing. But the roof wasn't on yet, and as hard as it was to believe, winter lurked right around the corner.

Expensive, over budget, and way overdue on the date I'd been promised for completion . . . I turned away from the sight.

"Why are you so sure the shoe is his?" I asked Sally as we got out of the car.

The late afternoon was as warm and humid as the inside of a greenhouse. Sally took the shoe back out of her satchel and fiddled with the heel, which after a moment slid aside to reveal a carved-out space about the size of a silver dollar.

"See?" When she slid the heel closed again, I couldn't tell that the hiding place was there.

Out in the backyard, the big rubber raft that the kids liked to use as a wading pool sprawled as if exhausted, under the maple trees shifting in a sluggish breeze. From inside the house, I heard a toy xylophone getting the life banged out of it, a radio broadcasting a ball game, and a child who wanted to know right now if flying squirrels were *flying?* Like *birds?*

"What do you think?" I asked when we got in, snatching my grandson, Ephraim, up into my arms. A sweet-faced, dark-haired four-year-old, he'd recently become a keen nature-observer.

"Do birds fly like squirrels?" I asked into his neck, which smelled sweetly of milk and peanut butter, and at his vigorous head-shake *no* I went on.

"Well, then," I said, putting him down reluctantly; he was snuggly but getting too big to hold on my hip for long.

"Well, then, why would squirrels fly like birds?" I asked, and with his hands stuffed seriously into the pockets of his new red swim trunks, he nodded wide-eyed at me.

"That," he pronounced solemnly, "makes sense."

Then with his little blue sneakers thumping the hardwood he

ran off down the hall; it was, I gathered from his shouts, his turn to play that damned xylophone.

When he'd gone, I found Ellie and Sally in the kitchen, where Bella Diamond, my housekeeper-slash-stepmother—yes, it's complicated—was making a chicken salad and rosemary biscuits.

From the top of the refrigerator the radio blared out a swing and a miss. I turned it down just as an outraged wail came from the living room; apparently that xylophone's ownership was a bit more contested than Ephraim thought.

Then my son's massive, ferocious-looking Irish wolfhound wandered into the kitchen—the tan, shaggy animal was as big as a pony and despite the breed's reputation about as dangerous as your average bunny rabbit—demanding either scraps of chicken or to be petted, and preferably both.

"Oh, poor baby," said Bella sympathetically to the animal, her soft heart much at odds with her somewhat forbidding looks. Skinny as a broomstick, rawboned and ropy-armed, she had a face like a hatchet and big, grape-green eyes surrounded by carved-looking wrinkles.

She tossed the wolfhound the skin off a chicken thigh. He snatched it out of the air with an audible snap of his sharp, white teeth, then smiled beatifically.

"Good dog," she told him, putting the bowl of chicken salad into the refrigerator; then, turning, she spied us at last.

"Oh, my dear," she said sympathetically, hurrying over and taking Sally Coates's hand in both her own. "I'm so sorry," she told Sally, glancing significantly at me; it wasn't the first time a woman had sat in this kitchen, asking for help, and Bella was as sensitive as a cat's whisker.

"You girls just sit and have your talk, now," she told us kindly, clearing the kitchen table of coloring books and crayons with a sweep of her bony forearm.

"Coffee's ready. I'll be in there." She angled her head toward the parlor where someone was positively destroying that xylophone.

Then she was gone, with the dog frisking along behind her. Once she reached the parlor I expected the musical-instrument bashing to cease at once, but instead I heard the atonal bleats and toots of a toy trumpet that my father had brought home. It would, he'd said, develop the kids' lungs.

I closed the door between the front and back halls; peace descended. Ellie had poured coffee and set out milk and sugar.

"So," I asked Sally when we were seated around the table, "if it wasn't him they brought in this morning, why are you so sure Paul's dead?"

Although of course I knew one of the reasons. If Wade had gone missing on the water and his boot washed up, I wouldn't be thinking he was still swimming around out there, either.

"And why do you think someone killed him?" Ellie added.

Ah, yes, let's not forget that little detail.

Sally stopped aimlessly stirring her coffee. "When Paul went out alone, he had a safety line snapped to his belt. He couldn't have fallen without unsnapping it."

"But how do you know he even—" I began.

"I bought it and he promised to wear it, that's why. Look, my husband was no rocket scientist, okay?" She took a shaky breath. "I know that, but I also know him. He said he'd wear the line and a life vest. And Paul kept his promises," she added, a hint of steel coming into her voice.

I was glad to hear it, because whatever had happened, she was going to need it. This was a woman with three children and—suddenly—no income.

"But that's not the main thing," she said, pulling the boot out again.

A faint, fishy aroma drifted up from it, mingled with the

smell of wet leather. Tipping the boot, she slid the heel aside, exposing the carved-out space once more.

"When Paul went out on the boat that morning, there was an antique gold coin in here. It was *always* there. He said if it was with him, no one could steal it. But now it's gone, and that means someone did take it, someone who knew about the boot."

She sniffled and went on. "And they'd have had to kill him to get it. He said it was for the kids, that it would give them a future."

"How much was it worth?" I asked.

She shook her head. "Paul inherited it along with a fancy Swiss Army knife from an uncle of his who'd been a diver in Florida, and he meant to get the coin appraised. But he didn't know who he should take it to, that he could trust. So he never did it."

She pulled a sheet of photo paper from her bag. "Here's a picture Paul took of it."

Not a good picture: The object was round, with letters and what might have been a face stamped into it, plus a cross shape. But you could get the idea; sure, it probably was a coin. No way of telling if it was valuable, but clearly Sally thought so.

"What if you don't get it back?" Ellie asked, and Sally looked up, stricken.

"Never mind college for the kids, I'll lose the house. And that's just the start."

Of bad things, she meant, and I agreed; no money and no way to get some is a terrible way to live.

"I'd work," said Sally, "but a job won't cover childcare, much less a car to get there. We'll be living on food stamps. In a tent, maybe."

I got up and took the chicken salad from the refrigerator, stirred it to distribute the mayonnaise, and put it back. Behind me, Sally began to weep softly.

"He knew. He knew something bad was happening. Just a few weeks ago he bought a lot of security equipment, put it all up, and even got a dog."

She rolled her eyes at that last part; apparently three kids and a missing husband were plenty, never mind dealing with a new pet.

"Paul had this little green book with lined pages, he was always scribbling in it. One fills up, he gets another one. He's written in one of them every day for just about forever."

"He kept a diary?" I asked. Because if he had, one or more of them could still be around, somewhere. Maybe he'd written something in it about where the coin went, at least.

"I don't know. He would never show it to me," said Sally. "I've gone all through the house looking for it, but—"

Then Ellie cut in with the words that I'd known she would say. "Sally, of course we'll help you if we can. But what is it that you want us to do, that the police can't do better?"

The widow—or was she?—looked up again, her face grim.

"The police won't help. Guy falls off a boat, where's the crime, right? I've asked them but they say I'll need to show them something more. Maybe if they found him and he'd been shot or something, then . . ."

Her voice nearly broke but she didn't let it. "Paul was no rocket scientist, but he was a good man. I'm asking you to find out what happened and get the coin back if you can."

She paused, straightening her shoulders. "I know how that last part must sound. But I've got to take care of the kids. It's what he'd want me to do."

She was a fisherman's wife, all right: practical even in disaster. In her place, I'd have been lying in a dark room with a cold cloth on my forehead.

"All right, Sally," I gave in finally, "why don't Ellie and I just nose around a little, figure out if there's even anything to investigate. Clues, or whatever."

A flicker of something that might've been hope brightened Sally Coates's blond-lashed blue eyes.

"No guarantees," I cautioned. "I'm not promising anything beyond that."

But she was already on her feet. "Thank you," she breathed, glancing at the beat-up Timex she wore. "Oh, man, the kids are at my mom's, I'd better go get them."

Minutes later she was out the door, followed by Ellie who said it was time she was getting home, too. Then Bella came back into the kitchen to warm the croissants we'd be stuffing with chicken salad, and the big Irish wolfhound returned and nuzzled his shaggy snout into my hand, begging for more treats.

The horn-tooting and xylophone banging had stopped. I patted the dog's head absently, torn between pouring myself a glass of wine and making a salad with the ingredients Bella had set out.

Both, I decided, and the bright, fresh greens and ripe tomatoes from Bella's garden plus the grapy, astringent Cabernet proved entirely welcome.

But even though at dinner I had another glass, plus two chicken salad rolls, a healthy portion of salad, and some very nice potatoes vinaigrette with homegrown herbs that Ellie had contributed, I felt obscurely troubled. And as I got up from the table and carried my plate to the kitchen, I realized why.

Sally Coates had wept three times that day; once at the Chocolate Moose and twice right here at my kitchen table. She'd sniffled once, also.

But I couldn't help noticing that each time, her eyes had been dry. No tears, I recalled unhappily.

Not even one.

Later that evening I met Ellie at Julio's, a no-frills, out-of-the-way little joint down on the waterfront where the fishermen and their cronies hung out.

Outside the long wooden building with the newer metal Quonset at one end, a small yellow lightbulb glowed sullenly over a steel door with a rustic rope handle and a lock like the kind they probably use at Fort Knox.

Julio liked authentic Eastport dockside atmosphere, but he was also a big fan of solid security; a realist, in other words.

Inside, the air-conditioning hit me like an arctic breeze, but the place still smelled like the salt water that had been seeping into its bones since 1898; the building was a warehouse, most recently for packed sardines, before Julio bought it.

On the mantel under the big TV behind the bar, photographs of Julio's family in Miami were ranged out like trophies. I'd heard about them many times from him: his mother, Marie, two sisters and their children, plus aunties and uncles galore.

As I crossed the sawdust-strewn plank floor, country music was coming out of the speakers mounted in the rafters. All his relatives had to eat, Julio said, explaining why he had to keep running the bar here in Eastport. He was the man of the house even if he wasn't living in it, and it was his job to keep them all fed, not to mention clothed and sheltered.

Now his waxy-pale face with its sharply receding hairline, hound-dog jowls, and thin, black mustache moved back and forth over beer bottles, shot glasses, and the ever-present bar rag he wiped his way up and down the polished surface with. The men at the bar were discussing sharks: who'd seen one, how big, and how to keep them from eating you. "Stay out of the water" seemed to be the consensus.

"A ten-footer," one of them was saying, "can bite you in half, no problem."

Great, I thought, hoping we wouldn't end up cutting Paul Coates's body out of one of the big predators, maybe along with the gold piece he'd supposedly had with him.

Ellie had already gotten our beverages, an orange soda for

her and ginger beer for me. I'd have been here earlier, but I'd
had a date with a four-year-old to read him his bedtime story.

"Okay, let's sum up what we know," she began as soon as
I'd sat down. But almost at once a big, half-drunk fellow came
over from the bar.

"Girls wanna drink?" he bellowed jovially.

It was a risk, here at Julio's. But the funky little dive among
the warehouses and wharves was a place where Ellie and I
could meet without being overheard; for one thing, none of our
friends would be caught dead there, and for another, Julio's was
too loud for eavesdropping.

"No, thanks!" I hollered back, trying to match the drunk
guy's level of good cheer despite my own stone-soberness.

But the good cheer swiftly evaporated; his brow creased as he
ambled unsteadily closer. "What, too good to drink with me?"

Oh, brother. Julio looked over at us, his balding head shining under the neon Coors sign behind the bar. As usual, the
plump, spaniel-eyed barkeeper wore black trousers and an
open-collared white shirt, the sleeves rolled up over his forearms.

I shook my head at him. Julio wasn't just a barkeeper; he was
a family friend, and always solicitous of me and Ellie. Then I
got up and stood in front of the drunk guy, who wore a gray
sweatshirt with the sleeves generously cut out and oil-stained
jeans that looked as if he'd had them on since he bought them
several years ago.

The guy at the bar—tanned face, yellow curls, white polo
shirt—who'd been talking about the biting ten-foot shark was
watching me. I ignored him.

"Listen," I told the drunk guy very seriously, "my friend
here is out on supervised release. I'm the supervisor."

I didn't say released from where. "If you want to talk to her,
you have to show me your driver's license and let me write
down your personal info, just in case."

The guy took an unhappy couple of steps back, looking as if he deeply regretted the ones he'd taken forward.

"In case she ... does something to someone," I persisted. "They'd ask you if she talked about it, first. I mean, assuming she hadn't done it to you."

I let him wonder what the "something" might be. Then: "Hey, it wasn't my idea to let her out in the first place. But when do they ever listen to us, right? So—"

I put my hand out as if waiting for his ID. He shook his head and returned to the bar, not looking back.

Julio looked over again, one dark, bushy eyebrow raised as if to say what a complete load of hooey I'd just slung, and that it was nicely done.

I nodded, accepting this, and sat back down where Ellie had been writing on a napkin, not missing a beat.

"We know Paul Coates went out on his fishing boat alone and never came back," she said. "We do not know for sure that he's dead. All we know is that his body hasn't been recovered, or not for sure, anyway."

She scratched off a list item. "Next, we know his wife thinks he *is* dead, murdered, and we know she believes whoever killed him took a valuable gold coin from him."

Julio came over with another orange soda for Ellie and a ginger beer for me and set them down with a flourish.

"On the house," he said. Stopping trouble before it started was a well-thought-of activity around here, even if it did come with a load of hooey.

"Thanks," I told him. "You still coming to our place for the barbecue next week?"

One of my son Sam's yard-work employees had gotten into the community college in Calais, the market town thirty miles to our north on the mainland, and we were throwing a party for him.

Julio's dark eyes crinkled with pleasant anticipation. "Oh, I wouldn't miss it. I'll see my little pal, Ephraim?"

My grandson thought Julio, who could fold elaborate paper airplanes and make very real-sounding duck noises with his hands over his lips, was the World's Best Human.

"You'll see him," I promised. "In fact, you won't be able to get rid of him."

"No problem," Julio replied, and went away humming the ABC song, which Ephraim loved.

"We don't know if Sally thinks Coates is dead and that someone took the coin," I corrected when Julio had gone. "We know she *says* she thinks so. But that's all."

Ellie looked up alertly. "And your reasoning there is . . . ?"

I told her about my no-tears observation. "Ellie, if it happened to one of our husbands, we'd be crying so hard we'd need salt tablets."

Ellie looked doubtful. I went on: "Or hey, maybe she's not the crying type. I'm just saying we only know what she says, not that it's a fact."

Ellie nodded ruefully. "Point taken."

In the dim light of the low-down little dockside wateringhole, her red-gold curls glowed fierily around a face that belonged on a woodland sprite.

She looked down at the scrawled napkin, frowning as she scanned it. "In fact, we don't actually know very much at all, do we?"

I drank some ginger beer. "Correct. So some general askingaround might be our first order of business?"

"Looks like it," Ellie said. "I mean"—she paused, then plunged on—"I mean if we're going to do this at all."

Suddenly the whole place erupted in joy and consternation as the Red Sox went up 1–0 on the TV. In all the noise, we got up together and slipped out; no sense alerting the drunk guy.

Or the shark guy either, for that matter. We turned away from the breakwater stretching white and empty out over the black water. A breeze still moved the air, gently warm after the staggering heat of the day.

On our way up to Water Street past Rosie's Hot Dog Stand and the small, white clapboard *Quoddy Tides* building, Ellie paused to gaze out over the boat basin and the dark water.

"Then there's the *how* of it," she said. "I mean, someone pushed him overboard? Or killed him and then pushed him?"

It was only ten o'clock, but Water Street was deserted, the streetlamps and storefront lights shining eerily in the silence.

"Sally said he wore his safety gear. Not just a life vest, but a safety line, too," I said. "So he'd have been hard to push unless you incapacitated him and then unhooked it."

We passed the Chocolate Moose, with the grinning, googly-eyed moose sign over the door. Ellie would return here later for what we'd begun calling the night shift.

"So to do the deed, you've got to get out there and onto the *Sally Ann*," she mused, "get Coates over the rail somehow, set the wheel and clamp it so the boat runs in circles, get *off* the boat, and get yourself back to shore again."

"While," I added, "also stealing a gold coin and not being caught doing any of it. Pretty tall order."

That last part meant also that it must have happened at night. There was nowhere you could go on local waters where you might not get inconvenient company, otherwise; while you were shoving a dead guy overboard, for instance.

"The gold coin part of it must mean that someone knew he had it," said Ellie as we turned onto Key Street and started up-hill.

"Except that we don't even know for sure there was a coin at all," I pointed out. "That photograph . . ."

She shook her head. "Yeah. Doesn't prove a thing. But I've known Sally a long time and I just can't believe she'd . . . well. You're right, we don't know yet what really happened."

At the corner she turned back toward the Moose. "But we'll look into it, then? Try to help her?"

Sally Coates, she meant, whose character I was a good deal less sure of than Ellie still seemed to be.

"Okay. We'll look into it," I agreed, just as somewhere out on the dark water a bell buoy clanked lonesomely.

"And don't forget, we need to deliver four dozen scones in a few days," Ellie said as we parted under a streetlamp, her to a session of midnight baking and me home to bed.

"Right," I said. We were already so swamped, I didn't see how we would do it, but Ellie had never let being busy stop her from doing more; it was why we had the Moose at all, and why we were a success.

Now as she hurried away back down Water Street, the spring in her step was so lively you'd never think she'd been up since five AM. I, on the other hand, trudged up the rest of Key Street like a zombie. The day's heat had sucked all the energy out of me, along with any possible scone ideas.

And I needed them, because chocolate scones are easy but raspberries are hard, mostly on account of the scones shouldn't have seeds in them but raspberries do. Also, whole raspberries can be unpredictably sour, another problem that needed solving.

Headlights brightened from behind me; then a car slowed and stopped just ahead. When I got up alongside it, the driver's face looked familiar.

"You okay?" It was the fellow from Julio's—blond curls, tanned face, polo shirt—who'd been talking about big sharks.

"Fine," I said. "Are you looking for something?" Eastport streets are safe at night, but sometimes strangers take a while to figure that out, so they offer assistance.

"Nah," he said. "Just headed home to Lubec." The car was a late-model tan Jeep with a smiley-face cover on the spare.

"I'm up here from Florida and I usually take my boat back and forth from Lubec, but she's laid up for a session of hull repair. Something," he added with a rueful laugh, "took a bite out of her."

The first part made sense. Lubec—pronounced Loo-BECK—is five minutes from Eastport by boat but an hour by car, because of having to go around the water instead of crossing it.

That second part, though. "How big a bite?" I asked.

He held his hands apart. "What's that, ten inches? So it's either a big fish or I hit a big rock that left tooth marks."

Even in the warm summer night I felt a chill ripple through me. Maybe all the talk around here lately about carnivorous fish was more than just idle chatter; those shark scientists weren't coming here for the scones, after all.

"Should we not dangle our feet in the water anymore?" I asked the guy in the Jeep.

Ellie had a boat tied up in the boat basin; we went out on it sometimes when we had time and she could talk me into it, or we just sat there and soaked our toes.

"Right now?" His sandy eyebrows went up. "I wouldn't do it, myself. I'm Peter Waldron, by the way, I'm what you might call a professional shark guy."

"Jake Tiptree," I said. "Are you here for the conference?"

He looked confused, but then his face cleared. "Uh, maybe. I'll see once it gets going. If it's, you know, interesting."

"Oh. Well, happy shark hunting, then. Hope your boat gets patched up soon."

His grin was properly toothy, very white against his tanned skin. "Thanks. Have a good night."

Then he drove off with a wave, leaving me wondering what a professional shark guy did, exactly, so when I got back to the house, naturally I googled him and found out.

But first, of course, I had to get into the house.

And past my father.

Three

Looking down Key Street from the end of my driveway, the bay was an inky expanse with a few late-night lights twinkling at its far edge, over on the Canadian island of Campobello.

I wondered if Paul Coates's body was floating around in that water somewhere, or maybe it was inside a shark. I wondered, too, if he'd ever had a gold piece at all, and if he had, whether he'd vamoosed with it.

Faked his own death, in other words, and yes, I'm the suspicious type. Only I call it prudent, and when I got inside, my father agreed.

"Oldest trick in the book. Fake your death, scram with the valuables," he said at once when I'd told him as much as I knew.

He was wizened and bent, skinny and very old, but he still had a mind like a steel trap. Now he sat in the parlor with a blanket around his shoulders and our black cat, Jinx, curled on his lap.

"For the insurance," I said, and he nodded agreement; his view of human nature was free of illusions. For his evening at home he wore a green flannel shirt and gray sweatpants, his usual pair of ancient, brown leather sandals, and a ruby stud that had belonged to my mother glinting in his earlobe.

"That is, if his wife can convince the insurance folks he ever had it," my dad said. "It would've had to be declared on the policy."

"I'm not sure Coates had theft insurance." When money's tight, the first to get ignored is stuff you can't eat. "Or even the smarts to plan something like fraud."

Even his wife had told us he was no Einstein. "Maybe he didn't plan it," my dad responded at once.

Someone else did, he meant. "Huh. Why didn't I think of that?" I said, and his smile looked like Jinx the cat's if Jinx had just eaten Mika's precious pet canary.

"An accomplice," I said, thinking already about calling Ellie. "To do the planning. Coates just follows instructions."

It would make the mechanics of the thing a lot easier, too: Coates could just set his vessel's wheel and hop over onto his partner's boat, which would be there to collect him.

"In the dark, you switch off the running lights, you'd have a decent chance of getting to shore without . . ."

Being seen, I'd have finished, but when I looked over again he and the cat were asleep; it's always a risk when you depend on the old folks for some of your best ideas. So I wandered out to the kitchen, where I found Sam folding a pile of laundry.

"Hey," he said blearily, pushing a heap of tiny socks and T-shirts across the table at me.

With his dark, curly hair, hazel eyes, and long jaw, he's the spitting image of my ex-husband, Victor, a brain surgeon and a philanderer so infamous that the nurses at his hospital called him Vlad the Impaler.

Sam waved at a newspaper lying on the table. "Did you read about the solar flare that's coming?"

The headline read SUN GOES BOOM, which I thought was a bit sensationalistic unless we were really in trouble. Underneath, the article backpedaled but still sounded scary: power outages, medical devices scrambled, communications all fouled up.

"Supposed to be tomorrow," he said, folding little jammies. "I'll have to warn my crew their radios might go dead for a while."

Fortunately, Sam hadn't inherited his dad's character. He'd started a lawn-mowing company ten years earlier, enlarged it to property maintenance, and now was one of the biggest landscaping outfits in the county.

All while not turning into a jerk. He'd bought the radios to make his landscaping and yard-care employees' lives easier when they worked big tracts of property. They could've used cell phones, except some didn't have phones and others wouldn't know how to use them if they did have them.

His people, he had remarked when I'd asked him about this, were all smart; it was just that some of them were smart about some things and some about others. Now he finished folding the remaining small nightwear while I made quick work of the doll-sized socks.

"Sam, have you run into the shark guy yet? Peter Waldron?"

The curtains at the open kitchen windows shifted lazily in a breeze that smelled like roses blooming.

"Who?" Sam asked, yawning. Like Ellie, he'd started at dawn, running his business and doing a good deal of the heavy work himself. And now here he was, folding little shirts with lambs and rainbows printed on them at ten thirty at night.

He gave his curly head a cobwebs-clearing shake. "Oh, wait, yeah, I do know him. At the WaCo the other day he was saying how sharks are in our bay like never before, prowling around. Bunch of 'em."

He saw my face. "But only underwater. Not, like, jumping onto boats or grabbing folks off piers," he said, hiding a grin.

"Very funny." I pushed the folded clothes toward him. "Did he say where he's from, or anything else?"

Sam thought about it, still folding. In the laundry room, the dryer rumbled; upstairs, the shower went on with a hiss. From the TV in the parlor the announcer declared that that ball was outta here.

That accounted for my where my daughter-in-law, Mika, and my husband, Wade, were, and from the pristine, I'd-better-find-it-the-way-I-left-it state of the kitchen, I thought Bella had probably already gone upstairs to bed.

"Nope," Sam said after a moment, yawning. "I know he's up here from Florida, but he only talked about sharks and his boat. Why, did the guy murder somebody?"

"No. I mean, not that I know of," I said. "Just curious."

With that I left Sam sorting more socks and went into the dining room, where the lights were all on but nobody was there.

With green tapestry panels draping the windows, wine-red cranberry glass lamps on the tables, and an elaborately carved old wooden mantel over the tiled hearth, the room smelled like lemongrass candles, Windex, and beeswax furniture polish.

I got out my laptop and opened it on the dining room table. Waldron was probably just a guy with a boat and wild hair; you wouldn't believe the characters we get here sometimes, saying they're experts on something.

But to my surprise, he had a Wikipedia page; seeing it, I revised my opinion. He had oceanography degrees and worked at research centers in Hawaii and California; then he'd gone off on his own to study great white sharks, mostly in south Florida.

So he was for real. I closed the laptop slowly. Outside the dark dining room windows, the still-warm breeze I'd felt earlier had risen to a steady wind, rustling through the maple leaves with a sound like rushing water.

Then I realized: it *was* rushing water. The air was so humid that when it cooled, it was like wringing out a wet sponge; rain hammered in the gutters and spat through the window screens.

And the Fiat 124 Sport Spider was sitting in the driveway with the top down; I dashed for the back door.

Outside, rain poured down. I flung myself past the skeletal outlines of the new construction and hurled myself at the car.

Fat droplets thrummed on the leather seats while I wrestled the heavy canvas top up over the passenger compartment. But then just as I was latching it, a gust ripped it from my hands.

"Hey," someone said. The familiar voice was so welcome, I could've wept. Then a pair of arms wrapped around my waist; it was Wade, here to help me.

"You take one side. I'll take the other," he said, and moments later the top was up and firmly latched. Then Wade got some towels and together we wiped down the soaked upholstery and the dashboard as best we could.

"Now what?" he asked when we'd finished; by then the rain had stopped as suddenly as it began.

But I didn't know *now what*. The towels had dried the car's hard-surfaced interior, but the upholstery was still sopping, as were the carpets.

"Hot again tomorrow," he said. In the porch light his hair gleamed wetly and his soaked T-shirt clung to his chest.

"How about I drive it over to Spinney's garage?" he went on. "He's always there late, he's got air-conditioning to help dry things out, and while I'm there I could use his vacuum to suck water out of the carpets."

I wasn't sure whether to hug him or kiss his feet. The leather needed to dry slowly or the heat would ruin it.

"And maybe start some fans running," Wade added, so we went inside and got into dry clothes, and I fixed him a thermos of iced coffee and a couple of blueberry muffins.

The muffins reminded me of the chocolate raspberry problem, which I'd decided was two-fold: how to make them,

and how to find the time to make them, and that of course reminded me of the Moose, which reminded me of Sally Coates.

Wade leaned over and kissed me, which he does so well that
it nearly made me drop the paper bag with the muffins in it.

"Listen, have you heard anything new about Paul Coates?" I
asked, stepping back with an effort.

"Uh-uh." He grinned, knowing precisely the effect he'd just
had on me. "Why?"

Walking him to the door, I summarized the story. "So Ellie
and I told Sally we'd keep our eyes and ears open," I finished.

He nodded slowly. Outside the screen door, June bugs
buzzed and clattered inside the porch light.

"Tell you what, after I'm done at the garage we'll go down
and have a look at Coates's boat," he said.

"The *Sally Ann*? The one he fell off?"

Wade glanced sharply at me, which was when I realized he
didn't necessarily think that's what had happened, either.

"Yeah. It's sitting on a trailer in the boatyard out at Moose
Island Marine," he said.

"We can do that?" I happened to know that the boatyard
was surrounded by a chain-link fence with a locked gate.

His answering grin as he got into the Fiat was tigerish; he jingled his big key ring at me.

"Hey, I'm the harbor pilot," he said. "I can do anything."

With that he drove off; inside, I wiped up the windowsills
where the unexpected rain had come in, turned out the lights,
and went upstairs with a mug of coffee and my laptop.

Peter Waldron's Wikipedia page was still open on the screen;
idly, I clicked a link, learning that in Australia he'd gone down
in a shark cage to see great whites and that after a cage malfunc-
tion he'd nearly been eaten.

And then he'd gone down again. So he had nerve, at least,
and who knew what else. Closing the laptop I wondered if he
might be boyfriend material, in case Lizzie Snow's trouble-
some relationship with Dylan Hudson didn't work out.

By now, my coffee had gone cold. On the way downstairs to warm it I passed the kids' room: Ephraim and toddler Doreen slept peacefully when I peeked in, while the baby, Laurence, still had a bassinet in his parents' room.

Cup in hand, I tiptoed to Ephraim's bedside. His book, *The Bobbsey Twins*, lay open beside him. He was already a precocious reader, and his habit of reading under the covers was one we all approved, but no one had told him it was okay, so as not to spoil the fun.

I picked up his SpongeBob SquarePants flashlight. His eyes opened sleepily. "G'night, Gramma," he murmured.

"Good night, sweetie," I whispered, and my heart didn't quite explode with love. In the other bed, little Doreen didn't stir when I kissed her. She slept like Sam, dead to the world.

A little later, Wade called. "Want to go boat-inspecting?"

It was midnight; five hours from now, I'd be due at the Chocolate Moose. There'd be coffee to brew and doughnut-muffins to bake for our early-bird customers; also, those scones.

But this was a chance to give Paul Coates's boat a hard look. "I'm ready," I told Wade, and ten minutes later we were in his old green pickup truck, headed for the boatyard.

After the warm rain, the night air through the open truck windows was as thick as syrup, heavy with the perfume of beach roses and salt water.

Puddles gleamed in the headlights. "I stretched the top up and pulled the carpets back, ran the vacuum and got the big fans going in the garage," Wade said of the soaked Fiat.

From Key Street, he took the right turn past the ballfield and the youth center. "Tomorrow I'll go by and check that it's not sitting in the sun," he added, and have I mentioned that my husband is a prince among men?

We passed the firehouse and turned onto Deep Cove Road, from there swooping down into a gully where a rain-swollen stream rushed through a culvert. On either side, stands of birch trees grew in clumps, their white trunks like tall, thin ghosts.

"You seem pretty interested in Paul Coates's boat, too," I remarked as we stopped outside the boatyard gate. Beyond it, boats of all sizes stood on trailers under the yard lights.

His lips pursed. "Just curious. I'd like to see that safety line he supposedly always used."

He got out of the truck and approached the gate; then his key ring flashed and we were in, construction gravel crunching under the truck's tires.

The lights on tall posts ringed the yard's perimeter. Under them I felt as if I had a sign on my back: TRESPASSER! But Wade led me confidently across the uneven gravel to where a large wooden boat on a rough-looking trailer loomed.

It was the *Sally Ann*. Wade stepped up onto the trailer's rusted fender and swung a long leg over the boat's wooden rail.

His square-jawed face shone damply under the yard lights. "C'mon, I'll give you a lift."

"Great." What I needed him to give me was a ladder. But I didn't see one, so instead I stepped up onto the trailer's rusting fender, reaching up for his hand.

Then: "Oof." Wade clasped both hands around my arm and pulled. The next thing I knew, I was belly-over-the-rail, then face-planted onto a deck slimy with fish guts and seagull poop.

Yeah, this murder-snooping was a glamorous business, all right. I scrambled up, wiping at my lips, which were now heavily smeared with the substances listed above, plus who knew what.

Wade looked around, picking up an orange life vest, then a pair of rubber waders. Then he found a small, rectangular gadget with a chain that fastened it to the vessel's control console; switched on, its lens flashed white.

"EPIRB," Wade said, switching it off again. "Electronic position indicating radio beacon, you use it if you're in trouble and need help. Or if you're sinking, it floats. Shows where you sank."

In case you were sunk, too, and couldn't tell anyone due to being drowned, he meant. Then he found something else.

"Look." A heavy spring-clip fastened a braided steel cable to an industrial-sized eyebolt screwed into the rail. The clip at the cable's other end wasn't attached to anything.

Wade examined the thing, using a flashlight he'd brought along. "See the wear on the eyebolt, here? That scratched area is where the spring-clip rubbed against it."

He turned to the rail itself. "And see here in this wood, this little hole filled with patching compound?"

I saw it. Epoxy, I thought; someone had packed it in, then smoothed it off and painted it.

"Bolt got loose in the first hole, Coates must've moved it and filled where it'd been," Wade said. "Took some trouble with it, too, to make sure his anchor point was good."

So the safety line wouldn't fail when Coates needed it, Wade meant. I peered into the shadowy wheelhouse, recognizing the wheel, the depth finder and navigation screens, switches for lights, pumps, and radio—the *Sally Ann* was much bigger than the boat Ellie had, but most of this looked familiar.

"No one's gone over the boat since it was brought in?" I asked Wade. "Not the police, not . . . ?"

"Not as far as I know," he answered, still peering at the rail as I stepped all the way into the wheelhouse. Coke cans, fast-food wrappers, and other trash half filled a black plastic trash bin, but there was nothing interesting in it.

I rummaged through the storage cubbies: boat registration, state permits and licenses, a state tax card, and an owner/operator certificate were all there in a watertight plastic envelope. A fire extinguisher hung on a bulkhead, a flare gun poked from a bin, and an orange cold-water survival suit was stuffed into another, larger bin.

Finally: What looked like a pair of heavy leather suspenders dangling from a hook by the hatchway was actually a harness for the safety line Sally Coates had told us about, and it appeared to be in good repair.

What it didn't appear to be was fastened onto Paul Coates's missing body, even though Sally said he always wore it. I went back up on deck.

"Survival suit's stowed," I told Wade. "Safety harness is still here, too."

"The suit being here makes sense," he replied, looking up from where he was scraping a fingernail over the rail's patch job. "There's no sign here of anything that'd make you want to put it on."

Like sudden bad weather, a breach in the hull, or maybe a fire; a boat was a big investment, and it would take a lot to get a guy to abandon it.

"So if he went overboard, it was because he wanted to?"

"Or didn't expect to. Didn't have time to put it on."

He straightened. "The boat was floating just fine when they found it, though, so that argues against a sudden emergency."

Beyond the boatyard's chain-link fence, fog drifted among the evergreens, making them appear and disappear as if behind a pale curtain. Nothing else moved, and the silence was suddenly full of . . . well, I'm not sure what to call it.

But it felt like eyes, watching. "Wade?" All at once I didn't like it here one bit.

But Wade had returned to the boat's rail, unconcerned. "C'mere a minute," he said.

I went over and looked, trying to shake off the chill I still felt despite the night's warmth.

"Um," I said, squinting. "The rail's got some scratches. So what?"

A fishing boat's no luxury liner, after all. Maintenance keeps it floating and the engine running, but dings, dents, and even a small leak now and then are all par for the course; hey, that's what bilge pumps are for.

"Now look up and down the rail, tell me what strikes you."

The yard lights made the paint shine. Other than the marks Wade had pointed out, its long surface was entirely unmarred.

Which meant the paint job was recent. "Fresh paint? But why . . . ?"

Like I said, cosmetic fixes weren't critical on work boats. But Wade explained why it probably wasn't just for looks:

"You'd do it if you got a little rot in there," he said, touching his finger to the surface. "Clean it, patch it, paint it. Recently, too. In the humidity it still almost feels tacky."

I went back to the wheelhouse and returned with a piece of trash that I hadn't thought anything of.

"Paint can," I said as I pried the top off.

A skim of white liquid moved thickly at the bottom; the smell of paint wafted up. "Pretty fresh."

I bent to the scratches again. Wade had been looking at them for a long time, and now suddenly he swung one leg over the rail, then the other, and slid across it so his middle scraped over the painted surface before he dropped to the ground.

Then he climbed back aboard again. "I could be wrong," he began, approaching the spot where he'd gone over the side.

But he wasn't wrong. The marks his belt buckle had just made in the paint were fresh and clear, and very much like the ones he'd found moments ago: scrape marks. Someone else had gone over the rail of this boat recently, willingly or unwillingly.

All at once the silence out here was like the stillness in the final moments before a pounce. *Don't be silly*, I instructed myself, but it didn't help.

"Got your phone?" I asked Wade mildly. But he heard the warning in my voice, and shared my belief that gut feelings are the best early warning system of all.

"Get it out, why don't you," I said, "take some pictures of those scratches."

Before we go, I didn't add, but he got it. While he swiftly got photos, I grabbed all the paperwork I could find: licenses, receipts, records, and permits. Finally, Wade took one more look around the boat, peering behind stacks of lobster traps and under the bait barrel, then opening the deck hatch that led down into the *Sally Ann*'s engine compartment.

He aimed his flashlight down there, squinted around, then closed the hatch and got up. "How long was this boat adrift?"

"I don't know. Not long, though." As a fisherman, Coates would've been out on the water at dawn, Sally had reported him missing at eleven that night, and the boat was found the next day.

"Wade, let's get out of here." By now I felt thoroughly creeped out, but I didn't think ghosts were lurking among the evergreens anymore.

I thought one was here with us; cans Coates had drunk from, tools he'd touched, the faint smell of tobacco, and the box of rags likely torn from his old shirts . . . all these things brought the man here almost as if he were present in the flesh.

Frowning, Wade bent again to the marks he'd made on the rail. "Funny. They're alike, but the earlier marks are cleaner."

He was right. The scratches his belt buckle had made were uneven, imperfect, while the earlier ones were so straight, they might've been drawn with a ruler.

And now I couldn't help wondering if someone had.

Four

So there I was, late at night in the middle of a boatyard full of ghosts. My task was to get back down off Coates's boat again, and you can probably imagine how much I enjoyed that.

"Wade?" I said, looking over the rail and noticing how far from terra firma I was. "Could you please give me a . . ."

Hand, I'd have finished, but when I turned he wasn't there. Not on deck, not out on the bow, not already down on the ground, waiting for me.

"Hey, Wade? Let's go. This place is giving me the heebie-jeebies."

Wisps of pale fog drifted from the trees like a procession of wraiths. A foghorn moaned distantly; nearby, an owl hooted. But then he emerged from the wheelhouse with a glossy brochure in one hand.

"Whatever that is, let's read it once we're in the truck," I said.

"You got it," he replied, moving to stand by the rail once more. "Now, how do you want to do this?"

I hesitated to say that I didn't want to do it at all. But standing on the deck of *Sally Ann*, I was about ten feet off the ground; twelve, if I stood on the rail.

Yeah, like that was going to happen. What I wanted was to be transported magically, then deposited gently. But that wasn't happening, either; also, there was still no ladder anywhere, not that I'm a big fan of ladders, either.

Seeing my hesitation, Wade took control. "Sit on the rail with your feet hanging over," he said, and I complied, but once I'd done it, I looked down, which was unwise.

"Now, I'm going to take your hands and lower you down to the trailer's fender," said Wade. "Here goes."

He knew better than to let me argue about it, and the next thing I knew, my butt had slid smoothly off the rail and my body dangled freely over the construction gravel.

And as a cure for the heebie-jeebies, may I simply say right here that being dangled by your arms is so painful, you'll forget all about ghosts. But being a dork in front of my husband is my least favorite activity, so I shut up even when he let go, and instead of balancing on the fender, I landed on my butt.

Silently, in the gravel, in the dark. But I was in one piece, and then Wade landed beside me. On his feet, of course; lightly, and with the glossy brochure in his hand.

He helped me up and waited while I brushed gravel bits off my backside, and in the truck he handed me the brochure.

"It's an auction flyer," I said as he pulled out of the boatyard onto Deep Cove Road.

He got out and locked the gate behind us. "Yeah, pretty fancy one, too," he said when he got back.

He turned on the windshield wipers as the late-night fog rolled in billows across the road, condensing on the windshield. Then in the clear wedges cut by the wipers, deer materialized; he slowed while the animals made their plodding way across the pavement.

I looked down at the flyer again, for an upcoming auction at a fashionable shop in Camden. Among the objects shown were a porcelain box once owned by Catherine the Great, a ruby-and-diamond tie pin worn by Joe Gallo the night he got shot outside Umbertos Clam House, Eleanor Roosevelt's favorite teacup—

The last deer made it over and vanished into the greenery lining the road; Wade pressed the gas pedal again.

"Wade, this is all historical stuff. Pricy and rare, but why would an Eastport fisherman be interested in it?"

He nodded, watching carefully ahead for more nocturnal wanderers. "Look at the back page."

So I did, and there in glossy, gleaming full color was a gold doubloon from a Spanish trading vessel, *Galatea*, that sank off the coast of Cuba in 1622.

"Wow," I breathed. The coin weighed twenty-three grams and had an elaborate cross stamped onto it on one side; on the other, a bunch of letters and symbols gleamed richly.

The marks looked familiar. The estimated value of the piece was $2500. "Maybe Paul Coates was checking out what his own gold piece might be worth," I theorized.

"Or maybe that one is his," Wade said. "And he's selling it already."

"Maybe." I looked at the brochure entry again. "Doesn't seem like it's worth enough to change his kids' futures. But who knows, maybe he's got more of them."

We started down Washington Street between the darkened IGA and the dollar store. At this time of night with the fog silent in the empty streets, Eastport felt nearly abandoned.

"So," I ticked off on my fingers, "no blood, no sign of a struggle, a safety harness and some faked-looking scratches that don't prove anything—"

"Not enough to take to the police," Wade said.

"Yeah." I gazed out, discouraged, as Wade turned onto Water Street. The Chocolate Moose was dark, which meant that Ellie had finally gone home for a few hours.

I should, too; five AM was approaching fast. A yawn escaped me. "Anyway, thanks. And for helping me out with the Fiat."

Wade smiled sideways at me. "No problem. This snooping stuff is kind of fun, huh?"

"I guess. If you like that sort of thing." As I spoke, my butt still hurt from landing on it, my hands ached from being gripped so hard, and my shoulders felt dislocated; also, the fright I'd felt turning in my gut was still there.

But hey, let him have his illusions. "Marine Patrol's going out again tomorrow," he said as we turned onto Key Street. "They'll find Coates's body pretty soon, they almost always do. And then maybe there'll be answers."

"Right," I agreed as we pulled into our driveway. When people went into the water around here, their remains—or, you know, what remained of their remains—were generally found floating or on shore, sooner or later.

We pulled into our driveway. In the truck's headlights, the new addition's unfinished structure looked like a stage set for a horror movie, full of shadows and harshly lit angles.

"I don't know, though," I said quietly as we got out. The house was all dark. "I'm not so sure it'll happen this time."

"Why not?" Wade held the door as we went in. The kitchen smelled like Comet cleanser, Ivory soap, and floor wax. He got a beer from the fridge, paused, and went back for sandwich stuff: roast beef, cheese, an onion from the garden.

"There are just too many unknowns," I said as a child cried out sleepily from upstairs and then feet padded overhead.

"Mmm," Wade agreed, "that's true. I'll be up soon," he added, carrying his plate to the TV room while I got a glass of milk and took it upstairs.

My daughter-in-law, Mika, was coming back out of the kids' room. With her glossy black hair hanging loose and a white chenille robe wrapped around her, she looked lovely as usual but also exhausted.

"Ephraim had a nightmare," she explained. "Someone at play group told him about the sharks."

The ones that the men at Julio's wanted to catch, he meant, and that I gathered scientist Peter Waldron was also studying. And come to think of it, those scone-eating conference attendees were coming because of them, too; those dratted raspberry scones flitted into my head again.

"Just what the poor kid needed," I said. Ephraim was a sensitive boy whose fears often crept into his dreams.

Mika smiled tiredly. "Yeah. G'night," she murmured.

"Sweet dreams," I told her, not adding that her mention of sharks had kick-started my brain back to wide-awakeness.

But it had, and now I had two unpleasant ideas to ruminate over as I tried to get to sleep, myself:

First, maybe there'd been no blood on the *Sally Ann* because some of it was in the water, and the rest was inside a shark.

Or—and this was the notion I'd been pondering with more urgency since Wade found the scratches and the auction brochure on the boat—

Maybe my dad had it right, and Coates wasn't really dead.

Five in the morning came criminally early, but the sunrise was worth it, like cherry juice splashed up into a marine-blue sky and rippling out across the water. I stood on Water Street, yawning and gazing at the glorious display.

"Good morning, Jake."

I dragged my gaze from the view. A police squad car idled beside me on Water Street with Lizzie Snow behind the wheel.

"You're up early," she observed. "What's new?"

Today she wore a crisp, blue uniform shirt whose perfect fit in the shoulders said it'd been tailored; below the short sleeves, her arms were trimly muscled.

"Work," I replied, aiming my thumb at the Moose. Her eyes brightened.

"Are you going to make coffee?" she asked hopefully, and of course I couldn't say no.

For one thing, I was planning to drink half a gallon of the stuff just as soon as I had it brewed. "Sure, give me a lift."

Maybe I could get some information out of her, I thought; what happened, though, was different.

Like, the exact opposite. "So what do you know about this Paul Coates guy?" she asked as she drove me the rest of the way down Water Street to the Moose.

I'd thought her cheery *What's new?* had sounded more like *What're you up to?* and now I thought somehow she'd learned that Ellie and I were snooping again.

And since she already knew that murder was all we snooped into, she'd figured out the rest. Once we were out of the squad car I let us both into the Moose, hung my bag on its hook behind the counter, got the coffee started, and turned to her.

"Did you really have your uniforms tailored?"

I gestured at the blouse, whose V-neckline lay perfectly flat and whose sleeve seams neither drooped over her shoulders nor cinched up into her armpits.

She shrugged. "A girl likes to look her best."

Yeah, I guess a girl did, but most of them didn't measure it to the sixteenth of an inch. I made a mental note to ask who'd done the alterations as she followed me to the kitchen, where Ellie had left me a note: an order for two dozen chocolate chip cookies had come in by text message.

To be picked up at 7:30 AM, the note said; two hours from now. "Sorry, but it turns out I don't have time to talk," I told Lizzie.

She'd poured coffee for us both; now she read the note over my shoulder, put her cup down, and grabbed an apron.

"What, you think I can't find my way around a bowl and a mixing spoon?" she asked.

Oh, what the heck, the morning was already going south;

why not let her help? So I got out the butter, eggs, and the sugars, brown and white.

"Pack the brown sugar into the measuring cup first," I told her, "it makes it much easier to pour in the—"

"The white sugar," she finished for me, "I know." Then, peering at the recipe card I'd handed her: "So, you want me to use as much flour as this says? Or a little less?"

"Less," I confirmed, surprised again; the gun on her hip didn't make her look at all like Holly Homemaker. Still she went confidently to the refrigerator for eggs and vanilla extract.

"Have you found a place to live, yet?" I asked. Rents were notoriously tight in Eastport, especially in summer, and buying a place was even harder unless you had *mucho dinero.*

"Yes. Bob Arnold's cousin's house? Out at the end of High Street? Bob put us in touch."

A pang of envy pierced me; the place she was talking about perched on a bluff overlooking a 180-degree water view. Just big enough for one, cozy and peaceful . . .

Yeah, I'd heard of that.

Lizzie looked at the recipe card again, then measured the butter into a bowl and put it into the microwave.

"Anyway, about Paul Coates," she prodded gently.

So she really did know how to do this baking stuff, and she knew how to keep asking until she got answers, too.

I sighed and gave in. "His wife, Sally, is a friend of Ellie's," I began, and while Eastport's new chief of police creamed sugar into softened butter I told her the rest:

The missing gold piece, the unused safety equipment, the auction brochure and the scratches on the *Sally Ann*'s rail . . .

"You saw them? That was last night?" As she spoke, she added the vanilla and eggs to the butter-and-sugar mixture and beat them in, first gently and then forcefully.

The memory of feeling that Wade and I were being watched

came back to me. "Was that you? In the fog, were you out there?"

Another shrug. "Well, first I took a walk on the dock after dinner. Stopped in at Julio's, the guys there were talking about Paul Coates. Seemed he was pretty well-liked."

A batch of doughnut-muffin batter awaited me in the cooler; while Lizzie measured the flour, I got the batter out and began slipping paper cupcake cups into muffin tins.

"His wife didn't have much bad to say about him, either," I said. "But what's that got to do with the boatyard last night? Were you following us?"

She smiled into the chocolate-chip cookie batter she was mixing very competently and efficiently.

"No. You and—who's that, your husband?—pulled into the boatyard just after I got there."

"Hmph. A likely story." But possibly true; we could have missed her easily if she was just sitting there in the dark.

"So you were watching the *Sally Ann?*"

"Yep. Just in case somebody messed with her."

She looked up at me and smiled sweetly. "And guess what, somebody did. You."

I only spilled a little batter; Lizzie laughed. "Don't worry, I don't think you swam out and killed a guy, stole a gold coin off him, and dropped his body overboard."

"Oh, good." I tilted the big glass pitcher over the first of twenty-four muffin cups. We had a big oven, fortunately.

Less fortunate was the fact that the muffins baked at 350 degrees, but the cookies that Lizzie was mixing chocolate chips into needed 375 degrees. So the cookies would have to wait.

Lizzie saw me preempting her use of the oven and went for the plastic-wrap roll; after covering her batter bowl she put it into the refrigerator without asking.

She'd also read the recipe, located the baking soda, baking powder, salt, and measuring spoons, and used them.

"Was Dylan Hudson with you last night, by any chance?" I inquired. He'd been bird-dogging her when she was in East-port several years earlier, too, but I didn't know the rest of his story except that he seemed not to be a state cop, anymore.

She just stared as I got out a stack of cups with lids, a handful of napkins, and some white paper bags from the supplies cabinet.

"Or am I not as good a snoop as I think?" I added as I put two sugar packets, two creamers, and two napkins into each bag, plus a popsicle stick for stirring. Then I loaded it all on two large trays and carried the trays out to the counter.

"Oh, come on, Lizzie." She sank into a chair at one of the café tables, looking as if some stunning new fact had just been revealed to her.

Maybe it was that I hadn't just fallen off the turnip truck yesterday. "You're here, he's here . . ."

I hadn't missed her expression a day earlier when she looked at him, either, feigning irritation. Maybe she was a good cop and would be a fine police chief, but she was no actress; where Hudson was concerned she'd been hit by the thunderbolt and that was that.

Then the little silver bell over the door began jingling non-stop; I kept on handing out coffee-and-muffin bags, taking money, and making change for the same twenty or so guys who came in every day, until a different face appeared.

"'Morning, Jake." It was Peter Waldron, the shark guy; after all my nosy googling of the night before, I eyed him with new interest.

"G'morning, yourself. You're out early."

In daylight his curly, sun-bleached hair, pale eyes, and tanned boyish face formed an appealing package, like he should be carrying a surfboard and wearing a necklace of seashells. He waved at the bay, already glittering fiercely with the promise of yet another broiling-hot day.

"My boat's fixed, and I'm following a fishing boat out to where the guy says he saw a shark. You wouldn't happen to have one more of those goodie bags you sell to the guys, would you?"

I didn't, but I put one together for him. "On the house," I said. "But now I've got a question for you."

It had been on my mind since last night at the boatyard. Waldron paused at the door. "Sure, fire away," he said, his face still cheery.

Or it was until he heard my question. "Do sharks eat dead people? I mean if a body fell into the water, would a shark—"

He tipped his head seriously. "Depends on the shark. Great whites don't like people meat, believe it or not. Mostly if they try to eat you, they'll spit you out."

He made a face. "Of course, by then the damage is done."

Of course. I averted my mind from the mental picture.

"Tiger sharks, though," he said, "those guys eat anything. Or," he added, "anyone. Bottom line, you can never tell what a shark will do."

He put a hand up, backing away. "I gotta run or the boat will leave without me."

"Thanks," I called, but he was already out and gone, and when I turned, Lizzie Snow stood in the kitchen doorway, her arms crossed over her aproned front.

By now I was feeling impatient and a little anxious; Ellie would be here soon and I hadn't done nearly as much as I'd hoped to before she arrived.

"What're you doing here, anyway?" I popped the sixty-four-thousand-dollar question to Lizzie as I brushed past her into the kitchen again. "I thought you were all settled up north."

"I was," she said, following me. "People were good, the job was fine."

She hesitated. "But my personal life took a hit."

Hudson again, I thought. Either he'd wanted her to quit, so she did it, or he didn't want her to quit. So she did it.

The cookies had been in our second oven, which we only fired up when we were busy. Now they were cooled enough to come off the cookie sheets; she took the spatula from me.

"And then Bob Arnold called me," she finished, "and said he thought I might be just weird enough to like it here, and did I want the job."

She finished sliding the cookies onto wire racks and took the cookie sheets to the sink. Ellie had baked enough cupcakes, brownies, and eclairs to nearly fill the display case.

But I still had a mountain of candied fruit, raisins, walnuts, and overripe bananas, plus more chocolate bits and the makings for cream cheese frosting, to turn into what we called fainting cake because you could faint from how good it was.

Lizzie finished rinsing cookie sheets, slid them into the drying rack, and changed the subject. "But about last night."

"What about it?" So much for questions. She'd clammed right up, and on account of it I knew not to ask about the child she'd been hunting, or at least not yet.

Just asking about the job had been nosy enough, I sensed, so instead I got down the big mixing bowl, four small loaf pans, and a heavy chopping knife.

When I turned with the knife in my hand, her eyes went to it instantly, reminding me again that with those tightly muscled arms she could've had the glittering blade in her own hand in a couple of heartbeats.

Then Ellie walked in and to my surprise, my daughter-in-law, Mika, was with her.

"Hey, Ma," said Mika cheerfully, then hung up her bag, pulled on a clean, white apron, and stepped behind the counter.

My face must've shown my confusion. "Ask Ellie," Mika said, shrugging cheerfully.

"Gotta run," Lizzie told us, waving toward the harbor.

"Coast Guard's looking, too of course, but I've got a boat waiting for me, little private search party of my own."

I was still looking at Ellie, who had on a pair of blue jean shorts, sneakers, and a blue striped top with a man's white shirt over it, the shirttails brought around and tied in front.

It was not her usual work outfit. Neither was the ball cap she'd jammed atop her reddish-blond curls, or the pair of gray sweatshirts she carried over her arm.

Also, her blue eyes shone with a kind of excitement that I'd come to know meant just one thing. The bell over the door jingled as Lizzie went to get onto a boat and go out on the water to search for a missing man's body. And then:

"Come on, Jake," said Ellie, "we're going, too!"

Five

Sunshine glared from the yellow-white ball overhead as we clattered down the metal gangway to the finger piers in the boat basin. Ahead, well-known local Captain Carl McFaul and a pair of gangly, tow-headed teenagers waited aboard Carl's 40-foot green-and-white lobster boat, *Frinch*.

"Look alive, now, boys, here comes today's charter!" he bellowed heartily, somehow not boosting my confidence. For one thing, a little voice in my head just now had reminded me that sometimes I got seasick on big vessels like this one.

Ellie's own boat, *Sea Wolf*, floated at one of the smaller piers nearby. A blue, 22-foot vintage Bayliner with an open deck, a sweet little cabin, and a new Tohatsu 180 outboard engine on the transom, *Sea Wolf* was half the *Frinch*'s size.

I rarely got seasick on it. But the larger, tubbier vessel had one thing *Sea Wolf* didn't: a captain who knew from long experience where things tended to fetch up after floating around for a while in these waters.

"I put up a poster in the WaCo Diner last night, looking for a charter," Lizzie had explained after we caught up with her. "Half an hour later, this guy called."

After fishing here his whole life, Carl was known in the area as somebody who could navigate blindfolded. I thought it boded well for Lizzie's future here that she'd hooked up with the right guy so quickly, since in Eastport, networking isn't just a business technique; it's a survival skill.

Once the three of us were aboard, she explained her plan for the voyage; while she talked, I peered nervously around, looking for the boat's safety equipment. And while seeing a row of life jackets and life rings with throw lines and hearing the marine band radio's sputtering reassured me, nothing else did. The *Frinch* was a fading old tub with extensively flaking paint, an anchor so rusty it resembled shipwreck material, and thick fiberglass patches on the hull, some pretty extensive.

Lizzie finished making sure we were all on the same page: We were going out to see if we could find Paul Coates's body, by following McFaul's suggestions about where it might be.

"Yep," Carl allowed agreeably around a chomped-on, unlit cigar. "If it's where I think, won't even take long."

Not waiting to explain his optimism, he stepped down into the *Frinch*'s ramshackle wheelhouse while the two teen boys—they were Carl's sons, and twins, I'd learned from them as we were boarding, and their names were Jeremy and Jeffrey—cast off the lines.

"This is great," said Lizzie, looking around in evident wonder as the boat slid away from the dock. Sky, water, gulls crying and flapping above—it's an experience, all right.

"Yeah," I breathed; I'd forgotten how much I liked this part. A seagull flapped down to perch atop a nearby dock piling. In the clear, greenish water, pinkish-pale jellyfish cast and recast their long, frond-like tentacles. Around me the warm, humid air smelled like boat fuel and sea salt, creosote and baitfish, the latter a stink so powerful, it was nearly visible.

I hauled a grease-stained life jacket from the bin of them and pulled it on. From the breakwater, tourists watched avidly as we passed: AUTHENTIC MAINE FISHING VESSEL HEADS OUT.

Probably they wouldn't be so charmed if they knew we were going to fish a several-days-dead corpse out of the drink. The *Frinch* motored smoothly past the old wharf with the tumble-down Fish Shack standing shakily on it; C-FOOD read the rusty sign atop the shack's age-blackened wooden shingles.

Next we motored between the end of the wooden fish pier on our right and the concrete-and-steel breakwater to our left (or starboard and port, for you boaty types). A tall steel winch stood at the end of the breakwater; below it, a lobster boat idled while her crew attached cables to a flat of traps.

Then we were all the way out on the open water, the breeze suddenly sweet and cool and the breakwater sliding away behind us. Turning from the wheel, McFaul drew his lips back in a toothy grin with the cigar sticking out of it.

"Ain't it just elegant?" he enthused, and even I had to admit it was. The contrast between hot, dry land and the water-cooled air made the *Frinch*'s open deck feel cold, though, and soon I was shivering.

Ellie shoved one of the sweatshirts she'd brought along at me. "Here. And put some of this on, too."

She pressed a tube of SPF 90 into my hands; dutifully I daubed myself with the white goo. I'd worn a cap and sunglasses, too, fortunately; it felt cooler out here on the water, but the sun still blazed with the white-hot intensity of a death ray.

Then: "Hey, you guys?" Lizzie called. "You know anything about reading these?"

She'd gotten the two teenagers, both shirtless and tanned to a deep bronze, to help her anchor a large sheet of paper to the deck using big lead sinkers, the kind that keep fishing nets submerged.

Ellie and I knelt on the deck by the sheet, which turned out to be a marine chart. Depth soundings, channel markers, icons for rocks and cables, and of course the international border between the US and Canada were all there . . . somewhere.

"Sorry, but I can't make head or tail of this," Lizzie began, and then Ellie reached past her.

"Here," she said. "You're looking at it upside down."

She straightened the chart, then pointed. "That's Eastport. Here's Campobello, and there's Lubec, where the bridge is."

Trust Ellie to catch on quick. She pointed south down the length of the bay at the bridge, shimmering hazily in the heat.

"And we're going . . . ?" I asked.

"There." One of the teen boys, I couldn't tell which—it was the one whose extremely curly blond hair was held back by a blue-coated rubber band—stood behind us. But as he pointed, his tanned face lost its good-humored look.

"Death's Head?" Lizzie queried doubtfully. "Really?"

It was small, isolated island, shaped, if we could believe the chart, like a grinning skull.

"Why there?" she asked as McFaul came up behind us to put a hand on the boy's shoulder; if you took away the wrinkles, the whiskers, and the cigar, the two looked just alike.

"See them pointy-like things?" McFaul put the toe of his boot on the chart.

The other boy—the one whose curly blond hair was stuffed into a ball cap—was at the wheel, now, pushing the throttle forward as we encountered an extremely lively patch of water.

In other words, he did the complete opposite of what I'd have done; I tightened my life vest.

"I've found stuff there before, that's why," said McFaul of our destination. "Boat cushions, crashed drones . . . once I found a perfectly good dinghy, nice little Evinrude on her. No numbers, nothing."

He turned to the wheelhouse as our vessel began pitching and rolling much more energetically than I liked.

"Jeremy!" he shouted while gouts of spray flew and I looked around a little wildly for something to hang on to.

"Give her a little more!" Carl shouted, and the *Frinch*'s diesel engine's rumble deepened; the boat plowed ahead.

"Lots of current through here," Carl said, waving at the abruptly roughened water. Behind us, Eastport shrank into the distance, tiny as a toy village.

"Tide hits the current and gets forced through one of the underwater canyons down there, it all goes— "

We hit more waves, and bigger ones; honestly, I didn't care even a little bit what caused them, only that they should stop.

"Throttle, dammit!" Carl shouted, "don't be afraid of it!"

I am. I'm plenty afraid of it, I thought. With a throaty roar, the engine began chugging and vibrating right up through the deck as if any minute it might erupt.

Satisfied, Carl turned back to Lizzie and me; Ellie had gone quietly over to talk to the other boy, Jeffrey.

"Youngster at the helm, now, he's learning," Carl confided. It was another bit of news I didn't welcome, like hearing that the flight attendant was flying the plane.

"Anyway," Carl went on, "there's a little inlet on the near side of Death's Head, looks like the entrance to a cave if you can find it. Hardly anyone ever goes in."

"But we're going to?" I asked. Oh, this was getting better and better.

First a skull-shaped island, now an abandoned cave . . . Lizzie listened with interest to Carl while I tried to hide my thoughts about Death's Head, all negative in the extreme.

Young Jeremy cut back on the throttle as we exited watery chaos into a sudden, glassy calm. Carl scanned the horizon.

"More rain's coming in, we'll want to be hustling right along before it gets here."

There wasn't a cloud in the sky but hustling along sounded good to me. "What's the water like in the inlet?" I asked.

But Carl was looking over his shoulder toward the helm again. "Throttle, boy, what're you, chicken?"

The *Frinch* surged forward as Carl turned back to me. "Oh, it's sweet there, you'll see. Nice, sheltered spot. You just go in-land a bit, you'll find a real pretty lagoon."

Relief touched me; it sounded at least as if Death's Head wouldn't bounce us around. Or, you know, drown us.

"You'll find him," Carl allowed confidently. "Getting in there, though. Lot of rocks and ledges around the shore, hidden at high tide."

Which was now. "Plenty of wave action, too," Carl said, and then, "Jeremy, will you lay on that throttle, please? We ain't out here to catch barnacles!"

The *Frinch* positively charged forward as Lizzie looked up from the chart at me. "Oh, goody, rocks and ledges."

"And wave action," I agreed, and was about to say more, but Ellie came running back from her chat with Jeffrey (the one with the ponytail).

"You guys, look!" She pointed at the water behind us.

Lizzie clambered up curiously. Carl and Jeffrey were at the rail, gazing in wonder, while in the wheelhouse Jeremy put a small pair of binoculars to his eyes.

"What?" Lizzie demanded. "Where? I don't—"

Unable to speak, I seized her head and turned it toward a triangular fin sticking up out of the blue water, moving fast.

Toward us. "Oh, my god," Lizzie breathed.

I'd have said something, too, but I still couldn't make a sound past the jagged chunk of fright stuck in my throat. It was a shark, a ridiculously large one from what I could see of its dark shape moving under the water, still coming straight at us.

The big fish slammed into the *Frinch*'s hull. A dull thud came from somewhere below the water, but nothing else happened.

Or I thought nothing had until Carl charged suddenly into the wheelhouse, then back out on deck again to yank up the trap door to the engine compartment.

Steam gushed up from the opened hatch. He dropped down into it anyway. "Take the wheel, Jeffrey!"

Jeffrey did, but he looked very unhappy. I was unhappy, too, because to make that much steam you need water.

Lots of water. The shark-bump must've broken through one of those patches on the hull, I guessed. Below us, an electric motor whined on, followed by loud gurgling sounds.

"Look over the rail!" Carl shouted hoarsely. But he didn't say who should, so I did it despite my sudden, overwhelming desire never to see water of any kind ever again.

Just as I'd feared: A hole bigger than my fist showed in a patch just below the *Frinch*'s waterline. Every time a wave hit us, or the vessel leaned to port—which happened often; boats don't just skim along, perfectly level—we took on more water.

"Dad?" the kid at the wheel called shakily. No answer, but a stream of the most astonishingly creative and varied profanity I'd ever heard now spewed up out of the hatch.

The kid relaxed; this, apparently, was par for the course. Still, I was pretty sure that a hole in the boat wasn't, so I felt reassured when thick gouts of water began pouring from the bilge ports, arcing out like the stream from an open hydrant. That meant the bilge pump was sucking up water and sending it elsewhere, in this case back into the bay.

I wished it would send me elsewhere. Carl clambered out of the engine hatch, his hands black with grease. No more steam boiled up, but the bilge pump still ran, its hum a high harmony note atop the engine's determined chugging.

"Stuck some patch material in it, threw a load of epoxy on it," Carl grated out. "Pump'll take care of it 'til we get in."

"We're going back now, right?" I said, but his answering look said I must be crazy to think so.

"What? We're almost there." He waved out ahead of us. "See? Right around that point there, that's the inlet entrance."

We'd nearly reached the shore on the Canadian island of Campobello. Along it, small year-round houses and larger summer homes nestled among trees now droopy with heat stress.

"If he's there at all, he'll be easy to find," Carl went on, "and I mean to help you do it."

He looked over at Lizzie. "Don't forget, I was told there'd be a reward. On top o' the charter fee."

"Don't worry, Carl, you'll get what I promised. Just stick close to shore when you can, okay?"

She put her hand on my shoulder. "My friend gets nervous. I guess we can't all be seaworthy old sailors like you, right?"

The woman could sweet-talk the poison out of a snakebite, I realized. Carl glowered briefly, but then an unmistakable twinkle crept into his eye.

"Jeremy! Lay offa that throttle, boy, you're shakin' up these ladies' delicate sensibilities!"

Jeremy half turned from the wheel with a smile, settling his cap smartly over his curls and seemingly none the worse for wear after our recent excitement.

To my surprise, I felt none the worse either. The shark had gone and hadn't returned and besides, the boat had quit bouncing at high speed. The pump had gone off, too.

Which meant we'd stopped sinking, this having been my most serious concern. Then Carl started handing out the grape sodas, Oreos, and peanut-butter crackers he'd brought along.

"So, Carl, did you know Paul Coates?" Lizzie asked as she opened herself a soda.

He shrugged. "Sure. I mean, the way you do meet guys on the dock. Twice a day, goin' out, comin' in. He was no Einstein, I could tell that much right off the pop, but he seemed like a nice enough young fellow."

"So you don't think he'd have just taken off, left his wife and kids behind? Just . . . get away from everything?"

McFaul snorted. "On what, his good looks? Like I said, he

wasn't a big thinker, far as I could tell. Except for fishing, he knew how to do that, all right."

He bit into his cracker sandwich, chewed, swallowed. "Shame about what happened. Heard he'd just recently picked up what the kids nowadays call a side hustle."

Another shrug, chewing. "Might'a made him some extra cash on top o' his regular fishin'. Heck knows he needed it, that young family and all."

"Really?" said Ellie interestedly; Sally hadn't mentioned anything about other jobs. "What was the side hustle, do you know?"

Carl nodded, his mouth still full of cracker. Swig of soda, swallow, then: "Hard not to. Big white boat called the *Consuelo* comes in from Lubec, picks a guy up off the dock, that's kinda difficult to miss."

"So he was working for . . ." I glanced at Ellie and Lizzie.

"That shark scientist guy, Peter Waldron," Carl said. "He was Waldron's guide, like, showed him around these waters. Not every trip, you understand, but pretty often."

After a final gulp of soda: "All I know, Waldron might'a been th' last to see Coates alive, 'cept his wife."

Which was fascinating as hell, but we didn't have time to savor it; as we rounded the north end of Campobello Island, Ellie glanced back over the *Frinch*'s transom for a last look at Eastport and saw something else.

"He's back." The shark, she meant. "I'll bet he's been out there behind us all along," she added nervously.

"Ah, he'll shear off," said Carl. He'd taken the wheel again while the boys sat cross-legged atop the wheelhouse to finish their lunch. Laughing, one of them flung the remains of his crackers out over the transom, into our wake.

The black fin rose briefly and plunged again. "Whoa!" the boys cried in unison.

Lizzie came to stand beside me. "I don't understand how

Carl can be so sure where the body will be," she said troubledly.

Unless maybe he knew because that's where he'd put it, she meant, right after he'd made it dead. It was the dime-novel explanation, but only because it was so obvious.

And the reason why it was obvious is that people did it all the time in real life. Guy knows where the body is, or says he found it, the real-life cops are going to take a good, hard look at him.

At minimum. But there was another, better reason. "Carl's granddad was Amos McFaul," I said. "Back in Prohibition times, he brought whiskey across the bay in his boat on moonless nights."

We passed between Deer Island and the lighthouse, a tall, red-and-white candy-striped column with a big glassed-in box at the top.

Lizzie glanced at it, then turned back to me. "So?"

Carl changed course, aiming the *Frinch* toward the light station's rocky shoals. I swallowed hard; probably he knew what he was doing.

"So sometimes he needed a place to lay low on the way," I said, trying not to gauge how fast we were approaching those rocks. "Amos did, I mean."

Lizzie nodded slowly. "He knew the good hiding places? And now . . ."

I nodded. "First place Carl worked was on his granddad's boat. The old man passed on his insider lore, I guess, 'cause Carl knows these coastlines inside and out."

He was modest about his findings, too: Just in the past few years he'd found lost children, a pair of lost sea kayaks, and in one particularly touching instance a white poodle puppy who'd jumped into the water and begun swimming to Portugal, for no reason anyone was ever able to discern.

"Ah," Lizzie said. "I get it." But then she frowned. "Only it doesn't account for how he'd know where *this* body went."

"Girlie," Carl grated, suddenly right behind us, "you drop one o' them cute yellow rubber duckies anywhere in this bay and tell me where you dropped it, next morning I'll go out to where it drifted and get it for you."

He grinned around the end of the cigar, still unlit. "Tides, ladies. Currents and tides, watch 'em close, pay heed to the wind, you'll find what you're lookin' for."

From the toothiness of the grin, I got the feeling he'd been standing right behind us the whole time.

"Bait bucket, camera gear, bag with a cell phone in it, even your mother-in-law, assuming you want her. Bodies, even," he added with a pirate-like grin.

Ellie called to us again from where she still perched near the transom. "Uh, guys? I think our friend, here, wants a ride."

The *Frinch* made a sharp turn to starboard; I sighed with relief. In the wheelhouse, Carl bent to Jeffrey and spoke. The boat slowed, bringing us even closer to the underwater carnivore who'd been stubbornly keeping us company.

Suddenly a gray, gleaming head with two blank, glassy eyes and a mouthful of pointy choppers lunged out of the water, and I can tell you for a fact that it had even worse breath than you can imagine.

I reeled back, my mouth producing sounds that in some less terrifying world might've been words. Ellie and Lizzie stared while the shark started trying to make friends—that is, if by *make friends* you mean *chew, swallow, and digest.*

I scrambled back to the rail to peer out at the new set of rocks we were approaching. At the wheel, Carl steered carefully while Jeremy read numbers aloud to him from a depth finder.

". . . twenty . . . eighteen . . . fifteen . . ." I read over the boy's shoulder. But those numbers couldn't be right, could they?

A crunching sound came from below, and now an alarm began warbling; Carl cursed even more creatively than before, putting the engine in reverse and easing the wheel to port.

In response, our stern moved a few feet sideways; then he did it the other direction. Moments later we were free, having backed off of whatever we'd gone aground on.

"And that," Ellie said quietly from beside me, "was nice boat-handling."

I had to agree, but it didn't make me feel any better. The little voice in my head that I thought I'd silenced earlier now roared back, directing me to lean over the rail, and I'm not going to say more about that except to report that I will never, ever drink grape soda again.

Meanwhile, an expedition I'd thought would be easy had turned out to feature sharks, rocks, and a boat with a hole in it, and that was just what we'd encountered so far . . .

Thinking this, I straightened, feeling a whole lot better, suddenly. Delighted to still be alive was what it was, probably, combined with the absence of that grape soda.

The salt-smelling air felt cool and fresh after the oppressive heat on land. Near shore, a family of ducks in a row paddled determinedly; above them a pileated woodpecker rat-tatted in a tree whose lowering branches dabbled the water.

Even the water itself was so clear I could see through it down to where tiny, transparent creatures darted among the seagrasses. Still, I hadn't come out here for a nature expedition; I turned back toward the others.

"Ten feet," Jeremy said; a scraping sound punctuated this.

"Yeah, an' you can bite me," Carl growled defiantly at the depth finder.

A stream of invective followed; despite it—or possibly because of it, I don't know—he freed our keel yet again from whatever it had gotten stuck on. But ten minutes later we were still creeping tentatively among the rocks that lurked under the waves around Death's Head, trying to get to shore.

"Almost there!" Carl called from the wheelhouse. Both boys sat out on the bow watching for even more underwater hazards, ones Carl had pleasantly informed us could rip the bottom right out of the boat.

"He's been saying we're almost there for a long time," I grumbled. "I guess it must be why hardly anyone visits there, you'd need a good reason to go through all this rigamarole."

Such as that you were hiding a body here, for instance. Carl had said Coates's remains probably washed in here, but now that I'd thought about it, I didn't see how that could've happened.

For one thing, past the final cluster of rocky obstacles all I saw was beach: a long, seaweed-strewn strip bounded at either end by trees. Nowhere did I spot Carl's promised lagoon or any channel leading into one.

Amidst a sudden grinding sound from below, the *Frinch* came to an abrupt halt. The number and variety of curse words pouring from the wheelhouse increased by orders of magnitude.

"What happened?" Alarmed, I headed for the wheelhouse to find out, but Jeffrey stopped me.

"We're stuck bad. Aground in a gravel bed, prob'ly. You better let him alone right now, maybe."

The boy spoke as if imparting a word to the wise. From the wheelhouse, Carl spoke, too: "You ugly freaking son of a—"

Only he didn't say *freaking*, and now he was actually munching on the cigar, its sodden length visibly shortening as he grimly manipulated the wheel, the throttle, and the cigar, all at the same time.

The boat lurched forward and back: *crunch, crunch.* We were stuck with nothing to do but wait until Carl got us freed up.

If he did. "Or until the tide comes in," Ellie said, "and we can just float back out again."

Small comfort, but it was something, anyway. It would be several more hours before the water here rose enough to float us free. But probably we weren't hopelessly stranded.

When I told Lizzie this, though, she took the idea and ran with it, eyeing the rocks remaining between us and the beach. "I bet we could make it," she mused.

The rocks, I mean, that I would most definitely fall off if I were standing on one, and the way I would get to be standing on one was that I'd haul myself up out of the water onto it.

With a shark right behind me, maybe. "I don't think . . ." I began doubtfully.

"Let's go," Lizzie said.

Six

From the *Frinch*'s rail to the wet, slick-looking top of the nearest big rock was only about six feet.

Not six miles, which was what it looked like to me. Also: again no ladder, or anything I could use as a ladder.

"Oh, just jump," said Lizzie impatiently, "what's the worst that can happen?"

I turned, and I guess my face must've told her that she should clam up, or else the worst that could happen would happen to her in about two seconds.

Ellie stepped between us. "Okay, Lizzie, let's you and I go first. Then Lizzie and I will catch you, Jake."

"Who's going to push her?" Lizzie asked. But then, "Don't worry," she said, meaning it. "We'll getcha."

Then in a single smooth motion she hopped up onto the rail and leapt from it.

"Wow, that was difficult," she called from the rock where she'd landed on both feet, not even staggering.

That did it. "Oh, yeah?" I said. Nobody was going to have to push me. Resuscitate me, maybe, but—

"Jake," Ellie warned, hurrying toward me, and Jeffrey got up, too, maybe to stop me. But by that time I was up on the rail and jumping off, and the worst that could happen turned out to be me landing in the water, and have I mentioned that it was cold water? We're halfway to the North Pole, here, despite today's evidence to the contrary.

Luckily I could scrabble up onto the rock where Lizzie stood, and then Ellie landed there, too.

It was a nice, flat rock. "You're wet," Lizzie observed.

"You're annoying," I observed right back, and it's possible that I thought about giving her the tiniest friendly nudge, just to see how athletic she was when push came to shove.

Luckily for me, probably, I didn't get the chance. "Hey," said Ellie, pointing toward shore. "Look."

Behind us, Carl revved that big diesel engine again, and the *Frinch* stayed stuck again.

"What?" I said, trying to wring out my dungarees while I was wearing them. But all I did was make them cling more soggily and clammily to my legs.

"I don't see anything," I said, and then Lizzie pushed me off the rock. Suddenly I was back in cold water, again, and only the fact that she'd jumped in behind me stopped me from, as Sam would've said, murderizing her.

Ellie splashed ahead of us, wading shoreward. "Come on!" she called back.

And I didn't want to be left there hip-deep in what felt like an arctic current, so I followed, stepping on, over, and around a slippery obstacle course of more wet rocks.

Then suddenly I put a foot down and then couldn't pull it back up again. *Stuck.* Between two large boulders, it felt like; Ellie and Lizzie both reached shore while I still stood there on one foot, trying to yank the other one up from where it was wedged. I hoped I wouldn't still be trapped here the next time the tide came in; also I tried not to think about what might be down there right along *with* my foot, getting ready to chomp. I'd heard that most shark attacks happen in shallow water. Like the water I was in, for example; this may have energized my struggles, which Lizzie and Ellie seemed to find hilarious. And oh, wasn't I going to get them for it . . . Then my foot came free suddenly, leaving the shoe still down there jammed in between a couple of unmoving boulders and sending me all at once staggering backward until I sat down.

In the water. Again. *This is getting old*, I thought as I put my hand down to steady myself; whatever it landed on wiggled slimily out from under it and shot away unseen.

A shudder of revulsion went rocketing up my spine and I was up on that rock again without even knowing how I got there. I didn't scream only because my teeth were biting down on my lower lip hard enough to draw blood.

All right, now, let's not make a spectacle of ourselves, I thought, gathering what few shreds were left of my dignity. Then I sat down, pulled on my soggy shoe—it had ended up floating to the surface on its own, somehow—and made my way to where Lizzie and Ellie still waited.

"I'm so sorry I laughed," exclaimed Ellie, hurrying up to me. "Are you all right?"

"Fine. No thanks to you two," I replied, dripping. She was clearly not sorry. She was trying not to giggle.

"Here," said Lizzie, untying the sleeves of a blue hoodie from around her waist, "you can at least get your head dry with this."

I rubbed it over my head. "Thanks."

"You know it's the function of some of us to amuse the rest of us, though, right?" she asked. "It's like, a natural law."

"Yeah, yeah." My ex-husband used to say I was the type who could trip on a bare floor, and for once he was right.

"Not much danger of my breaking that one," I said evenly,

meeting her assessing gaze as I handed back the hoodie; suddenly I felt that to her this trip might be a test of something, even aside from the whole body-hunting aspect of it.

Right, it was a test of my patience, is what it was. *Assess this,* I thought irritably, and then Ellie turned and waved from farther up the beach where she'd gone on ahead.

"I've been looking and looking, but I still don't see any canal or anything like one," Ellie said when we'd joined her. She waved at the thick, jungle-ish undergrowth straggling from between the trees edging the beach.

"So where is this lagoon Carl talked about?" I said. "And what's that humming sound?"

Venturing nearer to the trees, I turned back to the other two, who were staring past me at something.

I followed their unhappy gaze to where a shaft of sunlight slanting down through the leaf canopy backlit a pulsating gold cloud. Like . . .

Bees. Or hornets. Some of them zipped back and forth quite alertly, darting nearer, then retreating.

Lizzie and Ellie were already backing away. "Fabulous," I muttered, hastily doing the same. "Just so glad to be here."

As the angry humming faded behind me, Ellie's voice rose in a shout. "Hey! You guys! Over here!"

Lizzie jogged and I slogged to what looked at first like a cave opening behind a screen of tall grasses. But when we pushed through, it turned out to be the entrance to a watery channel roofed by tangled greenery, leading back into the forest.

Vines and branches curtained the opening; it had been invisible from the water. "And how's a boat even supposed to get in there?" Ellie said puzzledly.

You could see how the channel itself happened; it was like an instant Maine geology lesson. A granite boulder the size of a city block had cracked open, eons ago, likely from being pushed down on by tons of ice, melting and freezing again.

Eventually, salt water flowed into the crevice, and voilà! (or viola! as Sam likes to say), instant channel—that is, if by *instant* you mean a few million years or so ago.

Anyway, Ellie figured out the channel access question right away. "Oh, I see, it's tidal. You can get into the channel when the tide's high. The water's starting to come back already."

She was right; all the low spots in the beach were filling as we watched, foamy ripples lapping higher each time a fresh wave slid up the sand.

"Comes in fast," Lizzie observed as the space between the forest and the salt water narrowed steadily.

"Yup," I agreed distractedly. Again because of how far north we are, we have diurnal tides here; that is, four of each per day. So they have to go in and out in a hurry.

Meanwhile I was wondering suddenly what time it had gotten to be and thinking about my family in Eastport; they would be wondering about me soon if I didn't call.

But not quite yet, and besides, if I called I might hear some reason why I ought to go home. Elderly parents, the new construction, the grandchildren . . . anything could be happening.

But so far this morning I'd been tossed around on the high seas—well, high for me, anyway—been stalked by a persistent shark, lost my lunch over the rail, and nearly broken my neck jumping off that damned fishing boat of McFaul's, not to mention being slimed by some creepy unknown water creature. After all that, if Coates's body was here, I meant to find it.

Still, a lingering twinge made me try the phone—luckily it had been in its waterproof case—and this worked out because the phone didn't have any bars on it—cell phone coverage can be spotty on the water—so I couldn't call.

Which meant I was able to stick the phone in my pocket guilt-free, eyeing the path that ran along the canal: narrow, weedy, patrolled no doubt by mosquitoes and maybe more hornet scouts. I hoped nothing larger was patrolling it.

"Grab your hoodie," I told Lizzie, handing it over, "you'll want it." Then I pushed in through the vines and grasses.

And it was like walking into a fairy tale. Bars of gold sunlight slanting down onto emerald-green moss, birdsong and the smell of pine. The silent trees seemed to blot out all outside sounds; a shimmering peace descended.

Then very quickly the silence became unnerving, as if I were inside an enormous glass bell jar. The channel water, as still as a mirror, promised dark surprises in its depths.

Suddenly I was scanning the water's unmoving black surface for a pale, soddenly staring face . . . "Hey, you guys?"

No reply. The trees stood silently as if waiting to start tiptoeing up behind me once my back was turned. Then crackling and rustling sounds came from among the trees, like somebody coming toward me but not on the path.

Correction: some*thing*. *Crunch, snap* . . . and from the sound of it, it was a *big* thing.

I stood frozen for approximately two milliseconds, thinking that whatever it was, it was probably hungry and thought I would be crunchy and good with ketchup.

Or without. When the milliseconds were over I was already racing away down the path, back toward the beach. *Feet, don't fail me now*, I thought; I could already see the thinning-out of the trees, and the water beyond them. *Run* . . .

"Jake!" It was Ellie, sprinting up behind me. "What're you doing? Come on, we found a shortcut!"

I spun around. Lizzie was there, too, disheveled and with a fresh red scratch across her cheek. "Blackberry brambles," she said, wincing as she touched it.

"Jake, we found . . ." Ellie was all excited.

I, on the other hand, was hot, tired, thirsty, and charged up with adrenaline from the scare I'd just had. If we had come upon Paul Coates's body right then, I'd probably have punched it in the nose just for the sake of hitting something.

But: "Just show me," I said evenly, keeping a smile on my face. Because we were out here now, dammit, and we were going to find that corpse if it was here to be found.

Lizzie passed me a flask I hadn't known she had. "Drink," she told me, so I did, while Ellie handed us each a still-wrapped wet wipe that she'd had stuffed in her pants pocket. I gave the canteen back to Lizzie and dragged the cool tissue across my face.

"Thank you," I said, meaning it. The wet wipe stung, but in a good way. Then I noticed that they were already moving away toward the canal again.

"This trip," I muttered to myself as I hurried to catch up, "is not turning out as advertised."

I stomped along grumpily. "Sharks. Rocks. Slimy things that wiggle under your hand when you're just trying to . . ."

Never mind the jumping off boats and the ralphing over the side, the sitting down hard in cold salt water and the infernal itchiness of that same salt water drying on my sunburned skin.

Because, yes, I'd used the sunscreen and worn a brimmed cap. But I don't care how much of that glop you slap on or how well it works when you're on shore; on a sunny day out on the water you'll still fry like an egg.

Pushing aside low-hanging branches, tripping over roots, and slapping at buzzing insects, I tramped along behind Lizzie and Ellie until sunlight gleamed through a break in the trees.

And there it was, in the center of a small clearing just like McFaul had said: a lagoon, pale green around the edges and midnight-blue at the middle, where it looked deep.

Evergreen trees and wild rhododendron ringed the clearing. In the shadows at the far edge, a loon paddled, barely visible; beach roses perfumed the quiet air.

And a hat floated. Just sat there floating. A red hat.

"Who's wading in?" I asked, wondering if there might be a head under the hat. And a body under that, et cetera.

Ellie dragged over a long branch. "Maybe we can just walk partway out and snag it," she said, but then her face fell. "Or maybe not."

The branch probably looked long enough when she grabbed it, but now that she saw the lagoon again, she realized that to get out to that hat you'd need a branch big enough to float on, plus swim fins.

And speaking of swimming... "Oh, no," I said, backing away.

Over the previous winter I'd gone regularly to the pool in Machias, the college town to Eastport's south. There I'd taken lessons while my little grandson, Ephraim, learned to put his face under the water without panic and to paddle a few strokes.

And Ellie, who was not a particularly strong swimmer herself, knew it. "Come on, Jake, do you want what we've done just getting here to go to waste? And maybe have to come back?"

All she and Lizzie had suffered on the trip was possibly a stomachache from laughing so hard at my pratfalls, I thought. On the other hand, there was that canteen and the wet wipe.

"Oh, all right," I said crossly, mostly because the last thing I wanted to do was come back. Except for a few old filters from long-ago-smoked cigarettes here and there, this place was lovely, but there was still something very creepy about it.

Lizzie looked surprised when I stripped off everything but my underwear. But clothes aren't warm when you're in the water, only heavy; shoes, too. Then before either of them could speak and before I could have second thoughts, I plunged in.

We'll just skip the part about how, when I hit the cold water, I thought my heart would stop beating, just freeze up and quit. Also the part about how deep the lagoon turned out to be (very) and how far from shore that hat floated (way too far).

I did finally reach it, though; the sidestroke I'd learned in the pool over the winter hadn't deserted me. Treading water, I grabbed the hat, hoping not to see Coates's hair floating up beneath it.

And I got my wish, all right, just not the way I expected, because it wasn't Paul Coates in that lagoon, after all.

It was somebody else entirely.

The lagoon emptied into a short, deep channel that led out to a second beach, several hundred yards along the shoreline on the opposite side of the island. Lizzie and Ellie had simply walked around the island's edge, and found it.

"Because the path gave me the willies," Ellie told me when we were on our way back to the *Frinch* and her crew.

"Like it had a sign on it? THIS WAY TO THE CORPSE?" I asked grouchily.

Also shiveringly. And even more itchily than before; the lagoon water was as salty as the bay.

"No," said Ellie, sounding troubled. We'd left whoever it was in the water; the hair under the hat had been curly blond.

Not Coates's, and if it wasn't his body, I wasn't grabbing it; I mean, who knew if the head was even attached to anything?

Maybe it was just floating there by itself. Besides, Lizzie was our law officer, and she hadn't mentioned moving it.

"No," Ellie said, "it was more like . . . oh, never mind. Just my imagination, probably."

But the shortcut back to the beach where we'd first come ashore was not bad at all: plenty of gnarled tree roots to trip over, branches to slap me, and buzzing bees. Or hornets.

When we got there, the tide had crept in, the water now nearly reaching the pale green beach grasses whickering in the breeze. The *Frinch* was floating again, too, buoyed by the rising water out of the tight place it had been stuck in.

Beside it, though, another, larger vessel floated: a long, white Canadian Coast Guard boat, we could tell from its markings and flag. Seeing it, Lizzie ducked back into the trees, dragging me with her; Ellie came along on her own, looking alarmed.

"What's wrong?" I began. "Why . . . ?" But then I knew: Canada. You don't think of it as a foreign country when you live right next door, going back and forth often for errands and shopping.

But we weren't supposed to be here now. We hadn't passed through a border checkpoint or had our passports run through a computer; in fact, we could be arrested.

Nothing moved on the *Frinch*; through the grasses we crouched behind, the Canadian boat showed no activity, either. Meanwhile the tide went on rising, foamy wavelets fluttering higher and higher toward us.

"They're sure taking their time," I groused. Soon it would be too deep to wade through, to get back to the *Frinch*.

"They're probably on their radio, asking their bosses what to do about Carl," said Lizzie. "Boat's practically on shore, he can't very well say he got there by accident."

"But the Canadians don't know *we* came ashore," Ellie said, her eyes still on our only way off this island. "Or they'd be here looking for us. The only thing I can think of is it's some kind of a routine check, maybe because he is so close to shore. For smuggling or whatever."

"Maybe." Lizzie got to her feet. "I don't know. We'll just have to wait and see what happens."

Which didn't thrill me; all day long I'd been going around just seeing what happened, and it had not been working out well at all. In fact, right then I felt like crawling into my bed and seeing what didn't happen, for a change.

"So listen," I said after we'd waited a little while but seen no activity on the *Frinch* or the Coast Guard boat. "Have either one of you heard anything about the solar flare we're supposed to be getting? Tomorrow, I think."

It didn't worry me for myself, but Wade could be out on the

water when it happened, and piloting a cargo ship into our bay without any radio communications would be dicey.

Lizzie looked curious but Ellie nodded. "Yes, and that reminds me, we'd better figure out something so people can still use credit cards in the Moose."

"Remind me to get out a fresh spiral notebook to write the card information in," I agreed. That way we could run the cards later, once the internet came back on. Of course, some people wouldn't want their card info written down, but we'd deal with that if we had to.

I said as much to Ellie, who nodded. "If the card reader goes off at all," she said, not seeming to think any of it was a big deal, which it wouldn't be as long as I wrote all the numbers down correctly (don't ask how I know this). Anyway:

"So if it wasn't Coates in the lagoon back there, who was it?" Lizzie wondered aloud.

"Don't know. Didn't recognize him," I said.

I didn't know how long he'd been dead in the water, either, but it was a while and the weather had been very hot. Maybe somebody who knew him would recognize the hat.

"That Canadian Coast Guard boat's going to make reporting it a little dicey," she said thoughtfully.

I angled my head at the vessel. "Why don't we just go report it to them?"

Lizzie turned to me, her expression suggesting that people should be kind and patient with me.

"Jake, the immigration authorities take this stuff seriously. And I hate to say it, but if we tell them we found a dead body, how are they supposed to know we didn't— "

"Right, we killed him and then hung out here for a week, waiting for him to what, liquefy? Or we came back to visit him?"

She rolled her eyes, ready to retort, but Ellie put up a silencing hand. "Something's happening."

Three familiar figures had appeared on the *Frinch*'s deck:

Carl and his boys. While that was happening, the Canadian Coast Guard boat's engines rumbled and the vessel eased away toward open water.

"You missed seeing the Canadians going back to their own boat. Carl must not have told them about us," Ellie said.

"Fine," said Lizzie, "but what *did* he say? Because before I call the body in . . ."

Well, she pretty much had to, didn't she? After all, she was a cop, sworn to uphold the law.

". . . we need to get our stories straight," she finished.

By now, the Canadians were far enough away for us to try getting back aboard the *Frinch.* Hoping none of them were looking back with binoculars, we made our way over what little remained of the beach and waded in.

By now the water was quickly up to my waist, and those rocks were as slippery as ever, just less visible. "Oh, for Pete's sake," I said, wanting to say more.

Much more; worse, too, as what felt like a big rotted log and a boulder the size of Cleveland suddenly trapped my foot. The log squished spongily between my hands when I reached down under the water to grab it.

Then, as I lifted it from the water it broke gruesomely to let a million white, wriggling thingies spill out.

"Gah," I said quietly; the way this day was going I didn't want to wear out my scream machinery too early. But once I'd flung away the insect-larvae bomb I finally reached the *Frinch*, and Carl and Jeremy came shinnying down a knotted rope to me.

Then without stopping to explain, they tied the rope around me, looping it beneath my butt to form a sort of seat.

"What," I spluttered, "are you—oh!"

A motor whined, the rope tightened, and I began rising into the air, and have I mentioned how much I dislike carnival rides?

At the top, the seat I was tied into swung hard out over the water; my gut flip-flopped warningly. Next, Jeffrey grabbed me, hauled me in, and swiftly undid the rope, whereupon I leaned on the rail so I could pretend my legs weren't shaking.

Then Ellie and Lizzie scrambled up, both agile as monkeys, of course. Lizzie, I supposed, had learned it in cop school, but Ellie was just wired that way; I once saw her rescue a cat stuck so high in a tree, even the fire department wouldn't go up after it.

Finally, Carl and Jeremy climbed aboard and in moments the *Frinch* motored out of that cove like a diesel-powered bat out of hell.

"Carl," Lizzie demanded once we were under way, "why'd you put us ashore where you did when you could've let us off closer to the lagoon?"

Carl had his hand on the throttle, his eyes on the horizon, and a fresh cigar stuck in his mouth.

"See that cutter?" he said around the cigar. The Canadians, he meant, now a white dot on the horizon.

He pushed the throttle; the wind had shifted and so had the currents. Now we were battling back to Eastport through three-foot swells, so Carl was paying attention.

"You know what happens to me, I get hit for assisting in a border violation? Lose my captain's license, for one thing."

"That's not the worst of it," said Lizzie. She laid the news about the body on him. "And we're going to have to stay on the up-and-up about it," she concluded.

Carl shook his grizzled head. "You're reporting it, are you? The heck you want to get involved in that for? Somebody'll come along and find 'im, sooner or later."

"Carl," Lizzie said. "His family's probably worrying about him right now. Don't you think they deserve—?"

"Yeah, yeah," Carl grated out, eyes still fixed on the water ahead. "Do what you want. You will anyway."

He shifted the cigar from one corner of his mouth to the other. "After you do, they'll have me an' the *Frinch* under a microscope, though, wantin' to know what the hell we was doin' helpin' you out on this."

His eyes narrowed, squinting ahead. Suddenly our prow bucked upward and a swimming pool's worth of seawater slammed the windshield. Swearing inventively, Carl wrestled the wheel grimly; meanwhile I prayed to whichever gods help nitwits and numbskulls, and especially ones on boats.

The *Frinch*'s prow slammed down with a thud and another tremendous splash, but we didn't smash to bits, and I got my lip out from between my teeth eventually, tasting blood.

And then all was calm, suddenly. We'd made our way into the Old Sow whirlpool, just off Deer Island on the US side of the border, and at this time of day the water was as smooth as glass. Only an insistent nudging from below said how turbulent it was down there in the depths: like a hurricane, only wetter.

"Wouldn't 'a took the *Frinch* in that channel, anyhow," Carl said unhappily around the cigar, "an' I never said I would. I'm not that big a fool."

I didn't point out that nobody had asked him about the channel, only the other beach; don't antagonize your ride is a matter of common sense, I feel. The deck was tranquil suddenly, too, Lizzie scenery-gazing while Jeffrey and Jeremy explained to Ellie the winch they'd used to haul me up onto the boat.

Then suddenly: "Look!" Jeffrey shouted. "A shark! Man, he's a big one!"

"He's right down there!" exclaimed Jeremy, leaning out over the rail in a way I thought unwise, but then we all did it.

"Holy criminy," Ellie breathed from beside me. The *Frinch* moved right along, thirty knots, maybe; the shark kept up easily.

"That," said Lizzie, "is an impressive fish."

It came in right alongside us, massive and alien and way too up-close. "Yeah," I gulped. "Impressive."

But not in a nice way: dead-looking black eyes, a scarily large body, a tail you wouldn't want to get smacked by and a bladelike top fin that looked like it could slice you in half.

The eye closest to me rolled up, showing a sightless white membrane more appalling even than the choppers I glimpsed, when the shark suddenly rolled away and submerged. Then its dark shape dissolved in the deepening water and was gone.

"Wow," I managed faintly, just before I ran to the stern and lost what little was left of my lunch over the transom. Only this time it wasn't from seasickness; it was pure fright.

Lizzie came up behind me as I leaned, gasping. "Shark got to you, huh?"

"No shit, Sherlock," I managed, and then Jeremy hopped down off the wheelhouse roof, his boots slamming the deck.

"D'you guys know that the word *shark* makes people's blood pressure rise the most of anything you can say? They did a bunch of psychology experiments and—"

"Oh, can it, Jeremy," Jeffrey cut in dismissively. "You only know what you read in books."

"Yeah, maybe you should try reading one yourself," Jeremy retorted, "so you might at least graduate from high school."

That sent Jeffrey scrambling after Jeremy, who laughingly eluded his brother by scampering around barrels and gear and up onto the *Frinch*'s foredeck.

Suddenly Carl's voice erupted. "Hey! You two lookin' to go overboard?"

The boys side-eyed each other soberly and hopped back down, still nudging and shoving but grinning now, too, united against parental edicts. Which was probably the whole idea; my opinion of Carl went up a notch.

"So, here's how we're going to handle this," said Lizzie.

The body, she meant; any fun there'd been in the day had vanished with the finding of it, and Carl's obvious unease over his potential legal situation didn't help.

But we couldn't very well just not report the body in the lagoon. For one thing, when it eventually did get found—the cigarette butts back there said that Carl was right, it would be, sooner or later—the Canadian crew would remember him from today, and that would be worse.

The *Frinch* plowed steadily on toward Eastport, past Deer Island and the floating red channel marker, around a line of submerged lobster traps, each marked by a bobbing red-white-and-blue buoy, and avoiding a sizable hunk of a wooden dock that had broken off and floated from somewhere, with seagulls perched on it.

As we approached the breakwater, fishermen were casting mackerel jigs with multiple hooks that glittered as they flew. The boys tossed the *Frinch*'s bumpers over the side and prepared to land. Then Lizzie spoke.

"As soon as I'm ashore, I'll call the Canadian cops and let them know the situation. I know some people over there from when I worked up north. They might be able to help us."

Help us stay out of the clutches of the border enforcement people, she meant, which I thought was a fine idea; around here, lots of things get quietly taken care of at the local level, no official reports required.

Carl was unimpressed, though, and he let us know this by uttering swear words until Lizzie's raised hand silenced him.

"Look, I'm a cop, and they know me in Augusta, too. If you get in trouble over any of this, I'll get you out of it," she promised.

"Hah," said Carl, but there wasn't much he could do about it, and anyway he was busy getting us into the boat basin.

Not until we were all off the boat did Ellie sidle up to Lizzie and ask, "How will you get him out of trouble?"

Lizzie started to reply but an excited yell from up on the breakwater interrupted. People had put down their fishing poles and raised their binoculars, if they had them.

I looked where they were pointing, down into the boat basin where the waves glittered like mirrors through a slanting forest of masts and rigging. And among the mirrors . . .

Black. Bladelike. Cruising between the fish pier and the tall, concrete mooring block at the boat basin's entrance.

"How will I keep him out of trouble?" Frowning at the fin knifing through the waves, Lizzie repeated Ellie's question.

Personally, I thought we were all in trouble right now, as the fin zigzagged nearer.

"I have no idea," Lizzie admitted.

Too bad, although personally just now I wasn't too worried about Carl McFaul's legal troubles, if any.

"Shark!" yelled somebody up on the breakwater.

Yeah. Shark. I was worried about that.

Seven

The dock had never looked so narrow as it did with a shark swimming beneath it.

"One foot in front of the other," Ellie said from behind me as we made our way up the metal gangway.

He'd submerged, but that didn't mean he wasn't lurking.

"I'm lucky I still have feet," I grumbled. "That thing wanted them for a snack."

We stepped out onto the breakwater, across from the Coast Guard station with its red tiled roof, white siding, and large, waving American flag. The smell of fresh, hot onion rings wafted tantalizingly from a nearby orange hut: Rosie's Hot Dog Stand.

"No," said Ellie, steering me by the elbow. "You need to eat some real food. But first"—she looked wincingly sideways at me—"you need to wash your face."

What I needed, actually, was a working cannon, a couple of small antiaircraft guns, and some rocket launchers with rockets in them. And that was just for the shark.

Which, by the way, after all that sun, fresh salt air, and strenuous exercise I could've devoured whole; suddenly I was starving. A guy leaving Rosie's with a tray-load of chili dogs nearly bumped into me and it was all I could do not to trip him and take those chili dogs away from him.

But first things first. "Ellie. We said that we'd look into things for Sally Coates. And we have. We've looked, and we found someone else's dead body plus a large, toothy fish who's clearly ready to make trouble."

For me. With its teeth. I took a breath. "On top of which, we are now in trouble, ourselves, with the Canadian immigration authorities. They just don't know it yet, but they will."

Once Lizzie called them, the whole thing would come out. It would be up to the Canadians whether to treat us as trespassers.

"This was supposed to be a favor," I said. "It's already way more than that."

There'd been a bad moment when the guy in the lagoon rolled over and fixed me in his white, sightless gaze, so horridly like the shark's.

"I'm out, Ellie, I mean it. Tell Sally we're sorry but—"

"I wish you wouldn't." Lizzie's voice came from behind us. She'd caught up, and now she stood there with her feet planted apart, her hands on her hips.

"People talk to you," she said. "I've seen that already. And you know more about Eastport than I do right now. I thought you were lightweights but now . . ."

She looked at both of us. "I would appreciate your help."

The big, pointy teeth in that monster's huge jaws were going to haunt me in my dreams. Also, I really wasn't fond of finding bodies in lagoons, or anywhere else.

"Please," said Lizzie. Ellie was looking at me, too.

"Sally Coates is pretty well-liked here, I've gathered, and if I could help her it would go a long way towards other people in Eastport thinking I'm okay, too," Lizzie went on.

As, she meant, their new chief of police.

"Jake, maybe just think about it. Maybe decide what to do when you're not feeling so frazzled," said Ellie.

Frazzled didn't even begin to cover how I felt. Out on the breakwater, the mackerel-fishing had resumed under a sky so blue that you felt you were seeing right up into outer space.

Ellie was waiting. "Okay," I gave in finally. "I'll think about it. Not promising anything."

I meant it, too. That big fish was imprinted on the backs of my eyelids, which I felt sure he also would happily gobble down, and also I didn't like not knowing what killed the guy in the lagoon.

Or who. But for now Lizzie and Ellie seemed satisfied, and after that Lizzie gave me a lift back up to my house while Ellie returned to the Moose so Mika could leave.

"Want to stay for lunch?" I invited when she'd pulled the squad car to the curb. "It's jitterbugs."

Her tousled black head tipped inquisitively; maybe up there in northern Maine where she'd worked until recently, they called them something else.

"Spam, chopped sweet pickles, shredded carrots, and mayo," I explained, "on white bread with the crusts cut off."

She made an *ew* face; I understood. But: "Jitterbugs sound awful but they're delicious and they've even got vegetables in them," I said, "so how can you go wrong?"

She cracked a tired smile. "Thanks. Another time. I've got that phone call to make, and then a lunch date."

She checked her watch. "And oh, god, I'm so late."

I grabbed my bag and got out of the squad car. "With Dylan Hudson? Lizzie, did he follow you here?"

It was just a feeling I had, but her face said I'd guessed correctly. She eyed me levelly through the open driver's-side window.

"Yes to both questions. He's off the state cops, hasn't started anything else, yet."

Anything but pursuing me, her expression said. "And to your follow-up, no, I don't have any idea what I'm going to do about him."

She looked up at me. "Is that enough or d'you want a blow-by-blow of the whole relationship right out here on the street?"

Pain darkened her eyes; I'd been right about her feelings for Hudson and now I was sorry I'd quizzed her.

"No, thanks," I said. "Not right now. Maybe sometime if you feel like it, though. You know me, I'm all ears."

Her look softened. "Yeah. I've heard that about you. You did good out there today, by the way. See you around."

She put the squad car in gear and drove off, and I went on up the porch steps and into the house, where I thought it might at least be more peaceful than racketing around the bay evading carnivores and discovering dead folks.

Ha.

Inside the big old house on Key Street, I found my dad and two of his great-grandchildren playing an uproarious game of catch-me-if-you-can in the dining room among the chairs and table legs.

Toddler Doreen with her reddish-black curls and dark eyes wove in and out, giggling hysterically, while Ephraim, dressed in shorts and a Peppa Pig T-shirt, ducked and dodged my father's lunging grasp just quickly enough to evade it—until he didn't, to shouts of laughter.

Bella was in the kitchen with the radio blaring baseball, overseeing a kettle of bubbling raspberry jam, and she wanted me to stir it for exactly one more minute while she fetched a broom and a stepladder and got the parrot down off the chandelier in the parlor.

"Beano! Beano!" the parrot yelled, while Bella climbed up onto the stepladder, crooning. "Here, birdie, come birdie-birdie," she coaxed in her cracked, squeaking-screen-door voice.

Sam was at work, the dog was in the yard chasing one of the cats while the other cat yowled encouragement—they hated each other, those cats—and Wade was in his workshop upstairs doing something that sounded violently metal-on-metal with a power grinder.

Finally, once I'd finished stirring hot jam, I located and devoured some leftover potato salad, a cheese sandwich with a bite out of it, and a large chicken leg whose freshness date had probably expired but I was too hungry to care, I went out to the side yard where the new-addition construction was ongoing.

That's where I thought it would be more peaceful, and that's where I saw that sometime between early this morning and now, the new structure had collapsed; well, part of it had. One whole wall, previously upright and attached to the other three, now lay flat.

The building contractor, Buddy Holloway, put both hands up in a warding-off gesture when he saw me.

"Now, Jake, calm down," said the big, bald man in the blue coveralls and dusty boots.

I just love being told to calm down. "Buddy, the idea is to put the addition up, not—"

I gestured at the wall, which was most certainly not *up*, nor was it anything like *up*. "What the hell happened here?"

For as long as the addition remained unfinished, we were going to have enough people and animals in my house to fill and staff a medium-sized zoo, which was what the place resembled.

"Jake, Bobby Ingalls came by, and—"

Bobby was Eastport's building inspector. "Whatever it was,

it shouldn't have been a problem," I said. "He saw and cleared the plans and we've got the permits, so—"

"I know, I know. But he had a state guy from Augusta with him, going around to all the new construction in the county. And you know how Bobby agreed with me that the woodstove vents were up to code?"

"Yeah," I said cautiously. Bobby Ingalls was no slouch. He read building codes at the breakfast table and structural engineering textbooks in bed at night.

"State guy scampered up a ladder, tape measure in his hand, measured the vent clearances." Buddy sighed. "I didn't," he added, possibly noting my expression, "cut the holes myself."

Which was neither here nor there; they'd been cut and they couldn't be un-cut. Now they needed to be re-cut, and for that of course we would need new lumber.

"But why take down the whole—"

"Because," Buddy interrupted, "the way the holes are, they pierce a couple of supporting uprights. I told you I didn't cut 'em, right?"

So there was the real trouble: holes in the support beams that hold up the roof would be counterproductive, structural-strength-wise. There was no arguing with this.

"Fine," I said tiredly. "How soon and how much?"

I'd hoped we'd be finished by now, and under budget, too, but the answer Buddy gave me blew both those ideas not just out of the water, but into the stratosphere.

"I won't," he added once he'd given me the bad news, "be charging you for this here, of course." He waved at the partly torn-down structure, his hound-dog face sagging apologetically; he really did feel bad about this.

"Okay, Buddy," I said, relenting. "But this time do all the measuring and cutting yourself, okay?"

He was a lovely guy, Buddy, but he tended to hire screwups

on account of he wanted to give them a chance. Now his energetic nodding made his jowls bounce.

"I sure will. We'll git 'er done, don't worry about that."

I wasn't worried about that. I was worried about when. If we didn't make more space in that house soon, some of us would have to be freeze-dried and reconstituted later, when we did have room.

By now the cats in the yard had teamed up despite their earlier enmity and were chasing the dog in ways he'd apparently never dreamed possible; his outraged barks seemed to say that this cats-chasing-dog thing was not just unfair but also unnatural.

"Wait 'til you hear about 'man bites dog,' " I told him on my way back inside, where I found Bella at the stove again with the parrot on her shoulder, peering into the kettle.

"Beano!" said the bird, whose name was Dirty on account of what he usually said; *beano* was the only utterance of his that I can even repeat.

"I don't suppose Buddy was out there telling you he's ahead of schedule," Bella said mildly.

For her housework today—I'd have made her retire but she refused, determined to remain useful—she was wearing a ratty T-shirt and blue jeans so tattered that they were practically air-conditioned, a purple hairnet over frizzy, henna-red hair, and sneakers so ragged there was hardly any point in tying the laces.

"No," I said, "but he'll fix it."

Bella gave a short, communicative sniff that encapsulated precisely what I thought of the whole thing, too.

"You look," she said as she crossed to the counter with a tray of freshly filled pint jars the color of rubies, "like death warmed over."

Which naturally gave me an idea for the Moose: a chocolate

cupcake, still warm from the oven, drizzled with our specialty homemade chocolate sauce and with a scoop of chocolate ice cream melting against it. Death Warmed Over; Ellie would love it.

But it could come later. "I've been out on a boat," I said tiredly. "Got seasick. Fell in. Found a dead guy. Chased by a shark. And I'm probably in trouble with Canada's border guards."

Bella nodded judiciously. After living with me for years, she was hard to shock. But the more I thought about it, the more I thought that once the Canadians knew we'd thumbed our noses at their rules, prosecution would follow as night follows day.

And that made me rethink what I'd told Ellie about maybe giving up. "Bella, I expect I'll need to get out of the house later on tonight. I think Ellie's going out in her boat."

Bella used tongs to pick up the hot, lidded jelly jars and place them upside down on an old linen towel she'd spread on the counter.

"Thought you'd quit," she said with her back turned, and how had she known that?

She answered my thought. "Face like a thunderstorm, hands clenched tight, eyes like a couple of squinched-up raisins . . . you look like that when you've quit something. You hate quitting."

Bella and I had been friends for decades, and while she at times still seemed inscrutable to me, the reverse wasn't true.

"Yeah, well, I've changed my mind," I said.

I had to, because once that whole shark thing quit occupying my brain, I knew Ellie *wasn't* quitting. With me or without me, she'd try to help Sally Coates the same way she'd helped me out of a long list of difficulties over the years.

Besides, along with the idea for the new chocolate dessert,

another thought had popped up in my brain: How *had* Carl McFaul known about the lagoon, anyway?

He'd said he wouldn't take the *Frinch* up that canal; after seeing the dark, granite-sided groove in the earth for myself, I understood. So he'd gone on foot; his description of the place had been too right-on for anything else.

He'd been there, and that meant he'd had a reason to go. "I'll help," Bella said quietly.

"Thanks." Ordinarily, everyone in this house went out like a light at night, but with little Ephraim's sleepwalking habit still worrisome, nowadays if a pin dropped Sam or Mika got up to check on it.

"But I'm coming along," Bella added matter-of-factly.

I looked up from rooting around in the refrigerator some more. "No, you are not."

She was game for almost anything, but one of her hips needed replacement, a procedure she said she would undergo when ice cubes started pouring up out of hell.

"I'm coming," she repeated. "Or when you get back, we'll all be up waiting for you."

No way I'd get out of the house without her help: quieting the dog, the cats, and the parrot, shooing people back upstairs if they came down, and so on. But I didn't want to tell them about my plan, which was scary, dangerous, and most likely very unwise.

Also, it might work. "I mean it," said Bella, turning to me with her ropy arms folded implacably. "I'm coming, or you're not going."

When Bella put her long, flat foot down it might as well have been nailed to the floor. "Oh, all right." I gave in, and went to call Ellie right away to tell her my idea.

And just as I'd expected, she was all over it.

* * *

"It has to be now because we don't want anyone seeing us leaving," I told Bella for the tenth time that night as we made our way down the metal gangway to the boat basin.

It was nearly midnight, warm and windless with a few wisps of fog turning the house lights on Campobello to blurred sparks. Around us in the dark, chains clanked, docks creaked, and boats loomed, each dark wheelhouse looking as if a ghostly fisherman might be haunting it.

Ellie's boat, *Sea Wolf*, was tied to one of the finger piers; stepping carefully through the shadows under the dock lights, Bella and I followed Ellie down the floating dock to where the 22-foot Bayliner waited, bobbing on the black water.

"Hop aboard," she said, and went to do something with the lines holding the boat to the pier. Bella and I clambered over the rail and onto the clean, white deck, Bella swatting my hand away when I tried to help her.

"What do you mean, so no one can see us? Everyone in town can see us," Bella hissed, pulling on one of the life jackets from the boat's small cabin and handing one to me.

"Everyone in town," I retorted, "is sound asleep." Or I hoped so. "Anyway, you're the one who wanted to come."

She had a point, though; there was no reason for anyone to be looking down into the boat basin at this hour, but that didn't mean they weren't. This was just the best we could do.

Ellie returned, hopped aboard and opened the rear hatch to snap on the battery, then strode to the helm and started the engine with a turn of the key.

"On top of which that old engine of Ellie's sounds like a freight train," Bella began, then stopped because it didn't; if anything it was like a cat purring.

Or as if it was a brand-new, 180-horse Tohatsu outboard that Ellie had bought and had installed without saying a word about it. "Ellie! You didn't tell me you'd gotten a new—"

But just then Ellie threw the engine into reverse and we backed almost soundlessly out of the slip. Flipping on the radio, the running lights, and the depth finder with one hand, she steered the Bayliner out of the boat basin with the other.

Dark, seaweed-shrouded boulders went by on our right, then parked fishing boats on our left. Even in the dark, I knew she wouldn't hit any of them; Ellie could've piloted us out of the boat basin while standing on her head. I was just being a giant baby about it tonight, or my nervous system was.

But this time my nervous system could go suck an egg, I'd decided, because Carl McFaul must've had some reason to put us ashore where he had.

"He wanted us to find the lagoon," I told Bella. At our house there was barely any privacy anymore, so I hadn't had the chance to explain it to her until now. "And maybe the body, too. I'm not sure about that."

Bella listened intently, her frizzy red hair tied into a dark kerchief and her big, grape-green eyes alive with interest. In a black sweatshirt, black jeans, and a pair of black running shoes she'd filched off the shoe-rack in the hall, she looked like an aging punk rocker.

When we got out past the buoys floating half-visible in the darkness a hundred yards from the breakwater, Ellie hit the throttle.

"Ulk!" I uttered, and sat down abruptly. Behind me, Bella stood unperturbed, smiling and gazing out at the dark bay.

Then for a while it was almost pleasant; calm water, smooth ride, and of course there was not a large, black fin cruising in our wake.

I hoped. "So," I said, wanting badly to distract myself from that idea, "I think maybe our pal, Carl, didn't want us any-where near that canal."

"Then why'd he take us to the lagoon at all?" Ellie asked reasonably. "He was the one who said that's where Coates's body might've washed up."

"Because," Bella spoke mildly, "maybe a body is what he did want you to find."

In the light from the boat's instrument console, her green eyes shone. "Maybe he thought once you found that, you'd get so excited that you wouldn't look for anything more."

Or we'd get so tied up in red tape that we couldn't; he must've known he was dropping us on Canadian soil just as well as Ellie and I had. Wondering about this, I drank some hot coffee that Ellie had brought.

Then Ellie doused our running lights; darkness descended. "No sense advertising," she said as we approached Campobello.

By now I was extra-grateful for that new engine; the old one was so noisy, we'd have brought folks to their windows. There was even an elderly but still serviceable 5-horsepower Evinrude clamped to the transom next to the Tohatsu; a backup so if the Tohatsu quit, we could at least limp back to shore.

Bella gazed raptly at the dark shoreline gliding by, its gloom punctuated by dock lights or the glow of a cottage window. Soon we rounded the point and the lighthouse came into view.

"Oh," Bella sighed. The light's massive, slowly rotating beam was like a sword's blade slicing into the night.

"This what you wanted?" I asked quietly, and she nodded, drinking it all in: the dark sky alive with stars, the rank smell of seaweed in cold salt water, the hollow slopping of waves against our hull. Meanwhile the quiet rumble of the new engine went on reassuringly.

But then it stopped. "Darn," Ellie said mildly, turning the ignition key.

The engine didn't start, and have I mentioned that a boat without power is completely unsteerable? They just go where the tide and the currents carry them, which in our case was toward yet more rocks, their jagged tops like dark teeth.

Which reminded me: that shark. Nervously I scanned the waves. No black fin, no doll-like eye the size of a tennis ball, no big sharp choppers set in a hungry grimace appeared.

So we had that going for us, anyway, unless of course he was lurking under our boat. Wishing sincerely that this awful idea had never occurred to me, I joined Ellie at the helm.

"Trouble?" I asked quietly. She was turning the key again. This time the engine turned over but didn't catch.

"Yes, and I don't want to kill the battery trying to start it. Let's drop anchor and sit here a while, maybe it's flooded."

Whereupon she hopped out of the captain's chair, scampered out onto the foredeck in the darkness, and pulled off the bungee cords that lashed the anchor in place. When she dropped it overboard, the heavy chain rattled speedily out of its locker, following the anchor down.

After it splashed, we stopped drifting and floated in silence long enough for the surplus gasoline in the engine to disperse; when she turned the key again, the familiar rumble made us all feel a lot better.

But only briefly. Then another boat, bright white and very brightly lit, appeared out of the darkness, and that made us feel worse; well, except for Bella, still entranced by a night out on the water.

The boat approached slowly. We didn't want company, but we didn't want to get accidentally rammed, either, so Ellie snapped our running lights back on. In response, the other boat's own massive light show brightened further, and it pulled alongside.

"Ahoy!" came a cheerful voice from its helm, and soon a face appeared at the rail. It was Peter Waldron, the shark guy, on the brilliantly illuminated deck of his large, white vessel, *Consuelo*, looking like a cabin cruiser on steroids.

"You ladies all right?" He didn't seem surprised at our being on the water so late.

"We're fine," Ellie called back. "We had to drop anchor for some tinkering, but she started right up, afterwards."

Waldron nodded, looking impressed. Then before we could protest, "Here, lemme haul it back up for you."

The anchor, he meant; after swiftly lashing our vessels together, he jumped aboard the *Sea Wolf*, his sneakers hitting our deck with a solid thud.

I didn't like it, and neither did Ellie, I knew. It's more polite to ask permission to board. But there wasn't much we could do about it, and besides, he clearly meant well.

"Okay, keep 'er in neutral," he called from the foredeck, and then the anchor chain rattled back into the chain locker.

He came back dusting his hands together. "I know what I'm doing out here so late," he said cheerily, "what's your excuse?"

Fair question, but the answer was none of his business and despite his happily given help just now, I wished he'd go away.

Bella's bony old face had regained its usual severity. "We're invading Canada," I said quickly before she could deposit our visitor bodily overboard; those grape-green eyes could shoot daggers and Bella wasn't one to hide her feelings.

Waldron's blond eyebrows rose, surprised; I'd spoken more sharply than I intended. Swiftly, Ellie rescued me.

"Just a joke. We're out here stargazing. Right, Jake?" She shot a stern look at me. "Our friend, here, wanted a midnight boat ride," she went on.

Waldron grinned. "Great night for it. Have fun." He turned back to the rail, then hopped from it back onto his own boat, agile and quick.

"What're you doing out here?" Ellie called after him, and his answer sent a sharp-pointed icicle into my gut.

"Tracking a big one. White shark. Man-eater."

Now I took in the many satellite dishes, antennas, and other items of electronic gear mounted all over his boat's deck.

"Guys saw it, couple hours ago, out there past the light-house," he went on. "They said it might've been a ten-footer."

Fifteen, I wanted to say, but didn't, because Ellie looked hard at me over Bella's frizzy head and I got the message.

"Well, I guess we should head in before our husbands call the police," I remarked loudly.

"That's right," said Ellie, putting our engine in gear. By now he'd gone back up to the helm of the *Consuelo*, which looked way too fancy for one guy to own. Heck, with all those anten-nas turning, screens glowing, and who knows what else he had running electronically over there, the boat looked too fancy for a small university to own. If it had been any bigger, it would've been difficult for one person to run. But I gathered he managed it all right. "Miami Shark Institute," he said, answering the question he must've seen in my face. "So no, I didn't pay for it myself."

The answer shouldn't have made me feel nervous about him, but it did; besides him showing up so unexpectedly tonight, he was way too perceptive.

Midnight boat ride, my ass, he was probably thinking as the *Consuelo* glided away into the darkness. And for Waldron or anyone else to have lingering questions about what we were doing out here was the last thing I'd wanted.

"Now what?" Bella asked quietly as his lights shrank away.

"I'm not sure," I began, but Ellie was. Also, she'd noticed something that I hadn't.

"We're going in." She pushed the Bayliner's throttle and aimed us toward Eastport; the waves slid by.

"But—" I began. She pointed at the water alongside us.

I looked; Bella, too. "Oh," she said softly.

I didn't say anything, silenced by the sight of the black fin cruising patiently, waiting for one of us to dabble a hand in the water, maybe. Or to jump in for a swim, which I might never do again without a chain saw and a shotgun handy.

Eastport's lights brightened encouragingly as we approached and I thought we were home free. But then something bumped the boat solidly and purposefully, sending my heart into my throat, where it remained, thudding frightenedly against my tonsils.

Again: *thump!*

"What was that?" Bella gasped as Ellie pulled back on the throttle, hurried to the rail, and leaned over it . . .

"Ellie, what are you—?"

Sticking her head near a shark's mouth—or where one might be, any instant—seemed foolish in the extreme. But when she straightened, her head came, too, still attached.

"Lobster buoys," she reported. "I missed seeing them in the dark. We knocked them aside, is all."

Phew. As the Bayliner glided into the boat basin, Bella and I could've powered a sailboat with our sighs of relief. The water here was like a mirror, our boat's low wake rolling across it in ripples that reflected the dock lights.

Silently, we slid up against the pier. Ellie secured the lines while I shut down the radio, the depth finder, the running lights, and finally the battery, these being chores that Ellie had painstakingly taught me to perform. Then Bella and I stowed our life jackets and followed Ellie off the boat.

We didn't speak as we climbed the metal gangway to where we'd parked the car, Bella moving ahead of me with surprising speed considering her age and the late hour. Once she was in the backseat, she settled happily.

"That," she pronounced, "was fun. I can see why you girls enjoy this snooping thing so much."

The previous couple of hours had mostly reminded me of

why I didn't enjoy it. For one thing, *out on a boat at night* is as much fun as *in the dentist's chair*, if you ask me; add sharks and I'd much rather have a root canal.

On the way home, we drove past the Chocolate Moose, dark and quiet like the rest of Water Street. "Let's not forget about those raspberry scones," Ellie said.

A groan escaped me. "Can't wait. You're not going in early today, are you?"

She was even shorter on sleep than usual. She didn't reply as we turned onto Key Street between Peavey Library, the Old Sow Pub, and the Motel East, all overlooking the lobster pound, its wooden wharf, and the water beyond.

"I think you should cut yourself some slack tomorrow," I tried again as we climbed the hill and my old house appeared at the top. "I mean today, actually."

We crossed Middle Street with the Congregational Church's white spire piercing the wee-hours sky on our right and the old Planck mansion, its tenants now exclusively pigeons, stray cats, and the wandering ghosts of long-dead Plancks, to judge at least by its Addams-family appearance.

"I mean, those scones won't bake themselves," Ellie said as we approached my driveway and she began turning in.

Glancing sideways, I thought I saw the front door standing open a crack, but then it was behind us, and anyway it really wouldn't matter. Since Sam had brought his big dog to live with us, a burglar who broke in would get a scare and then get licked to death, or perhaps knocked down by a wagging tail.

The car's headlights lit up the partly built new addition to the house: dark, skeletal. Around it stood a concrete mixer, some aluminum sawhorses, an extension ladder, and a pile of sand with a shovel stuck in it.

The sand was from the driveway, unfortunately. The same geological past that produced the canal we'd visited earlier in the day had also left an underground sand dune here, and now the dune had a hole six feet deep dug into it, full of water due to the downpours we'd had the night before.

Buddy had promised that his guys would pack the hole with gravel to provide drainage, but apparently they hadn't gotten to it, yet. I wished they'd covered it, or at least blocked it with those sawhorses; in the dark, somebody could fall right in.

Meanwhile, still in the car: "I sure wish we'd managed to learn something out there tonight," Ellie said. "It's like the whole trip was wasted."

Bella sat up straight from where she'd been dozing. "What do you mean, nothing learned?"

Ellie shrugged. "We went to find out why Carl McFaul didn't want to set us ashore nearer to the lagoon," she said. "If he didn't," she added. "But all we accomplished was to get ourselves noticed by another boater, and we don't want Peter Waldron or anyone else getting curious about what we're doing."

"Because," I explained to Bella, "if Coates was murdered, we'd rather no one got curious about us nosing around in it."

"But Waldron was already curious," Bella said. "That big white boat of his had been following us."

Longish silence; I certainly hadn't noticed that. Finally Ellie spoke. "Why do you think so? He's out hunting for sharks and we could've been in trouble. So naturally he—"

"Then why didn't he find the one practically right underneath us? Isn't that what all the gear on his boat is for?"

I looked at Ellie and she looked at me. Bella was right.

"And," Bella went on, "you two might not've noticed, but *he* didn't have running lights, either. Not until he got close."

Entirely possible. Ellie and I had been busy at the helm when Waldron appeared.

"I was looking that way," Bella said. "I'd have seen him if he was lit up. Instead I saw the dark boat shape, and poof! he was there, hard upon us."

"That does put a whole new face on things," said Ellie, and I agreed, still wondering whether the front door had really been open, or if I was just so tired I couldn't see straight.

Ellie hadn't pulled all the way into the driveway, yet. Now she eased the car forward. "Bella, I'm glad you were with—"

She hit the brakes hard, jolting us against our seat belts as a figure about three feet tall, in pajamas with yellow ducks on them, walked barefoot out into the glare of our headlights.

It was my grandson, Ephraim.

Eight

I was out of the car and almost to him when Ephraim stepped blindly over the water-filled sand pit's edge, flailed as he lost his balance, and toppled. His head went under the water as I flopped down and grabbed for him, unsuccessfully.

Then he popped up again, wide-eyed and terrified, choking and trying to scream. I snatched him up out of the water so fast that he had no time to struggle, surprising him into silence for an instant, and wrapped my arms around his small, drenched form.

"Sshh, it's okay, Gramma's here, you had a bad dream. See? Bella's here, too."

Ephraim sobbed as Bella's face bent to us. "Here, give him to me." Sniffling, he reached out for her, and she swept him into her arms and hurried him into the house.

Once they were gone, Ellie and I stood peering into the sand pit, her thoughtfully and me furiously.

"I don't know who to be madder at," I said, "Buddy Holloway or yours truly."

Ellie sighed. "Yeah." As a mother, she understood that for

the rest of your life, no matter what happens it's always, always all your fault.

Or so you'll believe. "The house doors were all locked when we left?" she asked.

"Yep. I checked." But I still should've made Buddy fill up that hole, or at least I should have put some plywood over it . . .

A warm, tropical-feeling breeze moved the leaves overhead. "Well, then, take yourself off the hook," she said.

Easier said than done. "I should've done something. It's a death trap. *Buddy* should've—"

"Jake. Were you listening to Bella? About when Waldron and his shark boat showed up?"

The light went on in the upstairs bathroom window. Bella was putting little Ephraim into a warm bath, no doubt, and Mika was up, too; probably by now the whole household was.

So much for my plan to slip in quietly. "No, not really," I told Ellie distractedly. "Anyway, I'm not sure we can go by what she said, she was just gazing dreamily around, and—"

"Yes, and that's why she saw Waldron's lights snap on when he got close enough to see who we were."

The back porch light glowed, the back door creaked as it opened onto the decking, and Wade, in blue plaid pajama pants and a T-shirt, stepped out into the warm night.

Not happily. "You okay?" he asked, and when I said yes, he shot me a darkly communicative look and went inside again, very carefully not slamming the door.

Oh, great. I turned back to Ellie. "Or," I said, "Waldron already knew who we were. Saw us leave Eastport, maybe, gave us a head start so we wouldn't notice him behind us."

He could've been leaving Julio's, for instance, and spotted us when we were going out.

"But why?" Ellie wondered aloud. "I mean, the whole thing could also be a coincidence. Bella could've simply mistaken how far off Waldron's lights were; it's tricky, estimating distance on the water at night."

Inside, the kitchen light went on. "Okay," I said, "we'd better quit for tonight."

Ellie nodded. "Jake, I'm so sorry I got you involved in this Sally Coates thing. It's messier than I thought it'd be."

Missing men, guys in lagoons, sharks . . . "Yeah, you think?"

But she looked so woebegone I couldn't help adding, "Look, I wasn't on board with it at first. But it's obvious the woman's in deep trouble."

Sally, I meant. Three kids, no husband, no money and no realistic prospects of becoming self-supporting anytime soon . . .

"So let's keep poking around a little more," I said, "just in case we run into something that might help her, okay?"

Privately I didn't think that last part was very likely, but Ellie brightened, then went home to get whatever sleep she could between now and dawn.

After her car had gone, I turned to the house again, and to the many questions waiting for me within. From the open kitchen window I could hear Ephraim already jabbering brightly, probably over Oreos and milk, his favorite comfort food.

So I knew he was okay. And there in the driveway right next to the cement mixer was the Fiat; Wade must've brought it home from Spinney's.

Just then Sam came out, wearing rumpled jeans and a T-shirt that looked like he'd grabbed it up off the floor. Work gloves were on his hands, and as he approached, I saw his grim face and frightened eyes.

Haunted eyes. "Ephraim's fine," he said before I could ask. My son's lower lip wasn't trembling; not quite.

"He thinks he had a bad dream, is all. But if you hadn't been here, then . . ."

I was glad that's the tack they were taking and not, for instance, wondering exactly how I'd happened to be there or why.

Sam backed away when I put my hand out to him. "I gotta do this." With that he marched over to the garden shed and pulled out a shovel, and marched determinedly back.

As I got into the Fiat, he was approaching the huge mound of gravel piled near the hole that Ephraim had fallen into. As I backed out, he had just thrown the first shovelful into the pit and was turning back for more.

The house Lizzie Snow said she'd rented stood on a long point of grassy land overlooking the south end of Passamaquoddy Bay, with the town of Lubec and the international bridge to Campobello twinkling in the darkness beyond. When I pulled up in front, lamps still burned in the windows and two cars stood on the short strip of pea gravel that served as a driveway.

The moss-choked brick walk was a trap for the clumsy-footed, but I made it okay to the front deck, where large clay pots of marigolds, cushioned Adirondack chairs, and a portable firepit made a pleasant scene.

Then the red-painted front door opened. "Jake!"

Despite the hour—by now it was past 3:00 AM—Lizzie looked bright-eyed and not unhappy to see me. I'd been glad to see her lights on, because my head was full of what had happened on the water, earlier in the evening, and I needed to talk about it. But behind her in the front room, Dylan Hudson's unguarded glance said he hadn't been hoping for a visitor.

Still, he got up politely, we fist-bumped awkwardly, and after that first moment he grinned good-humoredly, showing a set of high cheekbones that . . . ye gods, but this guy was attractive.

"So Lizzie says you've already had an adventure together," he said when she'd brought me into the living room and sat me in a big, pleasantly cushioned wicker armchair.

A small, pot-bellied stove flickered, chasing the waterside

dampness from the room. Lizzie had put in a round wooden table, four ladderback chairs, a cushy-looking upholstered sofa facing the stove, and a green braided rug.

"More like a misadventure," I replied. "So what d'you think about it all?"

But at this Lizzie winced. *Don't get him going*, she mouthed from behind him; apparently Hudson could be . . . talkative.

"Or . . . wait. On second thought," I said quickly, taking her cue, "maybe you could tell me tomorrow? I apologize, but . . ."

I let my voice trail off. Lizzie jumped in. "Dylan, Jake needs to talk privately with me about something, I think, so . . ."

Vamoose, her expression said, and he obeyed amiably, his parting smile at her the equivalent of an embrace. I felt very strongly that I'd interrupted something.

But if Lizzie didn't mind, I didn't, either. "So," she said when the door had closed with him on the other side of it, "what gives?"

It was almost four in the morning, the sky beyond the room's big water-facing window paling from black to indigo, and now without Dylan Hudson in it the room seemed larger, emptier.

"I could ask the same of you," I said, and waited. Tears were in her eyes, and suddenly I felt that Paul Coates's body, wherever it was, could wait.

She turned from the lightening sky where the stars were dissolving from east to west. "He won't give up. He never has. He's trying to talk me into marrying him, for Pete's sake."

"And that's bad because? I mean, you two seem . . ."

She laughed harshly. "Right, until we're not, and then you might as well put two fighting fish into the same fishbowl."

I walked past her into the kitchen, where the coffeemaker was drizzling the last few drops into a fresh pot, came back with two cups and handed her one.

Then I sat her down and told her about my evening: Ellie's

boat, Peter Waldron showing up, the shark showing up. I didn't mention Ephraim.

"So you think he was already out on the water when you all left the boat basin?" she asked. "Or—?"

"Or did he follow us out? I don't know," I replied. "And I didn't see his running lights snap on, Bella did."

Lizzie knew better than I did how infallible eyewitnesses could be: like, not at all, and on the water at night it was worse. It meant that despite Bella's certainty, those running lights of Waldron's could've been on all along.

Then something else occurred to me. "Did you ever get in touch with the Canadian authorities?"

About the lagoon guy and the rest of it, I meant. Until now, what with everything that had happened since this morning, I'd nearly forgotten about our possible prosecution for illegal border crossing, Carl McFaul's legal vulnerability, and so on.

"Yep." Lizzie swallowed some coffee. "Funny thing, though. Before I could tell them anything, they told me a body had just been reported. The one in the lagoon," she added.

Though the day had been hot, nights near the water were damp and cool. A stick in the woodstove flared up with an explosive pop and fell into coals behind the isinglass in the stove's small, square window.

"Interesting," I said mildly, because what were the odds? Nobody finds the guy for days and then two people find him, both on the same morning?

Lizzie laughed, again without humor. "Yeah. Hell of a coincidence, huh? But at least it means we're not going to be visited by the Canadian Mounties."

"You think the Paul Coates thing is connected to the guy in the lagoon?"

"Well, Eastport's not a hotbed of crime," she said dryly, "so I'm gonna assume two croaked guys likely have some kind of link between them. But right now, we don't know for sure that one is really croaked, and we don't know who the la-goon guy is."

She took a breath. "So it's too soon for conclusions."

I got up. "Okay, then. Just wanted to keep you looped in as soon as I could. Now you know all I know."

I looked around. "Sorry if I interrupted something."

I moved toward the door, but she didn't give me a tired nod and send me off into the dawn, as I'd expected; instead she set her cup down with a sharp clink!

"Wait. There's someone I want you to try to talk to. You and Ellie." She found a yellow pad in one of the kitchen draw-ers and scribbled on it.

"This guy," she said, thrusting the paper at me, "might know something pertinent."

Glenna LaFarge, the paper said. No phone number or email; also no address. Grimacing, I stuffed it into my pocket.

"Yeah, I'm sure this guy will break it all wide-open," I said, not sparing the sarcasm. "Why don't you talk to him?"

Whoever and wherever he turns out to be, I didn't add; she knew.

"I don't think that'll work. For one thing, 'undomiciled' is the official term for LaFarge's living situation."

Homeless, in other words, which explained a lot; it was a tough way to live, here or anywhere else, and it stood to reason a visit from the law wouldn't necessarily be welcomed.

She walked me to the door. "The main trouble is, there's still no real evidence of a crime where Coates is concerned. If there were, maybe I could get officially involved."

And maybe not; the state's homicide and major crimes units handled all the big stuff in Maine's rural areas.

"But maybe he just took off," she finished. "And the city council doesn't want to spend cop money on goose chases, so . . ."

I opened the door. Outside, everything looked pale blue, the salty air full of birdsong and the kind of early morning warmth that signals another scorcher; the night's coolness was as gone as if it had been a dream.

"You don't think that's what happened, though," I said, and she nodded, tight-lipped.

"Correct. So far I just don't think the guy had the, uh . . ."

Right. By all descriptions, Coates hadn't been what you'd call a big thinker, likely to try to pull off some complicated scheme.

"Where'd you get this name?" I asked, patting my pocket.

"Julio's. Guys were in there, I overheard one saying that probably Paul Coates's bones were getting picked over for soup by somebody named Gwen LaFarge."

The light dawned, and not just on the horizon. "Could the name have been Glenna? Glenna LaFarge?"

Her eyes widened. "Yes! That's it, you know her?"

I knew about her. So did Ellie. But that was all. Everyone in Eastport knew the stories about the witch of Walk Island.

Knew them, and feared her.

Driving home with the top down and the soft, sweet air blowing gently into my face, I wondered what awaited me; the night before, Wade had looked pretty annoyed.

But when I got home and tiptoed inside, everything was quiet; even Sam's big shaggy dog only glanced up from his bed in the kitchen and promptly went back to sleep.

Which was all I could think to do, too, so after peeking in at Ephraim and finding him sleeping soundly as well, I got in a deep, dreamless three hours before struggling up, drinking large amounts of black coffee, and stumbling downtown to the Chocolate Moose.

To my surprise, Mika was already there, her dark eyes wide and her pale, drawn face showing the effects of even less sleep than I had gotten.

"He's completely fine," she said of Ephraim as soon as she saw me. "I checked him again this morning. Oh, Ma—"

She felt tiny and fragile in my arms.

"Listen, if it's okay with you two I'd like to stay here in the shop, today." She stepped away from me, took a deep, steadying breath. "I need," she said quietly, "a break."

From kids and dogs and Sam and Bella and my dad and sounds of construction going on right outside, she meant. I understood; when Sam was little, I'd have tried out for the Rockettes if it meant getting out of the house.

And if I didn't have two left feet. "You've got it," I told Mika without hesitation—we could really use her help—and Ellie called out her agreement from in the kitchen where she was working up a batch of . . .

Scones. I backed away from the kitchen doorway. In all the commotion I'd forgotten about them yet again, and now I wished I could go on forgetting them.

But the order had been placed, Ellie had accepted it, and so we were stuck. "Mika," I began hesitantly, "I wonder if you could possibly get started prepping for those . . . ?"

Mika was a high-end pastry chef before she came to Eastport and married Sam. She could do scones standing on her head.

"Already on it," she replied, her glossy, blunt-cut black hair swinging as she turned to grab an apron.

The rest of her costume consisted of blue-and-white crop pants, a navy T-shirt, and white leather moccasins with multi-colored beads on the fringes. Overall she looked sharp and wide-awake, especially considering what she'd been through the night before and the early hour.

I handed Ellie the slip of paper that Lizzie had given me, with Glenna LaFarge's name written on it. Ellie read it and looked up. "Please tell me this isn't what I think it is."

"I could, but I'd be lying my face off. Lizzie wants us to visit the witch of Walk Island."

The name people had given her was based on rumors that she kept toads as pets, cast evil spells, and in one particularly sensational story that she stole little children from their beds to make soup out of them.

"Why doesn't Lizzie go talk to Glenna, herself?" Ellie wanted to know.

"Because the city of Eastport didn't hire a new police chief so she could ramble around looking for bodies of people who might not even be dead," I said, summing it up.

Ellie blew a breath out through pursed lips to show what she thought of that idea. "What, she can't look for them before they're dead?"

I didn't answer this, but I thought it was fairly shortsighted of the city council, too. "Lizzie also thinks probably Glenna's no big fan of cops," I said.

"She's got that part right." Ellie pulled off her apron.

"Um, wait," I said, but she kept moving.

"Mika, you know the drill, right?" she asked, hurrying from the kitchen out into the shop area. She waved at the cooler; it badly needed filling.

"Fudge cookies, ladyfingers, chocolate rolls, the doughnuts for the early crew . . ."

Mika turned from readying the cash register and the credit card reader. "Got it, boss."

Her accompanying smile and snappy salute made me wonder who was doing the favor, here, us or her. When we went out, the opening notes of Bach's *The Art of Fugue* were on the sound system and Mika, whose moments of solitude were few and far between, looked pleased to see the back of us.

Up and down Water Street, shopkeepers swept doorsteps and watered window boxes, put out flags and banners and filled water bowls for dogs, and set chalkboard menus and clothing racks full of SALE! items outside their doors.

We hurried down the sidewalk among them. "Ellie, where are we going?" I called, trying to match her quick step.

But I feared I already knew. Down in the harbor, a few of the earliest boats' diesel engines rumbled to life, each crew hustling to cast off the bow and stern lines, secure loose gear, and swig from thermoses filled earlier in dark kitchens before putting out to sea.

It was high tide, I saw with a sinking heart when we got to the breakwater, perfect for getting Ellie's Bayliner out of the boat basin's rarely dredged channel with a minimum of fuss. More to the point, though, it was also high tide on Walk Island.

Wherever that was. "Ellie, we don't even know which way we should go to *look* for Walk Island."

That, according to one story, was where the witch had isolated herself years ago, after some kind of tragedy struck her; a different tale said a demon put her there after an unspeakably evil deed of her own. All the stories agreed that she might turn you into a garter snake if you annoyed her. Or make you into soup.

"You don't know," Ellie corrected me. "But I do." She stepped out onto the dratted metal gangway leading down to the dratted wooden finger piers.

And from there to the dratted water. "How?" I followed her out to where the Bayliner floated. "How do you know? Did you just look for it on a map, or what?"

She'd already hopped aboard. I stood on the pier looking down at her, while around us the pearly blue water lay smooth as a mirror, so clear I could see the minnows and jellyfish bopping around down there.

Gulls swirled above, scanning for food items, settled again with muted cries. "I know because I've been there."

She opened the battery hatch, then snapped on the battery and the other equipment. Finally she sat at the helm and turned the key; the new engine burbled to life at once.

She looked up expectantly. "You coming or not?"

I did not need this, I definitely did not—oh, what the heck, there was no use arguing; in the end I hopped aboard, and the trip, I have to admit, was pretty good. While Ellie drove the Bayliner toward Campobello, I watched porpoises leaping like salmon on their way to a fishy breakfast. The spray slapping my face felt restorative, too, filling me with gratitude for whatever huge cosmic mix-up had resulted in my being so lucky.

We were halfway across the bright bay when Ellie pulled the throttle back and dropped the transmission into neutral.

"What?" I asked, scanning the water all around. No one was near us. "You didn't see a shark fin, did you?"

Because if she had, I wasn't going to think I was so lucky after all, it being my firm belief that shark fins usually come with sharks attached to them.

"No, no. I just want to prepare you before we get to Walk Island," said Ellie. "Because first of all, it won't be there."

"Uh-huh," I said, deadpan, and waited.

"Anything higher than ten feet of tide, the island's pretty much submerged," she said.

The average high tide around here was about eighteen feet. "Does she have gills?"

Ellie rolled her eyes. "No, mostly she lives on a boat," she said, "that's moored to the island all the time.

"Except," she added, frowning in puzzlement, "last time I was out that way I thought I saw a shack of some sort, and how could that be?"

Because it should've floated away, she meant, most likely in pieces.

"I don't know, but how about we get going?" I suggested, angling my head toward a boat zipping straight across the bay toward us. The rooster-tail of spray shooting straight up behind it said it was fast, which to me spelled *purposeful.*

"Looks like somebody's taking an interest," I said, then grabbed the rail hard as Ellie kicked that big, new engine into action and we positively shot forward.

"So," I yelled as around us the waves grew and the other boat fell back; maybe it wasn't following us after all. "So what else should I know about Glenna LaFarge?"

Ellie piloted us around the point of land with the candy-striped lighthouse on it, avoiding the toothy-looking rocks and ledges sticking up from the waves crashing at its base.

"You should know that as far as I'm concerned," Ellie said evenly, "she really is a witch. Not the controlled-by-the-devil kind, but not just a story to scare children, either. And," she added, "not always the good kind of witch."

She eyed me seriously from the helm. "There are reasons why people don't talk about her, you know."

I just stared. "You're kidding, right? Ellie, don't tell me you believe in—"

"I don't." She aimed us toward open water. "But I believe in better safe than sorry, and after some of the things I've heard, that's how I deal with Glenna."

She checked the GPS and the depth finder, eyed the horizon, and turned back to me again. "Also, she's a scavenger."

By now we were in the open water between Nova Scotia and New Brunswick, Canada. I looked around at the vast stretch of glittering waves between us and land, and that's when it hit me.

"Wait, Walk Island is Canadian territory? But doesn't that mean we'll be—?"

"Border violators, again? Uh-uh." She consulted the GPS on the depth finder's screen again, and made a course change.

Now the island of Grand Manan was a hazy shape looming on the horizon. "We're not disembarking," she added. "Or at least not onto land, which is the illegal part."

"Okay," I said doubtfully, and twenty minutes later I got the chance to test her assertion. "Um, Ellie?"

We were approaching a crazily improvised-looking hulk, half barge and half paint-peeling old tugboat, called the *Carrie*. Her smokestack tilted, her decks ran askew, and her hull shed rusty tears behind rails fallen to piles of pipe.

Ellie tossed a line over a cleat and hauled us in toward a ladder bolted to the ramshackle vessel's hull. The ladder looked about as sturdy as spun glass and the bolts not much better, but before I could refuse, Ellie was shooing me onto it, and have I mentioned that both boats were moving very energetically on the waves?

Up and down, side to side . . . "You've been here?" I asked as I clung to the ladder like a clumsy monkey suspended over an especially wet jungle.

I reached up and grabbed the next rung. It bent like clay between my fingers. Startled, I scrambled higher, searching for something that would hold me.

Which turned out to be the tugboat's half-disintegrated rail, from which creaks and groans issued as if it, too, might simply give way at any moment. But the heck with it, I threw both arms up over it.

Then suddenly I thought about how I must look from below: like fresh meat, probably, if you were a big enough carnivore, and that thought pretty much lifted me bodily over the rail and onto the *Carrie*'s deck.

Where I collapsed while Ellie climbed up behind me, not even out of breath. "Let me do the talking," she said. "Glenna can be . . . grouchy."

"Uh-huh," I said distractedly, looking around. "Ellie, how come this deck is so slanted?"

Because it was, its port side lower by a couple of feet than its starboard, so that from right to left the deck tilted sharply toward the . . .

Water. And while I stood there, the deck tilted some more.

"Ellie, this boat is sinking."

And the Bayliner was tied to it, so if it went, so did our own transportation. "Ellie, I mean it, we're—"

A wave hit the *Carrie*'s hull, tipping us another foot. My

heart lurched as the *Carrie* heeled over sharply and threatened to capsize before righting herself precariously again.

Almost righting herself; the deck remained acutely slanted. "Come on," Ellie said, gesturing, "we'd better make this quick."

This was an understatement; I'd have said we should abandon ship, but it was already abandoning us, and Ellie had vanished through a hatchway leading to another ladder. Grumbling, I followed—at least this ladder wasn't hanging by a thread over shark-infested water—into what turned out to be the *Carrie's* roomy wheelhouse.

Two tattered leather chairs, a torn couch spewing yellowed stuffing, and a few ancient issues of insect-chewed magazines were the only furnishings. The electronics had been stripped and the floor was a shambles of broken tiles and old adhesive.

There was a bare spot in the tiling, though, and from it a worn leather handle poked up. Ellie tugged the loop and a hatch lifted; water sloshed somewhere below.

"Hello?" Ellie called down. "Glenna, are you there?"

No answer, just more sloshing, plus a new sound: *creak-thump.* Over and over it came, in rhythm with the waves that tilted the *Carrie* to starboard a little more each time.

"Glenna?" Ellie called again; still no answer, but the sloshing was louder and so was the creak-thumping, like someone trying to bash down a locked door and not succeeding.

Ellie looked at the hole, gritted her teeth, and vanished feet-first down into it. I hesitated, but I wasn't about to stay behind in a ruined wheelhouse with only a few moldy magazines and the ghosts of boat captains past to amuse me, so—

"Jake!" Ellie cried, and in response my feet dropped down into that hole so fast, it was like I'd been sucked into it.

The space below the wheelhouse had at one time been fitted out as a spacious cabin, with white pine paneling, a brass ship's clock opposite the wide bunk, and a chandelier made from a sailboat's wheel. I doubted that the inches of murky salt water covering the floor had been in the original design, but it did add to the atmosphere.

Of dread, that is. *Creak-thump* came the odd sound again, nearer than before, and now I could identify it: something kept bumping the hull from the outside, over and over.

A shark's nose, maybe. Then: "Ooh," someone moaned weakly. Alarmed, I peered around in the gloom and suddenly a face popped out of it: faded blue eyes, cheeks like red apples, short white hair going every which way. Age spots freckled her skin, and oh, wasn't she furious.

Wearing a zip-front blue hoodie and khaki pants, she was lashed down to a cot with wrappings of what looked like old electrical wiring. The water hadn't gotten in here, yet; the compartment must have been built to be watertight, maybe for storing valuables or documents.

But it would get in sooner or later. "Will you please," she said, way too calmly, "untie me."

It was the kind of calm you hang on to with both hands so as not to commit murder. But I wasn't too worried, figuring that if she really had any powers, she'd have used them to free herself.

"I thought you said she was a witch," I said to Ellie, now beside me. I'm rarely impressed by people's claims of special abilities, and this instance was shaping up to be no exception.

"Looks more like somebody's sweet old grandmother, to me," I said. At this, one of Glenna LaFarge's pale blue eyes swiveled toward me, not in a friendly way.

"I also thought I said keep your trap shut," Ellie advised me sweetly as the water around us kept deepening. It was up to my calves, now, and there was another, worse problem, too:

Glenna's restraints were of household extension cord–sized electrical wire, knots snugged tight. No way were we untying it in time, or hauling the cot with Glenna on it back up on deck.

But ever since I accidentally tied myself to a tree while walking Sam's big, shaggy dog on a length of clothesline, I carry a pocketknife. So: *zip, zop.* Glenna sat up in a smooth, ready-to-attack way, her face neither sweet nor grandmotherly.

"Where is he?" she grated out as we got her on her feet. "I'll make soup out of him."

Yeah, unless she drowned first. "Glenna, come on," Ellie urged, unfazed by potential witchiness. "Don't you hear that?"

Whatever was thumping the hull kept right at it, and now I heard cracking sounds, too, as if something was . . . suddenly the water rose around us, surging in.

"Ellie, go!" I cried as we lifted Glenna off her feet and propelled her ahead of us, then shoved her up through the trap door head-first and scrambled up after her.

By the time we got out, the deck was nearly vertical. Waves slopped between the *Carrie* and the Bayliner still lashed to her—which meant that if the *Carrie* went under, the Bayliner would, too.

"Jump!" yelled Ellie, then gave me a shove that sent me sliding downhill toward the port rail, now nearly submerged.

The deck was slippery, so I slid on my feet, then sat down hard. All at once I was skidding on my butt straight downhill toward the water, shoving with my feet like some demented cartoon character against gravity and the deck's slickness.

The deck's edge approached and went by underneath me; as I flew out over the gap between the *Carrie* and the Bayliner I was praying two things: that I wouldn't end up in the water between the two boats, and that if I did, I could swim out before they crushed me.

Instead, I flew off that deck like I'd been shot out of a cannon, then dropped to the Bayliner's deck with a bone-rattling thud. Chirping tweety-birds circled my head; then Glenna the Witch landed beside me with an "oof."

Finally, Ellie leapt down, yanked our lines off the cleats. Released from the sinking *Carrie*, the Bayliner rocked wildly, bouncing us all around until she was level again. Quickly Ellie started us up and got us a safe distance from the doomed barge.

Glenna sat up just in time to see the *Carrie*'s prow aiming skyward. Then the old hulk slammed down and vanished, sliding into the waves.

The depths change fast in these waters; it's basically a mountain range down there, with huge peaks and valleys that help make the currents treacherous. The barge could've been submerged forty feet deep, or four hundred.

Around where it went down, the waves boiled up into a massive, skyward-shooting geyser of water and barge-trapped air bubbles that momentarily blocked our view itself. Glenna watched the water settle where the barge used to be, muttering things I couldn't hear. Finally I turned away and went down to the Bayliner's small cabin, where Ellie kept dry clothes and where I barely resisted falling down onto one of the bunks, still quivering with fright and adrenaline.

By the time I'd pulled on dry clothing I'd calmed down some and no longer thought I was about to be drowned, crushed, eaten, or some creative combination of all three. I did, however, think that I'd better get some answers about all this, toot sweet, as Sam would've said.

In fact, I planned to insist pretty strongly on it—I was the one who'd had the jackknife and got shot out of the cannon, after all—but when I got back up on deck I found Ellie already questioning Glenna.

Quiet, Ellie's eyes warned me, so I was, even though a great many words were agitating to get out of my mouth. It's not every day that the choices I'm offered are grisly, gruesome, too wet, or all of the above, and I had feelings about it.

Ellie was more succinct. "Who hit you?" she asked as Glenna stood by the captain's chair at the helm. I hadn't seen the dark bruise around her eye before, but it was a no-kidding shiner.

"Never mind," she snapped. "Just take me home."

Ellie's eyes met mine questioningly. I shrugged; maybe our witch had hit her head somewhere along the way.

"But, Glenna," Ellie said, "someone tried to kill you. And as for going home—"

She waved at the still-bubbling place where the *Carrie* used to be. *Home is gone*, her gesture at the vessel's watery grave was meant to convey.

But then she stopped waving and simply stared with her mouth open, as what had been there behind the *Carrie* all along was revealed now that big workboat had sunk.

Nine

It was a shack, made from pieces of driftwood and roofed with an enormous heap of branches and dried seaweed. Canvas and blue tarps peeped from beneath the thatch sticking out around the roof's edges.

Ellie looked at the bubbles still surging up from below, at the shack and the ridiculously tiny scrap of rock it was perched on, and finally at me.

"I never even saw it," she said, shaking her head. "It must have been there all along, and we never even—"

Right, I agreed silently. *Some amateur sleuths we are.* We'd approached the *Carrie* from the opposite side and the slanting deck had kept us from seeing the shack behind it. If things had gone differently, that could have been disastrous.

If someone had been lurking in the shack, for instance. I reminded myself that someone still could be now. A small dinghy floated near it, tied to the shack's rough porch rail.

"All right, we'll take you," said Ellie finally. She waved again toward where the sunken *Carrie* still bubbled and blurped while the shack seemed to watch from the tiny island.

"Or we could take you to a doctor," Ellie added, "who'll check you out four ways from Sunday and set a bunch of social workers on you."

Ellie wouldn't do any such thing, of course; railroading people into help they didn't want wasn't her style. But Glenna the Waterlogged Witch looked apoplectic at the mention of social workers, and I could tell she was no big fan of doctors, either.

"But maybe instead you'll help us by letting us ask you a few questions," Ellie added, glancing at me.

A scowl was Glenna's only reply; you could've burned a hole through the Bayliner's deck with the look in her eyes.

"Not," Ellie added hastily, "questions about you. We're trying to help someone. Please, Glenna."

"Yeah," I broke in, unable to stop myself, "and it's not like we didn't just haul you up out of a sinking boat, so . . ."

Ellie's look shushed me. "There's a man gone missing out here on the water. His wife's my friend, she's got three kids, and we need to find a gold coin she thinks he had with him."

Long silence. Then, "Hmph," Glenna said, looking supremely unfooled. "How come it's never the wife that skedaddles with the gold, huh? Answer me that one."

Well, naturally I couldn't answer her that one, and anyway we were nearing the shack, so now I had other things to worry about. I wondered if it would be rude to keep my life jacket on when we entered Glenna's dwelling; the place looked as if one big wave could've turned it to floating splinters, none sizable enough to cling to.

Hope flared in me when at first Ellie didn't find anything to secure the Bayliner to; she certainly wasn't going to tie up alongside that little dinghy to a hut made of driftwood. But finally she found a place to get close enough without going aground, dropped anchor, and we scrambled from our boat directly onto the shack's tiny porch.

Rather, the other two hopped across; I scrambled. "How," I asked Ellie when I'd caught my breath, "will we get back?"

To the Bayliner, I meant; as the tide went out, the boat would descend until the receding water left it stranded on the rocks next to the anchor. Then we'd have to wait for hours until the rising tide floated us again.

"You don't stay here for long, that's how." Glenna LaFarge's sweet, grandmotherly voice contradicted what I knew of her so far, and so did her words. "Now come in here, and let's get this foolishness over with."

It was the best suggestion I'd heard today; crouching to follow Ellie into the tumbledown little shelter, I hoped hard that we'd be able to follow it.

Inside was nearly all one small, cluttered room, with corner posts, roof beams, and stringers of standard commercial lumber but otherwise built of driftwood, just as I'd thought at first. It was just like one of the Three Little Pigs' houses, I'd have told Ephraim.

So it wasn't as flimsy as I'd feared, but I'd gotten a look underneath during our watery approach and it wasn't anchored to anything that I could see; a high enough tide would float it.

Which was not at all a thought I wanted to be having as I stood inside, gazing at the many colorful and varied items that crowded the room: jugs of glass marbles, a vase bristling with eagle feathers, lobster buoys dangling in bunches, old clay pipe stems, life vests . . .

Wait a minute, *life vests*? A wooden barrel stuffed with them stood near the doorway. While we waited for Glenna to come back from wherever she'd gone while I wasn't looking, I wandered casually over to them. Most were old, heavily mildewed specimens whose owners likely hadn't minded much when they flew overboard.

But one of them was a newish inflatable model, the sort of

compact collar-and-vest contraption that inflated automatically and semi-explosively when the wearer hit the water.

Myself, I like my life jackets already inflated before I even leave the house, so I know right from the git-go whether or not I'll float if I hit water. Curious, I turned this one over in my hands, but no ID was visible.

"Put it down." Glenna reappeared in a dry sweatshirt and dungarees, wearing thick, warm-looking gray socks that I'd have killed to be pulling on, myself; by now my poor feet were a pair of Popsicles while the rest of me was frozen slush.

"I'll get a good price for that vest," she added, setting down a tray and three glasses plus a poison-green bottle that I hoped didn't hold toe of frog.

I put the vest back into the wooden barrel, then picked it up again so I could position it the way I'd found it.

"I *said* put it down," she snapped, and I don't know why in a day already so filled with scary, dangerous, and/or otherwise questionable events, that's what finally put me over the edge.

But it did. I grabbed a glass, dumped dark liquid from the bottle into it, and knocked the liquid back in a gulp. The stuff didn't quite put me flat on the floor, but close enough; when my vision cleared, the liquid in the glass had only fueled my fury, which erupted when I opened my mouth.

"Listen, you. We just risked our lives saving you out of a rusty old tub that should've been scuttled years ago, but now I'm thinking we should've left you there. And oh, by the way—"

I poured again, raised the brimming glass in a toast.

"You're welcome," I snarled, and drank.

Silence followed this. Glenna eyed me, looking as if she was mentally casting a spell that involved warts. But then: "So, there's a spinal cord in there. You may not be hopeless after all."

She filled her own glass and toasted me back. "Thank you for helping me out of there. Things were . . . complicated."

Yeah, that was one way to put it. "Right," I said, pouring for both of us again. The stuff was actually pretty good, like licorice-flavored rocket fuel.

Ellie came back from peering out the window, made from what looked like an old cabin-cruiser windscreen. "Who tied you down there, though?" she asked. "Glenna, we need to know."

Because it was too much to believe that this all wasn't hooked up some way or another with Paul Coates's disappearance. And even if some *other* villainy was going on out here, we needed to know so as not to get tangled up in *that*. But:

"None of your business," Glenna replied, the sharp tone and angry expression suddenly back in charge.

I kept trying to match her grandmotherly appearance with her junkyard dog attitude, and maybe she figured out what I was thinking about her. Or maybe she just knew; by then the rocket fuel was fully ignited and I'd have believed anything, even that she'd read my mind. Anyway:

"People can't help what they look like," she said. "You think I enjoy looking as if I came out of a nursery rhyme?"

She evidently expected an answer. I tried but found myself unable; my brain was just sort of floating around up there, not connected to anything.

"Although it does make good camouflage," she said, and just then lift-off happened; I was on the floor, suddenly.

I was still awake but I couldn't feel much of my body at all. Suddenly I knew why Ellie hadn't drunk any of that stuff.

Good Ellie. Smart Ellie. Her voice and Glenna's went back and forth over my head, which continued to lie motionless on the floor along with the rest of me.

"Glenna, Jake was right," Ellie said firmly. "You owe us. And we're just trying to help someone who's really in a tough spot."

"Hmph." The creak of the fraying wicker armchair by the woodstove was loud in my ears as she sank into it. "So?"

That sounded like an opening. Ellie took it. "So, who tried to kill you back on the *Carrie*, and why?"

Brief silence. Then, not sounding as if this was even a little bit negotiable: "I'll deal with them, myself."

Deep sigh from Ellie. "Okay," she gave in, and from my spot on the floor I was shouting mentally, *Are you kidding?* because the woman had just been nearly murdered, for Pete's sake.

But Ellie knew a real *no* when she heard it, and she knew how to pivot from it, too.

"Okay, but then what about that new life vest?" she segued smoothly. "Where'd that come from?"

It might not even be Coates's vest. Sally hadn't mentioned one like it. But finding it here, so clean and new-looking, was as Sam would've put it, an interesting co-inky-dink.

"Floated in on the tide," said Glenna, and I could hear her relaxing, probably from the drinks of whatever potion that was. At least, I hoped what knocked me flat had some effect on her.

"You want to see what else came in at the same time?" asked Glenna, accompanied by another wickery creak. "This."

I tried raising my head, but my head was opposed to this notion and somehow I also rolled onto my stomach and then fell down hard again, squarely on my nose.

"Ooch," I said, or maybe I imagined that part. You'd think I'd have learned about liquids in strange bottles from *Alice in Wonderland*.

On the other hand, I'd learned now. "Jake." Ellie shook my shoulder. "Jake, look. It's a man's boot."

I struggled and sat up. Ellie put the large, leather boot into my unsteady hands, and for a wonder not only did I remember what a boot was, I remembered what was supposed to be special about this one.

Grasping the boot's heel in one hand and the sole in the other—in my condition this was not easy but I managed it—I twisted hard. The heel turned, revealing a carved-out cavity: deep, coin-shaped . . .

And empty. "The boot washed up along with the vest?" I asked, thinking *Wow! My mouth works!*

"Uh-huh. First one, then the other," Glenna replied.

My head felt as if it were inflated with helium and would float off my neck any instant if I weren't careful.

"Anything else?" I managed. "Wash up on shore, that is? And how long was that before you got bonked by somebody?"

At this last part her face turned stony. "Nothing else. It was yesterday, mid-tide. I was out on the beach like usual and picking up whatever might be worth something."

Gesturing around at the many collections ranged out on every flat surface and hanging from the rafters, she went on:

"Lost buoys." The brightly painted markers hung on the rough walls. " 'Specially the wooden ones. I don't snatch 'em out of the water, but if they wash up, they're mine."

She angled her head toward an ancient tree stump, its top bone-white and smooth after someone had sanded it for hours. To my astonishment, a small laptop computer stood on the stump.

"Sell 'em on eBay, one o' them places," said Glenna. Then, seeing my surprise at the laptop: "Starlink," she added.

Cashlink, I called it; the service that put remote places like Glenna's online was so expensive that selling beachcombing finds wouldn't nearly cover the cost, I thought.

But Glenna's next remark changed my mind. "That life vest, fifty bucks easy," she said. "The shoe's worth something decent, too, with that handy hiding place in it. You'd be amazed what people will pay for beach glass. And antique marbles."

"The life vest," Ellie put in suddenly, "came ashore just like it is now?"

Uninflated, she meant. I'd wondered about that, too. But only now at Ellie's question and Glenna's affirmative nod did I realize just how odd a thing it really was.

They were supposed to inflate by themselves, remember. But this one had supposedly traveled in the water for who knew how long before being found pristine.

"And another thing," said Ellie, "was there anything still in the shoe's heel when you found it?"

"If there'd been something," Glenna retorted, "that'd be mine, too. But there wasn't." Her head cocked curiously at the boot. "What was s'posed to be in it?"

I got up shakily to peer out through the plexiglass window that someone had cut and glazed into an ornate old wooden frame. The woman was resourceful, I thought; clever, too.

"Maybe a coin," I said. "But maybe not. We're not quite sure, yet."

The tide was going out now, exposing a slope of seaweedy rocks. At the bottom, the Bayliner still floated; Ellie had a chain a mile long on that anchor just for situations like this. But we still didn't have all day.

"Ellie," I said, nodding at the window. She hopped up and looked out, too, and began moving toward the door.

"You're sure you don't want to tell us who tried to kill you?" I asked Glenna on our way out. After all, someone could try again; it didn't seem right to leave her.

But the look she gave me convinced me. "Thank you for your help," she said in a voice that warned me not to argue.

So I didn't. It had been too warm in the shack but outside it was as hot as hellfire, even with the water breeze; when the sunlight hit me I felt like an ant under a magnifying glass.

She followed us out. "We have," I added carefully, "some experience in that area. Finding out who did things, I mean."

And stopping them, I didn't add. By then we were making

our way down the rocky slope to where the Bayliner still floated.

"Oh, I know who you are." Glenna stepped expertly between jagged granite outcroppings and glistening seaweed patches so slippery, I could've just sat down and slid all the way to the water—that is, if I wanted my backside slammed repeatedly by those same outcroppings.

"But I'll deal with it myself," she promised darkly again.

"With what, your magic wand?" Her mulishness in the face of danger exasperated me. "Seems to me someone dealt pretty darned effectively with you," I added, "and if we hadn't come along—"

Ahead, Ellie strode into the water, waded waist-deep along the Bayliner's hull to the stern, and scampered up the swim ladder, which now I was supposed to do, too.

Glenna spoke again, softly, but somehow I could hear her clearly over the wind and waves. "You ought to know that it's easier to help other people than yourself."

I spun toward her. "What?" Here in the bright sunlight, her pale blue eyes were like opals.

She turned them toward Ellie, already waiting for me on the Bayliner. "We don't all get all the gifts," she said obscurely. "Her, though. She might be a different story."

"Yeah," I said, unable to dispute this. Ellie could charm the birds out of the trees when she wanted to, but she was a tough little nut and after all we'd been through, she was about to take us home unharmed.

Honestly a bit of witchery in her wouldn't have surprised me. Then she called from the Bayliner's deck.

"Jake! Come on or I'll have to back out into deeper water!"

Which would mean a longer wading-and-swimming trip for me; I drew in a breath, preparing for the plunge.

"All right, Glenna," I began, "I just hope . . ."

But when I turned the grandmotherly old woman with the

sour manner, junk-filled shack, and unsavory reputation was already halfway up the rocky, seaweed-strewn slope, moving fast and not looking back.

If a shark did attack, at least I wouldn't feel it, I consoled myself as I sloshed through numbingly cold salt water toward the Bayliner. It sobered me up, but next came clambering up the swim ladder, then tumbling tail-over-teakettle over the transom, past the engine, and onto the deck.

Then Ellie slammed us hard into reverse, swung us around, and got us the heck out of there, before the falling tide could maroon us; soon Walk Island was a dot on the rear horizon.

"So, what did you think?" She scanned oil pressure, fuel level, and RPM gauges as she spoke.

I swallowed hot coffee and passed her the thermos. "I think something's funny about that life vest she found. Why wasn't it inflated? And who's paying for a Starlink internet connection?"

Now that I was sober I realized that even the high prices that Glenna mentioned wouldn't make it profitable. "Her whole story doesn't make sense," I finished. "You'd think she was doing it all by . . ."

Witchcraft, I didn't say, but Ellie nodded her understanding, meanwhile scanning around for boat traffic as we passed the lighthouse again, this time on our left.

"Only takes four inches of water," she agreed. To trigger the vest, she meant. "A big wave would've dunked it that much."

"And if it *wasn't* really ever in the water, then it didn't get washed up on the beach like Glenna said. So then where *did* she get it, and why is she lying about it?" I went on.

"Somebody put it there?" Ellie theorized, steering sharply to avoid a patch of floating seaweed with a dock piling caught up in it. A seagull perched on the dock piling aimed his bright eye at us as we went by.

"Same with the boot," she said, steering us back on course. "Maybe it didn't float ashore, either. Maybe she just found it there and thought it had."

Ahead in the distance, Eastport spread like a toy town, its steeples, storefronts, and houses all looking idyllic, as many will do when they're far enough away. The new engine ate up the distance, though, and in a few minutes, we were entering the boat basin.

Vessels in their slips slid by smoothly as the rush of relief that dry land always brings me swept through me; intense and fleeting, but somehow the pleasure of not having drowned never gets old, and I luxuriated in it.

Until: "Take the wheel," Ellie told me, and I had little choice since she'd already let go of it.

"Why?" I slid into the captain's chair. Soon it would be time to cut the engine and make a quick turn, one that would bring us very gently right up against a short wooden finger pier.

The important word there being *gently*. "Ellie?"

The turn loomed, coming up faster than I'd expected. Making it perfectly was the key to a good landing, by which I mean one that doesn't demolish the pier, the dock pilings, and the dock itself, probably right along with whatever fishing boats floated nearby.

"You're doing fine," Ellie called; she was crouched out on the edge of the Bayliner's bow, getting ready to jump.

I was ready to jump, too; overboard, if possible. But the wooden pier we were meant to slide neatly up to, got closer and more aggressive-looking by the moment.

"Now," said Ellie. "Turn the key off, turn the wheel, and if we die, we die."

"Wonderful," I uttered grimly, knowing for sure that we were going to be crashing into something solid. But with my hands on the wheel and Ellie nowhere nearby, I was stuck.

Then: *Oh, the hell with it.* I switched the engine off and

turned the wheel. The Bayliner veered starboard, but not enough; I turned harder and suddenly we swung fast.

"Jake?" Ellie inquired sweetly. "You okay?"

"Fine," I grated out, although this may not have been a perfectly accurate description of our situation. We were heading straight at a pretty little vintage Chris-Craft runabout, all teak and brass and red leatherette seat covers.

I turned away; we slid past the Chris-Craft with inches to spare while the men fishing on the breakwater watched the woman trying to dock a boat.

Amuse the rest of us, my great Aunt Fanny, I thought grimly at them, then recalled something that Ellie had said to me once, back when I was still firmly refusing to steer the Bayliner at all: that it's like driving a car.

So just as our bow kissed the pier's edge, I swung the wheel again. We had good forward momentum—too much, if you asked me—so in response our stern swung in neatly.

And presto! We were parked. Or *landed*, for you boaty types; at any rate, we were safely lined up against the finger pier and I hadn't taken out half the fleet.

"Wow," I said breathlessly. Ellie had already jumped from the bow to the pier, tied the lines, and now jumped back aboard.

"Good," she commented on my boat-landing triumph as we went around turning things off. "Now you can do it every time."

Oh, great.

Back at the Moose, we sent Mika home with our thanks and enough money to make a morning's work worth her while, though she protested that for her, it was like a vacation.

Some vacation, I thought when she'd gone and I'd confronted the evidence not only of a midmorning rush, but of a noon hour that must've been well-nigh apocalyptic.

While I bagged the trash, Ellie filled the dishwasher with pots, pans, mixing bowls, measuring spoons, and enough cookie-baking sheets to put a new metal roof on Glenna LaFarge's tiny island shack.

Speaking of whom: "Somebody tried to kill her," I said.

"Right," said Ellie, scrubbing the kitchen's big butcher-block worktable. "But she won't tell us who."

Somehow, Mika had not only waited on a zillion customers, she'd also filled our display case with peanut blossoms, mocha tartlets, pinwheel cookies, and a really spectacular-looking German chocolate cake whose frosting bristled with coconut.

I craved a piece. In fact, I realized suddenly, if it were a cake made of cardboard I'd still be tempted, I was so hungry.

"Go home. Eat, rest a little. Then come back," Ellie said when she saw me eyeing the cake.

"You're sure?" I looked around skeptically. There was still a lot of cleanup to be done and there'd be more customers, too.

"Scram," she replied, so after putting on a fresh pot of coffee and emptying more trash, I got out of there, the little silver bell over the door jingling merrily behind me.

Hurrying along in the heat, I dodged groups of tourists lingering under shopfront awnings, kids on bikes arrowing by on both sides, and a guy leading a German shepherd so huge, a small child could have ridden it.

The dog smiled; distracted, I smiled back. All I could think of as I quick-stepped up Key Street was that soon I could get some lunch and maybe even a moment's peace.

Fat chance.

From inside came the *bangity-bang-bang!* of a wooden spoon hitting a saucepan's copper bottom, and have I mentioned that my grandson was a talented percussionist? Too bad that by the time he was old enough to take lessons, I'd be in a padded cell.

Bang! Even the dog had fled the kitchen where Ephraim was showing off his chops, and when I went to get a beer, the cat was on top of the refrigerator looking frantic.

"Ephraim," I said gently when he'd finished with his new riffs, "why don't you go let Grandpa listen awhile?"

Ephraim trotted off agreeably, still banging. I guzzled cold beer and thought about life vests, shoe heels, and the kind of person who would leave a person to drown on a sinking vessel.

Just then Mika came in looking troubled. "I need," she said unhappily, "a small harness. The kind that you tie a person into bed with."

I must've stared. "Ephraim's decided that last night's bad dream was a wonderful adventure," she said.

His near-drowning in a sand-pit full of water, she meant. "So he says he's going to try to do it again," Mika added.

I'd told him it was a dream. It seemed right to say, at the time, but he'd taken my words too much to heart. Now he marched bangingly back into the kitchen and around the table, then out again, and despite my tortured eardrums I still had to hand it to the kid; he could definitely keep time.

"Mika," I said when he'd gone; the unholy racket he'd made had given me an idea. "His bedroom door opens outward, correct?"

I was pretty sure I remembered this. Over its two-hundred-year life, the house had undergone many changes; Ephraim and Doreen's shared room had been part of the no-longer-existing back stairs.

Mika nodded. "Well, then," I began, "what if we . . . ?"

The plan was simple, if perhaps not the most sophisticated, and it would make the din of the pot-and-spoon combo sound like a whisper by comparison. But I thought it would work, so the kid wouldn't have to be trussed up like a turkey.

Then, just as Mika and I had agreed on our tactics for the evening, Sam's truck pulled into the driveway and he came in.

"Ma? Did you tell the carpenters to"—he spied my beer, grabbed it, and swallowed the last gulp—"pull down the rest of it?" Sam finished, wiping his mouth with the back of his hand, whereupon a loud crash sounded from outside, and then another one.

By the time I got out to the yard, the second wall of the new addition to my old house had already bit the dust. Also it had bitten the rhubarb patch, some ornamental grasses, and a few of Bella's raspberry bushes.

Buddy Holloway strode across the driveway toward me, one hand wiping sweat from his brow with a blue bandanna and the other already making calming gestures in my general direction.

"Jakeia, now, it couldn't be helped, we didn't find out until after we'd—"

I was too mad to talk on purpose so I just opened my mouth and let the words come out all by themselves: "First the framing was down, then it was up, then *some* of it came down, and now—"

"Jake." He knew I was mad. "Jake, there was nothing we could do. As soon as he knew, the shift foreman called up the mill operator, operator called the yard, the yard called me."

"Knew what?" I waved around at the framed-up walls lying flat on the ground. Some of the crew were already power-sawing the brand-new, fragrantly fresh two-by-fours into pieces.

"That the lumber wasn't to spec," Buddy said resignedly. "Not building-grade material."

I just stared at him. "This stuff," he waved behind him, "might be good for deck railings and such-like."

He sucked in an unhappy breath. "But not for structural, not for bracing and load-bearing and so on."

Another deep inhalation. "The new yard kid," he went on to explain, "just put the wrong stuff on the truck, that's all."

In other words, the lumber we already had wouldn't keep the new addition from collapsing under a heavy snow burden, or in a windstorm. Or maybe if it just happened to take a sudden notion and fall down.

"How much?" I sighed. It would be over my budget, I knew that much, because we already were over budget, and late, and who knew what this would cost?

But Buddy surprised me. "Nothing. Yard's error, they make it good. But it will take another . . ."

He named a length of time: not forever, but it wasn't next week, either. And we needed it; if nothing else, we needed the extra bathroom before Doreen got out of diapers and began lining up for it with the rest of us.

And Buddy knew this, but he still didn't look optimistic. "We'll do what we can," he promised, and since I'd heard this so often already—about the windows that seemingly had to be built one by one, for instance, and the floor tiles that had arrived in pieces—I didn't have much hope, either.

Turning away from the spectacle of a perfectly good house-addition being demolished—well, except for the might-fall-down part, of course—I dragged my hand across my damp, sunburned forehead. The few puffs of hot, sultry breeze tasted metallic, and the leaves on the maples sagged limply as if in surrender.

I had just turned away from the latest carpentry debacle and decided to go inside for a cold shower when it hit me: those scones, the chocolate raspberry ones that Ellie and I had said we'd bake for tomorrow.

I'd forgotten all about them yet again, and so had Ellie, I was willing to bet, or at least she hadn't mentioned them. Now the promised delivery date was less than twenty-four hours away, and we hadn't even finished inventing them yet.

Yeesh, I thought, and headed for the porch, giving up my hope of a shower for the promise of another beer and a speedy return to the Chocolate Moose.

My hand was on the screen door when a car pulled into the

driveway. Without looking I knew that the car needed a muffler, at least one wheel bearing, and very likely a valve job, too. That's what you learn when your son likes to fix things—ones with wheels, mostly—in your backyard.

Just what I needed, I thought tiredly, a visitor to muck up my day even more than it already was.

But then I saw who was in the car.

"I'm so sorry," Sally Coates wept as I led her inside. "I was driving home from work and the car started making noises . . ."

I brought her into the kitchen and sat her down at the table, which was covered in drawings of deep pits with laughing children falling into them.

Or . . . no, that kid in the drawing wasn't falling. He was jumping gleefully, his grin running off the edge of the paper. I swept the drawings away and got two beers out, figuring that if Sally didn't drink hers I would.

But first she'd have to stop crying. "Sally. Come on, you can't get anywhere that way."

It's another thing I've learned over the years: You can cry all you want, but it doesn't fix anything; when you're finished, you still have to get up and do something about whatever it is.

Besides, if she went on sobbing, I'd have to give her salt tablets along with the beer. "Whose car is that?" I asked.

She hadn't had one the day before. Sniffling, she looked up. "Neighbor kid's. I traded him some of Paul's fishing gear."

Well, at least she hadn't handed over any cash, and at this point I doubted that Paul would be using the gear again. From the sound of it, though, she wouldn't be using the car for very long, either.

"And the car made you start crying? The noises coming from it?"

They'd have made me cry, that was for sure; a wheel bearing alone would cost hundreds of dollars to repair.

Sally nodded brokenly. "It was too much, all of a sudden. Paul, the car . . . but that's not all."

She pulled an object bundled in newspaper from the canvas tote bag she'd brought in and began unwrapping it. The smell of fish wafted up.

"I found this fastened to the back porch step early this morning," she said, uncovering a whole mackerel with an extra-long galvanized roofing nail driven through its gills. A few drops of fish blood had oozed up around the nail.

It was as if someone wanted to frighten her, perhaps so she'd ask us to quit snooping. Suddenly little Ephraim galloped into the kitchen wearing a purple construction-paper crown and not much else.

"Fishy-fishy! Inna brook!" he yelled, spying the mackerel, and fell to the floor giggling before Mika came in and swept him up into her arms.

"All right, buddy," she said, "let's go."

She tried very hard, and Sam did, too, to keep things from getting too uproarious around here. But they could only do so much, and there were so many of us . . .

"Fishy!" I heard him bawling as she carried him off, and then Sally was talking again.

"I have no idea who put it there," she said, meaning the dead fish. "But I'm worried about my kids. I applied for a job at the dollar store this morning, and what if someone comes to the house when I'm at work and—"

She stopped suddenly, probably at the look on my face. Her kids weren't old enough to stay alone, and she knew it. But she couldn't afford a sitter on dollar store wages, I felt sure.

"Anyway," she finished, "maybe it was a prank. And I guess the kids could stay with my mom," she added with a glance at me. "But it still seems threatening."

I pressed the cold beer bottle to the side of my head. "It seems kind of threatening to me, too," I said.

In the living room, Ephraim had cheered up and was busily testing the high-volume limits of the xylophone, and if you ever give a xylophone—or a drum, or god forbid a kazoo—to a kid, then I wish you the joy of it.

"But is that why you came?" I asked Sally. "You happened to be in front of my driveway when it all just . . . hit you?"

She shook her head. "No. I remembered something. I went by the Moose but Ellie looked busy so I came here."

She dug in the satchel again, found a scrawled-on scrap of paper and thrust it at me. On it was a man's name and an address way out in the boondocks on the mainland.

"Paul's half brother, Bailey Lyman, he used to fish with Paul," she said. "But just recently they had a bad falling-out, Paul wouldn't say why."

"When was that?" The name on the paper sounded familiar but I couldn't put my finger on why. "And was it about the same time as Paul got so security-conscious?"

Upstairs, the baby began crying, while out in the yard Sam's big dog had seen a squirrel or a chipmunk—or possibly nothing at all—and was having conniptions over it.

Sally nodded. "A few months ago. Paul was upset."

She glanced at her watch, a beat-up old Timex, then tipped what was left of her beer down her throat and got up.

"You think Bailey Lyman might know something useful about Paul disappearing?" I walked her to the door.

Her shoulders moved in a shrug. "Maybe. But maybe not. I don't speak to Lyman myself anymore, he's such a creep, so I don't know."

She stopped in the doorway. "And he's the kind of guy, I don't know how much he'd say even if anyone did ask him questions."

We stepped out onto the porch. Out in the yard, a pair of men loaded sections of cut-up lumber into the bed of a pickup truck; two others hauled heavy four-by-fours, sweating in the heat.

Sally crossed the driveway past them and got into her car, which was loaded with more silver duct tape than chrome and so rusted that just looking at it could probably give a person tetanus.

I watched it back out, spewing smoke from the tailpipe, then examined the scrap of paper she'd given me. The address was in Lindville, a town of about five hundred spread over some of the most intensely rural territory in the county, and the name— Bailey Lyman—still sounded familiar.

But why, I wondered as in the parlor the xylophone banged, upstairs the baby howled miserably, and the dog outside went on barking—that animal could've given the Baskerville pooch a run for its money—while power saws snarled their way through more of the now-worthless junk lumber outside.

Along with it all came the haunting strains of somebody in the house next door playing scales on a trumpet, missing the third note each time, and I had an instant of hoping that it was the angel Gabriel over there; if it was, at least afterwards maybe I'd get some peace and quiet.

Then Bella came down the hall toward me with her hair in messy pin curls and a pair of flip-flops on her feet, wearing a cotton housedress and looking as if she too needed an aspirin, an ice pack, and a stiff drink, not necessarily in that order.

"Ephraim is such a wonderfully *energetic* boy," she managed faintly as the xylophone's repetitive clanging began resembling a medieval torture tool.

Clang! Bong! Bang! She winced, then she looked down at the paper I held and gasped in unhappy recognition.

And that's when it came to me, why Bailey Lyman's name was so familiar. It was also when I realized that not only was I going to find this guy and get him to tell me whatever he knew about Paul Coates's disappearance—

The trumpet-tooting and xylophone-clobbering grew louder and more insistent, the baby's cries settled into a rhythm like an ice pick being jammed monotonously into my ear, and in the yard the dog sounded as if he wanted to kill somebody so please, *please* won't we just let him at them—

Not only that, but I was going right this minute.

Ten

Lindville was on the mainland, fifteen miles from Eastport on a narrow, twisting, two-lane blacktop road. It was a part of down east Maine that visiting tourists rarely glimpsed.

Small mobile homes stood on dusty, roughly cleared quarter-acres surrounded by forest, baking in the sun. Lakes shone blue through screens of evergreens in the pine-perfumed heat. I'd put the Fiat's top up, but the air rushing through the windows felt as if it were coming out of a furnace.

The road, though: zoom. The Fiat ate up the sharp curves and sudden inclines, and by the time I reached Lindville—no town hall or post office, just a crossroads and a road sign pocked with .22-caliber bullet holes—I'd blasted a lot of my anxiety about this trip straight out through the zippy little sports car's twin carburetors.

But not all of it. Bailey Lyman was what Sam would've called a bad dude, with a history of crimes—fighting, assault, bad checks, breaking and entering—culminating in his arrest a few years earlier for vehicular homicide.

He'd mowed down a guy in a parking lot; accidentally, he

said. A jury agreed, and only afterward did it come out that Bailey's earlier interactions with the victim had been worse than anyone had wanted to testify about.

Much later, I'd heard in Julio's that the whole thing was over a girl Bailey fancied himself in love with. He'd been stalking her, learned that her boyfriend was hitting her and otherwise abusing her, and took swift action.

But people were too afraid of Bailey Lyman to say that, so they didn't. Thinking about this, I turned in onto an old dirt driveway that curved in toward a big old white house with a long screened-in porch. Upstairs, gables looked out in all directions and four redbrick chimneys pierced the roof.

Five, if you counted the one on the ell, which I guessed held the kitchen; now that part of the house looked abandoned, and a flat granite slab sank unevenly into the earth where its doorstep had been.

I parked the Fiat in front of an old, falling-down barn and started through the unmown grass to the porch door, whose torn screen I now saw was as neglected as the rest of the place.

By now I was realizing that I should've at least let someone know where I was going. I even had my phone out to call Lizzie, give her my location in case I didn't return from it.

But then came the sound that I least enjoy hearing when I'm approaching a strange house: a dog, running and barking at the same time, getting rapidly closer. The creature's voice sounded like a Doberman's, or maybe a mastiff's.

But where? Everything else in the summer afternoon was still and silent. Even the birds had shut up, too hot to chirp, and no cars went by. Only the dog went on barking frenziedly; then the porch door flew open and a brown blur burst out.

It wasn't a Doberman. It was a German shepherd and I'd seen it before, somewhere. Just recently, even.

"Hey, bud!" I called. The dog kept coming but slowed as it neared; then it stopped, sat, and tipped its head inquisitively as

I began walking again. Finally it got to its feet again, its tail wagging, but tentatively.

Just keep walking, I told myself, hoping the dog wasn't thinking *just keep biting*. But as I passed, meanwhile wondering about whether or not I'd be able to tie a tourniquet one-handed, the big canine swung around and loped alongside me, looking up at me every few steps as if leading me.

At last the big house loomed over us, its broken shingles and mossy siding, rotted sills and dangerously swaybacked roofline presiding over the lawn's shady silence. Not until I'd made my way past the grime-clouded kitchen windows in the back section, their flowered curtains now fallen to graying rags, did I see the police cars.

Lots of police cars, parked in the yard behind the barn; I counted two county squad cars, the sheriff's white SUV, and one car each from the neighboring towns of Machias and Dennysville.

But no actual cops were in evidence. I stopped in the dusty driveway between the barn and an open shed with a rusting tractor in it. Farmall, said the name through the corrosion on the machine's once-red hood.

On the wall nearby were a bunch of hooks; from them hung an old wetsuit, some ancient-looking goggles, and the mask-and-hose air regulator contraption that divers use to breathe.

Which I thought were interesting. "Hello?" I called into the silence, then turned from the barn and went up onto the back porch, found the door unlocked, and opened it a crack.

"Hello? Anyone here?" A warm funk of rotting trash, old bacon grease, and wood smoke came out at me.

The dog pushed inside, then turned to look anxiously at me before hurrying away down a hall. I could hear it whining, and its toenails click-clicking.

I looked back once more toward the barn and the weeds and tall grasses in the field beyond. But no one was out there, and now the dog was back, whimpering urgently and tugging gently but insistently at my sleeve.

"All right." I gave in, following him down a long hallway that was furnished with a long hat rack, a bentwood coat stand, a wall-mounted thermostat, an ornate cast-iron radiator, and one of those Jesus paintings with the eyes that follow you around.

The dog disappeared around a staircase into what I assumed would be the dining room, since it was directly adjacent to the kitchen. But when I reached it, I got a surprise.

Several, actually. The room, graciously proportioned with high ceilings and that big bay window, had in recent years been turned into a man-cave, with plaid-upholstered heavy furniture, a braided rug that might at one long-ago time have been green, and a TV screen covering the space above the fireplace mantel. Fast-food wrappings, snack bags, and beverage cups littered the room.

I stepped further into the room. The mantel was crammed with what looked like Navy memorabilia; a young man in uniform, the same guy in swim trunks and goggles, grinning at the camera, and again in full diving regalia. There were commendations and certificates in frames, metal ID tags on a chain, more IDs for the base's mess hall and gym facilities and so on.

Also, there was a dead guy on the floor. Bailey Lyman, I presumed, and the shepherd must be his dog.

Although once I'd found the body, the animal lost interest and wandered away. I felt like doing the same, and forgetting I'd ever seen any of this. Helping Sally Coates was turning out to be even more trouble than I'd anticipated.

Although something had recently troubled Bailey Lyman more severely. The fireplace poker lay on the floor; from the nasty-looking perforation in his head, I guessed it had taken just one poke, but that one poke had spattered the wall and ceiling.

The dog returned, sniffing inquisitively. "Damn," I said to it after checking for a pulse again, but it was still absent. So why weren't those cops already in here?

Somebody had called them to the property, clearly, making me wonder how anyone had known they should come; there was no sign of trouble from outside. But all I'd seen were vehicles.

I started to think about taking a look around the rest of the house now, while I had the chance. But before I could snoop into anything but the rolltop desk in the corner, loud voices came from the kitchen.

The shepherd whirled and ran toward the voices in a way that made his teeth look even bigger and sharper than they were.

"Dog's friendly!" I yelled. "Don't shoot him, he's—"

I hurried to the kitchen, stopping at the sight of half a dozen cops' service weapons, all aimed at me. To their credit, though, the cops realized pretty quickly that I was harmless.

I might've taken issue with that notion, but this wasn't the time. "Look in the dining room," I said, lowering my hands.

The shepherd's tail wagged. Somehow he'd gotten the idea that I was letting them in, so now it was okay.

Still, the cops eyed him worriedly. "You'll keep him under control?" one asked.

"You bet," I promised, fingers crossed behind my back; if this dog wanted to do something, I might as well try to control Godzilla.

What the dog did want, though, was to go back outside, so I went along and a little while later the officers came out again, too, all serious-faced, a few already on their phones. A county deputy, young and with brush-cut, baby-blond hair, came over to me with a notebook open in his hands.

Yes, I'd found the guy. No, I didn't know him; I was here to ask him about his half brother's disappearance at the request of his sister-in-law. Yes, they could have my contact info.

Then he told me why they'd stayed outside, at first: the dog wouldn't let them in. Why he'd allowed my own entry, I had no idea; maybe I'd just smelled good to him. But at any rate the snarling canine had held them off, so they'd been waiting for an animal-control staffer to arrive.

As he told me this, a white pickup truck pulled up. A young woman in a Town of Dennysville T-shirt and jeans hopped out, and the dog galloped toward her.

"What, is Barney giving you trouble?" she asked, bending to scratch the dog's noggin affectionately.

There was a big, gray, dog crate in the truck's bed, plus a long pole with a stout wooden handle at one end and a snare at the other, for uncooperative customers. Meanwhile it was clear that if Barney wanted to, he could've eaten the snare, the pole, and the girl, too, without trouble.

He just didn't want to. One of the officers filled the girl in on the situation.

"Oh," she said regretfully. "So you want me to take him?"

To the pound, she meant. Where he would languish, and wonder why. "Wait," I heard myself saying, and they all looked at me.

Oh, good heavens. But, "I'll take him," I said, still not quite believing it—to this day I don't know what got into me—and they relaxed; nobody else wanted him in the pound, either.

And that was it: When I brought the dog home, my family might decide to put me in the pound, we were so crowded already. But I'd worry about that later; for now—and still very much to my immense, somewhat terrified surprise—Barney was mine.

After a couple of minutes of back-and-forth with the police officers, the young woman drove off. The officers finished with me by checking my contact details again, then sent me away, too.

I don't remember the ride back to Eastport.

* * *

"They didn't ask me if I'd killed him," I answered Ellie half an hour later in the Chocolate Moose.

I'd come straight here from finding Bailey Lyman dead in the sprawling pile of disrepair he called home, and of course it was way too hot to leave a dog in a car, so I'd brought him in with me.

"Everything else nearby had splatter on it except me," I went on, "and I suppose it didn't hurt, either, that I've got on a white blouse."

"Mm-hmm. That makes sense." Ellie cast a doubtful glance at Barney, sprawled in the corner of the kitchen near the window, where the air conditioner emitted a coolish breeze now and then.

"What's Bella going to say about him, though? There's already enough animals in your house to populate the Ark."

"Bella's not our problem right now." I whisked us past the subject of the tongue-lashing I expected. Bella liked animals, but not hordes of them; her squawking about another new one was inevitable so why dwell on it was my attitude on the subject.

"The problem is"—I returned us to the subject at hand—"somebody killed Bailey Lyman before I got to talk to him. But how'd they *know* I was going to talk to him?"

Ellie pulled dough out of a mixing bowl and plopped it onto the flour-dusted worktable. She kneaded the dough strenuously a few times, then applied her rolling pin to it.

"Maybe they didn't. There are lots of reasons someone might decide to kill a guy like him," she said. The dough mound flattened swiftly to a pie-plate-sized circle about an inch thick.

Watching Ellie work, I realized suddenly what she must be doing. She'd worked up a new recipe for the shark scientists' chocolate raspberry scones, and now she was trying it out.

"Besides, Coates has been gone a week, now," she said, cutting the flattened dough circle like a pie into eight reasonably equal wedges. "Maybe someone thought that with us snooping around, they'd better tie up loose ends. And them getting to him just before you did could be coincidence."

"It was like somebody knew I was going to Lindville," I mused aloud, only half-listening to Ellie. "But I didn't tell anyone I was going. It was spur-of-the-moment. So how . . . ?"

Ellie moved the dough wedges to a baking sheet and slid it into the oven, then turned, dusting her hands together.

"Look, Sally told you about him," she said. "She might've talked it over with her mom, too. Or a friend, and who knows who they told? Anyone could have known, and like I said, deciding to act on that knowledge just when you went out there to see him could've been a . . ."

"Right, a coincidence," I finished for her, because she was right: sure it could've. And I could be the Dalai Lama, too.

But I'm not.

Ellie checked the oven temperature. "Jake, all I'm saying is that it doesn't mean Sally set you up to find Bailey Lyman's body."

Possibly by killing him, herself, I added silently; I've always been much more bloody-minded than Ellie.

On the other hand, she was smarter than me. "The thing is, though, his house will be empty tonight," she said, setting the timer on the oven. "I mean, won't it? After the coroner takes the body away and the cops get done, it'll all be . . ."

See what I mean? Brilliant. "Dark and quiet," she went on. "Fairly easy to get into, too, I'll bet, even locked up."

She was right. The place was in such poor shape, you could probably break pieces off with your hands and get in that way.

"Maybe we could find out what Bailey Lyman was up to in the days before his demise," I mused.

"Like maybe disappearing his half brother, Paul Coates, and stealing a gold coin from him?" Ellie suggested.

"Just like that," replied somebody who wasn't me.

The voice came from behind me; I jumped about a foot, and Barney the German shepherd got up alertly.

Lizzie Snow stood there. I don't know how she managed the bell over the door; carefully, I suppose.

"Planning another expedition?" she asked, glancing around.

I didn't know how much she'd heard. "Are you kidding? Do you not see how busy we are?"

The work area resembled an explosion at the flour factory, raspberry juice stained one whole end of the butcher-block worktable, and the dishwashing sink was heaped.

"You do look like this all will keep you out of trouble for a while," Lizzie conceded.

I couldn't tell if she really thought so. "Anyway, I've got news," she said.

She pulled a sheet of paper from her back pocket and spread it on the worktable where the scone dough had been; Ellie and I peered at the photocopied page from a book called *Treasures of the Caribbean.*

The page showed a photograph of a large, not-quite-round coin, obviously very old. The text was in French, which I used to know from reading restaurant menus, but not anymore; Ellie shook her head at it, too.

I did see the words *magnifique, sans prix,* and *très précieux* sprinkled through the text, however. And I saw very clearly also that this was the coin whose photo Sally had also shown us, the one she said Paul had been carrying in his shoe when he disappeared.

"The book says the coin was recovered from a Spanish wreck off the coast of Florida in the mid-twentieth century," Lizzie said, "and it's been missing pretty much ever since."

I looked up, surprised. "Oh, I learned French quick when I went to work up in the county," Lizzie explained.

Sure, I realized belatedly; she'd have had to. Plenty of people in Aroostook County speak French at home, and some of the oldest are more fluent in it than in English; a few don't speak English at all.

"What's it say about the value?" Ellie asked, frowning at the photo and back at the photocopied page again.

Lizzie replied, "Priceless, the article said. Or it would be, if it ever came up for sale. See how clear the letters on it are, and the sun rays behind the crown?"

She refolded the page. "I went over to her place and looked at Sally Coates's picture after you told me about it. Then I scanned it into my phone, sent it to a coin guy I used to know in Boston. He emailed me the article about it."

Ellie and I looked first at one another, then at Lizzie. We'd both expected she'd probably be doing things differently from the way Bob Arnold had done them when he was police chief.

But at best I'd hoped for benign neglect. This looked like actual help. "That's good," I said, too surprised to say more.

"Anyway, it's hundreds of years old, but it looks brand-new because when the ship sank, it was new. Never circulated."

Ellie squinted puzzledly. "So where's it been all this time, and how'd Paul Coates ever get hold of a thing like that?"

Lizzie shrugged. "The article says the coin dropped out of sight within days after divers found it in a shipwreck," Lizzie said. "There were theories about who took it. None proven."

"So . . . it's never been sold?" I asked. "Publicly, I mean, like at an auction, or something?"

"I guess not," said Lizzie, "although I'm still hoping my coin guy can tell me more once he's had a chance to ask some of his colleagues about it."

Which still left Ellie's question: How did a struggling fisherman with a family to feed come to possess something so valuable?

Something occurred to me. "Maybe we're looking at this from the wrong end," I mused aloud.

They looked blankly at me. This made me wonder if perhaps

I'd just said something stupid. Also, I was in that common but annoying situation of not knowing for sure what I thought until I heard it come out of my mouth:

"We're wondering if somebody killed Paul Coates," I said, "then took the coin. But what if all of that's backwards? What if he handed it over willingly and *then* someone killed him?"

Lizzie's lips curved like the Mona Lisa's as she moved to the door, looking like she'd gotten what she wanted.

"Nice talking to you," she said. Then the little bell over the door jingled and she was gone, lowering her sunglasses as she moved past the shop's front window.

After that, business picked up again, so we didn't have time to discuss Lizzie's visit. Time passed in a blur of baking and serving, cash-registering and cleaning up. By closing time we'd sold every crumb of what had been in the display case, and I never got even a morsel of that German chocolate cake.

Ellie's scone recipe turned out well, too. The samples were delicious and the trick turned out to be fresh raspberry puree with the seeds strained out, a pain-in-the-tail process that started with fresh raspberries and that I ended up doing.

When I got done, my hands were so stained with red juice that I looked as if I'd been committing murder, myself. But the raspberry part of the program was *fini* and now all that remained was to find a way to get the chocolate in there.

"A not-boring way," Ellie specified firmly as we cleaned up and prepared to go home. "I'm not inventing a whole new recipe just to dump store-bought chocolate chips into it."

Out in the kitchen, Barney the German shepherd still snoozed under the so-called air conditioner. When I called him, he lifted his head but made no move to rise.

"That," Ellie observed as I called again and he finally got up, stretched, and walked out to us, "is an unhappy dog."

Tail down, shoulders slumped, brown eyes mournfully looking at nothing in particular . . . I thought most likely he'd witnessed the deadly event in Lindville, and now that he wasn't quite so amped up with anxiety, he was processing them.

Outside, he climbed back into the Fiat dutifully while Ellie got out the keys to her own car. "I doubt Lizzie's coin information helps us much, unfortunately," she said.

I looked at her over the Fiat's hood. At five thirty in the afternoon, the sun still beat down like a fiery hammer.

"I don't know," I said. "Maybe it's helpful."

When Lizzie said the coin had been found off the coast of Florida, a puzzle piece in my head snapped into place.

"Because," I went on, "before he came home and set his foot on the path of unrighteousness"—by which of course I meant assault, breaking and entering, bad checks, car theft, drunk and disorderly, and the absolute capper of them all, vehicular homicide—"Bailey Lyman was a Navy diver," I said. "In Florida."

The pictures of a younger Bailey in the room where I'd found him dead had told me, along with his other mementos: I'd learned the rest from the old diving gear hanging in his shed.

I just hadn't realized it until now.

Ten minutes later when I pulled the Fiat into the driveway at my house, music was thundering out the open upstairs windows so loudly that I couldn't even tell what it was.

It shut off abruptly as I slammed the car door a little harder than usual. In the silence that followed, I stood staring at what the builders of the planned new addition had accomplished that day.

Which was nothing: no walls, no rafters, no plywood sheets waiting to be nailed down as underlayment for the floors. Also there were no work trucks, toolboxes, lunch pails, energy drink bottles, nor any actual workers of any kind anywhere on site.

"Okay," I pronounced softly into the complete absence of activity, then got the big dog out of the car and led him to the fenced backyard where Sam's equally big dog liked to hang out. There was fresh water there along with plenty of shade, and he made a beeline for them while Sam's dog watched calmly.

Then I went inside, where the baby was crying and Ephraim was applying himself to the piano with enormous gusto. Bella ran the vacuum cleaner in the hall, Sam cranked his music back on again upstairs, and my dad started the blender out in the kitchen where he was pureeing, apparently, a lot of ice cubes.

"Hi," I said faintly to Mika, whom I found walking steadily back and forth in the dining room, jouncing the wailing baby and wearing a fixed look of calm under pressure.

One thing you could say about that baby; she could find your last nerve. "Mika?" I said over the din. "Do you happen to know why the carpenters didn't work today?"

Suddenly the baby stopped crying, babbled cheerfully, and produced a spit bubble. Mika and I blinked, startled.

But just then the blender started up again in the kitchen, sounding this time as if it was laboring through something thick, and Ephraim returned to pounding the xylophone with, it sounded like, a jackhammer.

The baby whimpered warningly. "No lumber," said Mika. "It didn't get delivered."

I was ready to call the lumberyard and give them a piece of my mind when Mika spoke again.

"Truck driver's mom was in an accident," she said. "She's fine, but he went to Bangor with her to make sure, and the other driver's in the ER with leg cramps from working in the heat."

See, this is the level of detail you get around here, not just what but who and why and whose cousin they are. I put the phone down as, in the parlor, the piano fell silent and little sneakers thumped up the hall stairs.

But at the same moment, the shower went on up there—

Sam, probably; his music, his boots in the hall—its faint hiss diminishing as the bathroom door closed.

"Hey! I gotta get in there!" Ephraim protested.

Mika looked vexed. My dad ran the blender again, its metallic snarl like a jagged blade in my eardrum, and Bella chose that moment to dump the whole silverware drawer into a metal trash can.

Or that's what it sounded like, anyway. "Give me that baby," I told Mika. "And tell my dad whatever he's making out there, I want one."

I took the baby, kicked off my sandals, and sat down in the padded rocker by the parlor fireplace. The tiles around it were cool on my feet.

"A big one," I specified to Mika, and soon after that my father appeared with a frosty mug containing the largest frozen strawberry margarita I'd ever seen.

His wrinkly, age-spotted face creased in a smile when he saw that the baby was asleep. Later, Mika relieved me of baby-duty and brought me my dinner: chicken salad, homemade French fries (Bella was a whiz at these), and a small pile of greens from the garden, so fresh they were practically still growing.

Sometime after that, Ephraim climbed up into my arms and conked out, his dark eyelashes resting sweetly on his soft, pink cheeks. Wade came in and kissed me when he got home; I eyed him questioningly. We hadn't spoken since he'd shot me the evil eye the night before.

He shrugged, not evilly. "Yeah, yeah. Just try not to scare me, all right? I'd looked for you earlier, is all. Before you got home."

So that's why he'd been up and in a bad mood already when I did arrive, I realized; he'd been worried about me, not without reason given my snooping history.

"Oof. My bad," I said, and agreed (not for the first time) not to terrify my husband any more than I could help, and then he kissed me again and went upstairs to take his own shower once Sam got out and the water heater had boiled more hot water.

A little later with Ephraim still out cold in my lap, Bella patted my shoulder and asked if I would like some dessert: fresh apricot pie, still warm from the oven, with a scoop of vanilla ice cream melting on it. Then Sam peeked in, saw the sleeping boy, and gave me a thumbs-up, tiptoeing away again.

At last the dogs arrived, curling up at my feet like old friends. Outside the windows, evening darkened; a breeze, warm but welcome, puffed the gauzy curtains inward. Around me the house quieted except for the old wooden clock ticking hollowly in the hall.

And that's how I ended up sitting there with a dead-to-the-world Ephraim in my arms until the clock struck ten, which is when I got up, handed him over to Mika, and changed my clothes for the night of fun and frolic still to come.

Something warmer than a blouse and shorts, I thought as I rummaged through the hall closet; darker, too. Finally, I found a navy-blue sweatshirt and a pair of Levi's and pulled them on.

And then I went out to break into a dead man's house.

In the moonlight at the north end of the island, Ellie's paved driveway was as bright as a landing strip; she was waiting at the end of it when I pulled up.

"Here, it's what's left of the margaritas my dad made," I told her as she got in and I handed her a paper cup.

Holding it, she settled into the Fiat's passenger seat. For our expedition tonight she was wearing a navy-blue hoodie, dark jeans, and black high-top sneakers because, as she said, in this life you never know when you'll need running shoes.

I hoped tonight wouldn't be one of those occasions. "Sorry the ice is melted," I said as we pulled away from her house.

Beside it in the rearview mirror, the little barn where she

kept goats and hens was a flat black cutout against the marine-blue night sky. Ellie swallowed some of the drink and coughed.

"That's okay," she managed. Then she knocked back the rest of it; maybe she was as nervous about this trip as I was.

Because I mean seriously: a dead guy's house? Nevertheless, minutes later we crossed the long causeway that links our island with the mainland. Soon after that we sped through the moonlit landscape of lakes, fields, and trees all perfumed by pine trees and new-mown hay, on our way back to Lindville.

"I still absolutely don't get why Glenna LaFarge won't say who tied her up in that barge," I said as I drove.

"So she can deal with them herself," Ellie replied.

"What, like she did in the first place, when they stuck her down there to drown? And why would anyone do that, anyway?"

Ellie shrugged. "Maybe to stop her from talking to us?"

"Yeah, well, she didn't do much talking. Or not much that I believe. *Found it on the beach*," I scoffed. "Sure, she did." We didn't even know if the life vest belonged to Coates. It could have come from anywhere, blown off a boat or a ferry. The shoe was a different story, sure, but Sally hadn't talked about Paul having both shoe-heels carved out. Just the one.

"I don't suppose anyone will be there now, do you?" Ellie asked. At the late Bailey Lyman's place, she meant.

"Not unless they left him there," I half joked. Handling victims' bodies may go right to plan in big cities, but out here at the back end of beyond we did our best with what we had.

Limited morgue space, blistering heat wave, only a few funeral homes in a county the size of Connecticut . . . if too many other people had passed on around here recently, we could get to Lindville and find Bailey Lyman's remains packed in ice from a convenience store.

But: "Don't worry." Packed in ice was my worst-case scenario. "It'll be just us chickens," I predicted confidently.

We drove in silence again. With the top down, the moon up, and nobody else around, despite our errand it was heavenly out here.

"Those cops are all home watching the ball game," I said as bugs darted and dove zigzaggedly in our headlights. Finally we reached the crossroads and the stone wall enclosing the old Lyman place.

The massive pile of rotting clapboards and ragged shingles shone a moldy greenish-white in the moonglow, and the windows were black holes where bright eyes used to be.

"Yeesh," Ellie said expressively. "Did you bring any more of those margaritas?"

"I wish." Now that we were here, the trip suddenly seemed nuts. I pulled slowly up the driveway. No movement anywhere . . . but there wouldn't be, would there? If someone was waiting for us. Out of nowhere I wished we'd brought the dog along.

But there was no sense saying any of that. I got out of the Fiat and we strode through the moonlight toward the house.

"When we get in, look for anything more about Florida, or diving, or rare coins," I said.

I had no idea how or if Bailey Lyman had been involved in Coates's disappearance. But I doubted he could've missed out on knowing about the valuable coin his half brother had inherited. And if he'd known about it, maybe done something about it.

I'd left the Fiat halfway down the drive, figuring it would be too visible from the road up near the barn. As we neared the house, I wondered if I'd left it too far away, in case we needed a fast getaway.

But out of sight was better, I decided. "There was a desk in the kitchen and another in the dining room where I found him. We'll want to check those," I said.

My toe slammed into a rock sticking up through the driveway dirt. "Ow," I said woundedly to the rock while I bent to rub the toe; no blood, I noted, dismissing the injury.

But when I straightened, a dark shape was flitting across the driveway, at the top where it widened out.

Between the barn and the house. Flitting and vanishing; I thought it had gone into the house. Ellie'd seen it, too. Neither of us said anything stupid, though, like *What was that?*

Because we both knew what was that; it was a person, and the person was sneaking around. The warm night air felt thick with humidity and menace, suddenly.

Because look: We already had a man missing plus the obvious murder of another, so somebody around here was dangerous. Meanwhile the shape didn't reappear, but we hadn't imagined it. "Do you want to leave now?" I whispered.

"Sure do," Ellie replied, squinting at the place where the shape had most certainly been. Then her lips tightened, her brow furrowed, and her chin lowered mulishly.

"But the heck with that." She started toward the house.

"Wait!" I whispered. She didn't. I trotted behind her until we got to a patch of moonlight shimmering in front of the barn.

I didn't want to cross it to the kitchen door I'd gone in earlier. Ellie, either, but then she spied another way.

"There's an ell," she said. It's a sort of breezeway off one end of an old house, used for cool storage, coats and boots, and wintering-over geraniums, spring bulbs, and so on.

This one ran between the house and the barn, and the barn door was open; quickly we scuttled into warm, stagnant darkness that smelled like old motor oil and dust.

Moving cautiously, I walked face first into a cobweb and felt something skitter across my hair, swatted madly at it, and stopped when my hand slammed into something solid; one of the barn's support beams, probably.

Cradling the hand, I moved forward again, trying to keep up with Ellie, whose flashlight beam kept bobbing away ahead of me.

"Okay," she whispered, turning the knob on the old wooden door that suddenly loomed out of the darkness. "Here goes."

Whereupon the old hinges let out a *skee-reek!* like a cat having its tail stepped on. Too much like it, in fact; I looked down and sure enough, a cat was having its tail stepped on.

"Yikes, sorry." I lifted my foot and the cat streaked off, tossing back a glare before vanishing into the barn's dusty darkness. Then the door that Ellie had been fiddling with swung soundlessly open.

Moonlight slanted in through the ell's windows, falling in pale gray squares onto the concrete floor. On the windowsills, a trio of African violets had long ago withered and died. Between the windows hung an Eastern Fuel Oil calendar from 1992.

At the ell's far end another door led into the house, this one locked. "Darn," Ellie said, eyeing it, "I'm not sure . . ."

The door opened. Lizzie Snow's cop boyfriend, Dylan Hudson, stood on the other side, smiling amiably.

And pointing a gun twice the size of mine at us.

Eleven

"Step into my parlor," Dylan Hudson invited wryly, and we did, of course; that big gun, and so on. But being intimidated never fails to annoy me and now was no exception.

"Oh, put that thing down," I said crossly, standing in the awful kitchen. The room was dark until he flipped a switch; then a fluorescent overhead cast a bluish flicker onto the stained sink and overflowing trash bin. A strip of flypaper thumb-tacked to the ceiling spiraled hideously over it all.

"What the hell are you doing here?" I demanded, my heart still thudding wildly. A patch of old motor oil from the barn smeared my shirt front; I brushed angrily at it.

Hudson eyed us both. "I could ask the same about you," he replied, slotting the gun back into a shoulder rig under the navy-blue polyester jacket he wore.

"Lizzie told me you were both too nosy for your own good," he went on, and at that I might've lost my temper a little.

"Listen, you," I said, jabbing a finger at him, "when I need a character assessment from a low-grade Lothario who thinks he's god's freaking gift to women *and is mistaken*, I'll—"

His lean face fell. You'd think I'd just kicked his puppy. "Is that what she said about me? That I'm a—?"

Lizzie came in suddenly from the hall leading to the front of the house, stopping short when she saw Ellie and me.

"Oh, for Pete's sake," she breathed exasperatedly, taking in the situation. "I should've known you'd—"

Apparently she hadn't thought our snooping into Paul Coates's disappearance would involve housebreaking. I reminded myself that she didn't know us very well, yet.

Meanwhile, Ellie's sharp gaze bopped efficiently around from the desk shoved in between the ancient stove and the old, round-shouldered Frigidaire to the linoleum-topped counters full of opened envelopes, bills marked *past due* in red magic marker, and containers of Super Glue, turpentine, and 3-in-1 Oil.

Finally she wandered across the kitchen to sit carelessly in the old metal folding chair pushed up to the desk.

"You," I told Lizzie, "are an Eastport cop. You have no business here any more than we do. And neither"—I pointed at Hudson—"does he."

Ellie slid a desk drawer open and poked a finger into it. She was good at fading into the woodwork when she wished; now she peered at the items her finger had stirred around.

"We," I pointed out further to Lizzie, "have just as much right to be here as you do."

Which was none, but never mind. Something about my argument gave Lizzie pause. I wished I knew what, but for now:

"Okay," she told me finally. "We're here, we might as well try to cooperate."

This was the last thing I'd expected to hear. Hudson looked disapproving and started to say something but she shut him down with a look, adding:

"Hey, Dylan? I just got this job and I'd like to keep it. What do you think the city council would say if it got out that I'd been breaking into houses?"

Oh, now I got it, or thought I did. "Lizzie, for Pete's sake," I began, "we're not going to—"

Tell anybody about this, I'd have finished, but instead Ellie's swift look silenced me: *She knows that.*

So now I really got it: Lizzie didn't want Hudson to know that she was—sort of, anyway—on our side; I still wasn't sure why.

Still, I'd take it. "Okay," I said hastily before she could change her mind, "how about we take the downstairs and you go upstairs?"

Let them be the ones to check the bathtub for ice and a body. Also there were still two desks down here, stuffed with who knew what kind of information, and I wanted at them.

"We're looking for anything having to do with rare coins, diving, any kind of treasure, or—"

"Or murdered men," Hudson muttered sourly. He didn't like it at all that Ellie and I were staying.

"Or murdered men," I agreed as he and Lizzie went away down the front hall together, both wielding flashlights; Hudson had snapped off the kitchen light switch he'd turned on, earlier.

We didn't want anybody going by on the road to see lights on in here, after all. Practically rubbing my hands together as I watched them go, I turned to the desk Ellie had been looking into. But then she called to me from a small, dilapidated alcove off the kitchen, half-hidden behind the water heater.

"Jake, look at this." A path around the heater into the alcove was worn right through the old kitchen linoleum; only a few steps in, I felt the unstable floor moving beneath me.

Water damage, I realized right away, and as the long-time owner of a very old house I don't even want to talk about how I knew this. When I looked up, a droplet quivered on the ceiling: from a pipe upstairs, most likely, which had probably been leaking for a long time.

Then another thought hit me. "Hey, Lizzie?" I could still faintly hear her and Hudson talking in the front hall.

"Listen, that was you outside, right? Going from the barn to the house a little while ago?"

Lizzie appeared in the kitchen doorway. I'd tiptoed very gingerly into the alcove; now I took a drawer from the beat-up wooden desk in there and slid it out across the floor, nearly to where she stood, then did the same with the other two.

"This whole floor feels like it wants to fall into the cellar," I explained, then turned for a final look around before stepping back out into the kitchen.

But then I saw Lizzie's face and took an unthinking step back. Unfortunately, without warning my foot went straight on through the worn linoleum, busted the spongy-feeling rotted floorboard beneath it, and didn't stop until it plunged into a cottony gray mass of ancient spiderwebs.

With, I could see through the hole my leg hung through— the wood kept tearing away like wet cardboard at the slightest touch—spiders living in it.

"Enghhh!" I said. Or something like that. The hole enlarged steadily as my attempts to escape just broke off more of the old floor; soon there'd be none within reach for me to cling to.

"Don't come out here," I warned as another hunk of linoleum broke off in my hand. With it came a small scrap of paper, but I didn't care about that; at the moment, just breathing felt like it might send the rest of me down through the floor.

Hudson hurried in looking as if this whole evening was making mincemeat out of his last nerve.

"Floor's bad," I gasped at him. My other leg was readying to follow the first one and punch through into spider world, and then my body would follow.

And who knew how far? I couldn't see past the spiders to

the floor below them, assuming it really was a cellar down there and not an old well, or worse.

"A broom handle," I managed, "or a piece of clothesline."

But sweeping a floor or washing laundry had both been way outside Bailey Lyman's wheelhouse, apparently, and nothing else that I could grab to get pulled out of here was in evidence, either.

So in the end Dylan Hudson lay down, wincing as his jacket met the layer of grime on the kitchen floor, and stretched out his hand. "Grab it," he said flatly.

Not that I needed urging. But couldn't quite reach it and if he came any closer he'd go through the floor, too.

He inched nearer anyway, his shoulders now inches past the alcove's threshold. The floor sagged again; I squeaked in alarm.

"Now, Jacobia," he said, and that's when I knew he'd done some kind of a background check on me; nobody calls me Jacobia but Wade and my father, and only when they're annoyed.

"I'll count to three." His gaze held mine. "On three, you'll throw your weight towards me hard, and grab my hand, okay?"

No, it wasn't okay. Below me, a legion of darkness-dwelling arachnids were sharpening their mouth-parts, and below that—

"Jacobia." His voice drew me back to reality while his eyes said don't worry, none of this was really a big deal.

Yeah, easy for him to say. "One . . . two . . ."

His hand reached out, his eyes locked again with mine, and for an instant I thought I saw what Lizzie must see in them; plenty of flaws, but when you need him, he'll be there.

"Three!" he finished, and there wasn't much else I could do so I gave up and hurled my upper body sideways, as per his instructions. He did the rest, seizing my shoulder in both hands and pulling hard.

A moment of being dragged helplessly up out of the hole and I was free, half expecting to see masses of spiders boiling up out of it behind me, but they weren't.

I got up. Hudson brushed at his now-filthy jacket; clearly, now that I wasn't in danger anymore—danger of my own making, his face said, and in this he was regrettably correct—I was of no interest to him.

Then he went grumpily off to look some more for anything that might link the murdered Bailey Lyman and that darned coin, whose very existence I was beginning to curse.

"Anyway, what did you mean, what you said before?" Lizzie wanted to know while I'd checked myself for injuries, like maybe a spider-bite or a severed artery.

"About someone coming in here?" she added, so I explained what Ellie and I had seen from the driveway, right after we'd arrived here.

"Sprinting toward the house," she repeated thoughtfully. Then she was out of the squalid kitchen and down the front hall, calling urgently up the stairs.

"Hudson! Watch it, we've maybe got another visitor."

Hudson appeared on the stairway landing. "Not up here." He patted his shoulder rig. "We checked."

Lizzie let a breath out. "Of course you did." Still, my question meant the house had to be gone through from attic to cellar, and Ellie and I were forbidden to join in.

"We don't need four people running around up there with flashlights in the dark," said Lizzie.

We were to stay in the kitchen, stay out of trouble, and not touch anything, which was all just fine with us except for the parts about staying in the kitchen and not touching things. After all, there were still two desks to search and I meant to search them no matter what.

As for staying out of trouble, we were already in trouble, so the heck with that, too. Ellie took charge of the desk drawers I'd removed from the alcove while I cautiously tiptoed down the hall to Lyman Bailey's long-untidied man cave and the desk in there.

But as I approached the doorway, a shadowy figure, moving in equally cautious silence, tiptoed out of it.

"Hey!" I shouted. In my shock and surprise as the figure rushed past me, it was all I could think of.

But it was enough. Hudson and Lizzie came flying down the stairs while Ellie charged out of the kitchen like a linebacker barreling at the ball carrier.

The intruder faked fast, right and left, then dove hard, skidding and scrambling up again, pounding across the kitchen with the two cops close behind.

Their feet crunched the driveway's pea gravel outside and a couple of halfhearted shouts came from the front yard, but soon Lizzie and Hudson returned, disgruntled and empty-handed.

"Why didn't you tell me sooner that you thought someone was here?" Lizzie demanded under her breath.

"Didn't give me a chance, did you?" I gritted back. "Too busy teaming up with your boyfriend, there."

She shot me the kind of evil eye that suggested I might've struck a nerve. Behind her, Hudson was giving the kitchen a last looking-over, key fob in hand.

Then we were all outside and the place was locked up tight. *We'll never get back in there,* Ellie's face said as she watched Hudson try the door.

Then we got ushered down the driveway to the Fiat, whose engine when I started it let out a feral snarl that instantly made me feel better. Hudson was still ticked off, though.

"You ladies need a hobby," he grated out, and of course I didn't hop from behind the wheel and sock him in the kisser; for one thing, Lizzie seemed to think it was a pretty nice kisser, and for another he was bigger than me.

Also, he'd just hauled me out of a hole. But: "Yeah, we'll

give that idea some strong consideration," I said, not sparing the sarcasm—hey, saving my life doesn't mean you can be a jerk to me for the rest of it—and he rolled his eyes.

"We'll talk tomorrow," Lizzie said, then turned to follow Hudson to his car. I put the Fiat in reverse under the big yellow moon now shining through the trees along the driveway.

"You look," said Ellie, glancing over from the passenger seat, "like the cat that swallowed—"

"Ellie, I found something." Getting a hand into a pants pocket while wearing a seat belt is not my favorite activity but I managed it, then thrust the crumpled scrap of paper at her.

I'd thought little of it when it came up out of the hole in the collapsing floor along with me. But just now I'd glanced at it by moonlight as we got into the Fiat, and—

"This looks like a phone number," Ellie said, peering at it.

"It must've been tucked under the worn-through linoleum and when Hudson dragged me up, it snagged on my pants or something."

It would've been easy to slip a bit of paper down in there where nobody would look: easy, and unnoticeable afterward.

"You have your phone with you?" I asked.

Nodding, Ellie dug it from her bag, squinted at it, and seemed satisfied at the number of bars on the screen; just like on the water, out here at the back of beyond a dead spot is not only possible, it's common.

Ellie looked questioningly at me, her button-pushing finger poised. I shrugged, turning my gaze back to the road.

"Might as well give it the old ring-a-roonie," I said as we wound sharply downhill and over the Dennys River toward Route 1.

"Find out who's so mysterious that Bailey Lyman had to hide their number," she agreed.

And why would a person do that, anyway? I wondered as Ellie punched in the digits. "It's ringing," she reported.

I turned left onto Route 1, smooth and straight with a good bright yellow edge-line. Ellie took the phone from her ear and looked troubledly at it, then hung up, slowly folding the phone back into her bag.

"Well?" I demanded as headlights appeared in the oncoming lane; a sudden rush of air shoved the Fiat forcefully sideways as the eighteen-wheeler roared by. Next came two cars crammed in tightly behind the truck, waiting for a chance to pass.

So it was a little while before I glanced at Ellie again.

"Did anyone answer?" She was frowning at the windshield, looking as if she was doing some tricky arithmetic in her head and the numbers weren't adding up.

As we swung down the exit ramp onto Route 190 toward home, she turned to me again, still looking mystified.

"Jake, I just called the number you found in Bailey Lyman's house."

The very much dead Bailey Lyman, I thought. The murdered Bailey Lyman, since it was pretty certain he hadn't stabbed his own head with a fireplace poker.

"And Sally Coates answered," Ellie said.

The moon lit the mists drifting ghostlike on Carrying Place Cove. "Interesting. But you didn't recognize the number on the paper?"

Ellie shook her head. "No. It's not Sally's usual number, I know that one by heart."

Ellie was the kind of person who knew phone numbers after using or seeing them just once. So either Sally had a second phone, and Lyman had the number to it—and hid the number, for some reason—or it was someone else's phone that Sally had just answered.

Coming into town, we detoured past her house: dark windows, that junker she'd just bought parked outside, everything quiet.

"Maybe she's at her mom's," said Ellie.

Which was possible; she'd have heard about Bailey Lyman's death by now, most likely, and maybe she was upset about it.

But that was all we had: lots of maybes. I eased the Fiat away down the street, keeping the engine noise to a low growl as much as I could; it was past two in the morning.

"Okay," I told Ellie when I dropped her off in front of her house, "later we'll find Sally and just ask her why Bailey Lyman had her number, and why she thinks he'd hidden it."

Ellie sat unmoving in the Fiat's bucket seat, staring out into the warm summer night as if turning a new thought over and over in her head.

"No, we won't," she said, opening the car door at last.

"Why not? It's the simplest way to—"

She got out and closed the car door. "Two reasons," she said. "First"—she held up a finger—"the scones. Have you forgotten them? The chocolate raspberry ones?"

I had forgotten them, all four dozen of them. Didn't want to remember them, either, but I had little choice.

"What's the other reason?" Out on the water, the Cherry Island beacon flashed red.

Ellie smiled sadly. "We're not going to ask her because we don't know the answer. And . . ."

The beacon's red beam jabbed the darkness. "And all of a sudden," she said quietly, "I'm not sure I want to find out."

Nobody was awake by the time I got home, the house all dark and even the dogs curled up in their bed, unmoving.

"Some watchdogs you are," I said as I heated some coffee. I took it into the parlor where I wandered around aimlessly for a minute, exhausted but unable to settle, then decided I'd better force myself upstairs and at least try to rest.

In the upstairs hallway I padded quietly on the carpet, moving through my usual nighttime bed check before I lay down; not that I'm a control freak or anything (insert my family's hearty laughter here), but I do find it soothing to see everyone safely under the covers before I lie down, myself.

Not that there'd be many covers on a night like this, the air warm and muggy no matter how many windows were open. Even my dad's knitted nightcap, worn both winter and summer to keep his brains warm, he said, hung on his and Bella's tall bedpost when I peeked into their room.

Meanwhile the littlest two kids wore only diapers, Sam and Mika slept with a single sheet pulled over them, and Wade—

Wade, who sleeps like a dead person, wore only the gauzy moonlight slanting in through the window. I'd have joined him if I could, but I had one more bed to check, so I tiptoed down the hall to Ephraim's room.

Inside, it was very dark and too warm; he didn't like open windows through which monsters might climb, or nightlights that might show monsters the way to his bed.

And forget about moonlight; monsters, he had informed me seriously, could ride on moonlight. Still, I crossed to the window and opened it a crack; by the time Ephraim noticed it would be daylight, which was when monsters slept.

His stars-and-planets mobile, turning lazily now in the few puffs of warm air coming in the window, glowed faintly. His stuffed bear peeked from beneath his Snoopy blanket, which he'd pulled up over himself despite the room feeling like a sauna.

I bent to adjust the blanket so at least it wouldn't strangle him, and also for a soothing whiff of his clean-little-kid smell, like a faintly soapy sugar cookie.

But when I reached down for the blanket's edge in the near-darkness, I noticed something odd; beneath it, he wasn't shaped like a little kid.

Or breathing like one. "Ephraim?" I murmured, knowing the truth already but trying not to. "Honey?"

No answer. I ripped back the blanket and felt frantically

around the bed, then fumbled for his Felix the Cat bedside lamp and pulled the cord.

The room sprang into light: the Felix lamp, his dresser, painted in primary colors, his Little Engine that Could clock. Even his beloved stars-and-planets mobile—*Here comes Jupiter, there goes Mars!*—went on turning very calmly and unhurriedly as if all was well.

But a thorough search of the house—soon everyone was awake, and we each took a room to hunt through yet again while Wade and Sam searched the yard and the neighbors' yards—didn't locate my missing grandson.

I couldn't believe it. It didn't seem possible. But Ephraim—our stoutly stubborn, meltingly sweet little boy, his smile just heart-stoppingly lovely and his eyes so wide and guileless you could practically fall right into them—

Ephraim was gone.

If I'd ever had doubts about Lizzie Snow's cop skills, they vanished that night.

"The sheriff, the state cops, an Amber Alert, every deputy in the county, and all the guys from down at Julio's, even Julio, himself," she said. "Julio called them in, had them call the ones whose numbers he didn't have, to help search."

It was nearly three hours, now, since I'd found out Ephraim was missing. We were under the fluorescent overhead light at the table in my kitchen, and the first light of dawn was brightening the black sky to gray outside the windows.

"And a squad of volunteers from the fire departments in the surrounding towns," she finished. "I've got them assigned to grids so they don't duplicate effort."

She told me a lot of other things, too, but I couldn't take them in. Then a realization hit me belatedly, that he would never have arranged his bed to look as if he were still in it. He wouldn't even know how. Someone else—someone who was taking him—would have to do it.

Still, maybe there was another explanation, I told myself desperately. He could have sleep-walked down Key Street to the edge of the bay, and into it. He could be in a backyard swimming pool.

Or hit by a car. Anything could have happened. "We'll find him, Jake," said Lizzie. "Kids wander off all the time."

Yeah, but how many wander back? I wanted to retort, but I didn't; she was trying to help.

"I'm going out," I said instead, "I can't sit here."

She followed me out to the Fiat. The few salvageable pieces of the unfinished new addition lay at the rear of the driveway, looking in the half darkness like sections of a wooden monster's enormous skeleton.

I wondered if Ephraim had worried about it. But mostly I wondered where the hell he was.

"Tell them I'm driving around," I said to Lizzie, who stood there looking like she really wished I wouldn't do this.

"Jake, there are a *lot* of people searching," she began. But she couldn't stop me, could she?

No, she couldn't, and at that moment a speeding locomotive couldn't have, either; I shoved the key in the ignition.

"Jake," Lizzie began again. The Fiat started with a growl very much like the one I wanted to emit.

She stepped to the car's side, holding a clipboard whose top sheet was already very much scribbled on. She was, just as she'd promised when I'd called her in a panic, doing everything she could.

"What?" I demanded. "What's so important that I should stay here instead of going out searching with the rest of them?"

She looked down at her feet, then up again at me, her gaze direct and entirely unsparing.

"Someone," she said, "needs to be here in case there's a

phone call. I want it to be you. You or Ellie might recognize a voice, or a turn of phrase . . ."

But Ellie wasn't here. On the other side of the forsythia bushes edging our yard, Wade's bobbing flashlight moved farther away from us.

Lizzie's look bored mercilessly into me. "In case," she made it perfectly, terribly clear, "there's a ransom call."

Twelve

Dawn on the breakwater in Eastport was blessedly cool and damp—it had rained, just as McFaul predicted—and silent except for the creak and groan of fishing boats moving against the wooden dock pilings, and the crying of gulls.

Through the high, barred windows of the disreputable-looking Quonset hut in the alley behind the Coast Guard Station, I could see that the lights were still on inside Julio's. The big steel door was locked, but I rattled it and went on knocking until Julio himself came to the door and let me in.

Inside, chairs were upended on tables and barstools pushed aside. Floor sweepings were in a pile at the center of the rough plank floor, ready for the dustpan.

Julio had been on the phone when I knocked. Now he spoke into it once and hung up, then turned to me, clasping my hands.

His dark eyes were mournful. "Jake. I'm so sorry. My guys and some of the customers are going through the yards in North End."

He nodded toward the phone. "That was one of them," he said, and sighed heavily. "No luck so far. Little Ephraim, oh, I can't believe this, he's such a good boy. Sweet boy. But they'll find him, Jake."

"Thank you, Julio." My heart softened toward him; he was almost like family around our house, even staying with us for a few nights once when a nor'easter flooded him out of his living quarters at the rear of the bar building.

Now despite his clear misgivings he made it sound as if there would be good luck soon, of course there would be, that it was only a matter of time.

But I knew too well that the longer missing people are gone, the more they stay gone.

"Listen, Jules, that's wonderful of you." He was like an uncle to Ephraim, giving him horsie rides when they met on the breakwater and letting him pound the piano in the bar on the few occasions when Ephraim was inside.

"But I need a different favor from you now," I said, "and you're not going to like it."

The wary narrowing of his eyes said he knew what I wanted. There was just one main rule here at Julio's and if you were in here with any regularity, you knew it: What happened at Julio's stayed at Julio's unless it was cops asking.

Otherwise, ut-up-shay. But: "What?" he asked.

"Paul Coates," I said. "His wife, Sally. And . . ."

"And Bailey Lyman?" Julio made a face of distaste. "I've heard what happened to him," he added. "Few of the county cops were in. But what's that got to do with your missing boy?"

"Maybe nothing. But I need to know about those three, how they were . . . anything you can tell me about their interactions."

Julio pulled down a pair of chairs and sat back to front in one of them. "Okay. I probably shouldn't, but . . . Bailey would come in when Paul and Sally were here. Try to buy her drinks, make her dance with him. Paul didn't like it."

"That's it?" I stood despite the offered chair.

Julio nodded. "All I ever saw." His face changed. "Couple of bruises on her, once or twice," he added reluctantly.

I felt myself straighten. "Really?" Sally hadn't mentioned anything like that. Julio got up and fetched two club sodas with ice, and I drank some gratefully.

"They were arguing about Bailey," he went on. "Couple of weeks ago. Paul had changed his tune for some reason, said they both had to be nice to him, that he was family."

Huh. "And she said?"

"She said Bailey gave her the creeps, and if he put his hands on her again she was going to punch him."

Another *huh*. "What else, anything?"

"She said it would be great if Bailey could get a diving job again, that there were plenty around here and he could be some use to himself for a change."

That made sense. Julio went on.

"Dishonorable discharge, but he used to be a Navy diver."

Without warning Ephraim's absence slugged me in the solar plexus again. "Jules, I've got to go. Is there anything else about the night they came in together I should maybe know?"

His balding head tipped sideways. In the right light, his face resembled a mournful spaniel's.

"Like I said, sometimes she had a bruise. But that night it was a black eye. Makeup on it, but still."

"Oh. Okay." I thanked Julio for the information and the seltzer and promised that I wouldn't make a habit of violating his saloon's confidentiality arrangements.

"Listen," he said, "you want me to cook for you tonight? All of you? I've got some great T-bones stashed in the walk-in freezer, I could—"

I managed a smile. "You're the best, Julio, thanks very much for the offer. But I think we'd better wait until—"

Sobs threatened suddenly; I headed for the door but when I got there, I turned back.

"What about that shark guy, Peter Waldron? Do you know him? Any impressions of him?"

Julio's face cleared. "Oh, him. Yeah, he's a nice enough guy, I guess. Got a real shark fixation, and he's kind of what they call nowadays socially awkward."

He got up. "Seems okay, though, what little I know. He was in here the night Paul Coates went missing, in fact. Got a little loaded, as I recall. But no problems."

Julio looked sharply at me. "Why, you have trouble with him?"

"No, just wondering. I heard Coates had been working for him, that's all. Thanks, Julio."

I stepped out into the early morning, where the boat basin had come alive with idling diesel engines and the breakwater was full of parked pickup trucks. I got into the Fiat, backed out around a refrigerated box truck and a boat trailer with a wooden dory strapped to it, and made it at last to Water Street, where I faced a decision.

Dylan Hudson was answering the phone at my house; he'd suggested to Lizzie that maybe someone with cop experience should do it. The slim chance of my recognizing a voice or a phrase was nothing, he pointed out, next to the possibility of bungling a ransom call, and Lizzie agreed.

Meanwhile I'd called Ellie, whose husband, George, was now out searching the island with Wade, and of course she didn't expect me at the Moose; Sam and Mika were searching too, while Bella and my dad watched the rest of the kids and the animals.

All of which helped me decide, as I gunned the Fiat out onto Water Street, to turn right, toward Sally Coates's house.

The sun was high enough to be warm, now; it would be another hot day, I thought with the part of my mind that hadn't gone crazy with worry. In the front yards of the small, white-clapboard cottages I passed, small children had already tumbled out to play before the temperature got prohibitive.

Sally's house was the last one on the left before the yards and houses got bigger and farther apart. I pulled into the short uphill driveway between two elderly lilac bushes desperately in need of pruning, turned off the ignition, snapped the key off, and yanked the emergency brake.

A sign in the yard said the place was wired to a security company. Gazing around, I spotted the cameras on the picket fence surrounding the yard and on the utility pole; similar wires encircled the doors and windows of the house, a small gray factory-built structure on a concrete-block foundation.

On either side of the concrete back steps, heat-stroked marigolds drooped defeatedly. There had been an attempt at a vegetable garden, now baked to dust. I strode past it to the back door and rapped on it, noting the cameras and security wiring here, too. It seemed that Paul Coates had really, really wanted to feel safe from something.

Or someone. Inside on the TV, John Wayne was telling somebody to listen up and listen up good. A small child lisped out the first line of "Zip-a-Dee-Do-Dah" over and over while another began crying, stopped, and started again.

Finally the door opened—not all the way, but hey, I could work with it. By now, politeness was a vanishingly small speck in my rearview mirror.

"Let me in, Sally. We need to talk right now."

She stepped warily aside; I might just possibly have looked dangerous. At least I felt that way; this woman had omitted several important facts from the tale she'd told Ellie and me, and Ephraim might—*might*—be missing because of it.

A burst of raw fury boiled through me when I thought that maybe somebody took Ephraim to distract me from finding out what happened to Paul Coates and his gold piece. A far-fetched idea, maybe, but once I had it, it wouldn't let me alone.

But then from the chipped Formica table in the kitchen, three small children in bright cotton play clothes and pint-sized Crocs looked up at me from their sloppy bowls of cereal and smiled, and suddenly I was ready to cry.

"My grandson's gone," I said, and let the wave of fright wash over me. "Ephraim. He wasn't in his bed. I'm afraid someone might've taken him."

I sat down in the kitchen's unoccupied chair. Sally poured coffee without asking and set it in front of me, and I sipped it and thought about how much I wished for fright to let go of me.

And then it did; enough for me to go on, anyway. "So I want to know about the black eye Paul gave you," I said.

I didn't care if she liked the question or thought it made sense. "And I want to know right now, along with the reason why Bailey Lyman had your phone number."

"You kids go watch TV, now," she told the children, all of whom climbed obediently from their chairs and scampered off.

"Wow," I said, startled. When Sam was that age, if I'd said go watch TV he'd have shoved the TV off the terrace of the big-city penthouse we lived in, just to show me again, dear god, yet again, that I was not the boss of him. Meanwhile, though:

"Whatever," Sally said tiredly. Now that the kids were out of earshot, she didn't have to put up a brave front. "I really don't see why you can't explain why you're asking about this, and if Julio told you about it, I'm going to kill him."

I thought that last part was an unfortunate choice of words under the circumstances, especially given what I knew, now: that Sally might've had a fine reason not just to kill Paul, some-how, but also to get rid of a creep who'd been harassing her.

Plenty of things didn't add up about that, but once I knew more, maybe they would. Glancing around again, I noticed a pair of dog dishes on the counter by the sink.

One for food, one for water. The name BARNEY was painted

onto the dishes. One of the kids toddled in, saw me looking at them, and piped up:

"Mommy sent Barney to live with Uncle Bailey."

"Oh," I said. "Do you miss him?"

The child shook his head. "No. He was too big, he pushed me down all the time."

He turned and toddled away. Sally looked up at me. "The dog was just too much," she said. "With the kids he was just too . . ."

She stopped again. Then finally, "Okay. Yeah, Paul hit me." She glanced into the living room where the kids sat staring at an animated sponge on TV.

Sally bit her lip. "A few times, actually. I even went back to my mom's twice. But we got through it. We worked our way through it, we both made changes, and he's never raised a hand to me again. Or even his voice."

Which didn't correspond at all to what Julio had said, that the black eye had happened recently.

"I guess then you must've decided being nice to your half brother-in-law, Bailey, was worth it to save your marriage?"

She drew back in distaste. "Absolutely not. What, are you kidding me?"

"Fine." I wasn't going to waste time arguing. "Then how come I found your phone number—your *other* number— under the linoleum in that grease-pit of a kitchen he had out there?"

She looked shocked. "I have no idea. He shouldn't have, I didn't give it to him. The whole reason I got the new phone was so he couldn't call me anymore."

I pursued this tentatively, sensing that a hard push might shut her down altogether. "He was pesty, was he?"

"Pesty isn't even the word. It was like he was obsessed with me."

She glanced over again at the three small heads unmoving before a big TV screen now showing a pair of animated teenaged numbskulls being . . . well, numbskulls.

"I don't want them to hear this," she said quietly as the kids giggled along with the laugh track. "Paul used to get mad when Bailey got handsy with me. Sometimes even mad at me, like I'd encouraged Bailey, somehow."

Sure, because his half brother's piggishness was so clearly his wife's fault. Sometimes I feel like beating people about the head with a tightly rolled newspaper, you know?

"But then Paul changed his mind all of a sudden, decided Bailey didn't mean any harm, that I should humor him and so on." Her face said what she'd thought of that. "But Bailey never put a hand up my shirt when Paul saw it, did he? Paul would've backhanded him across the room. But I was supposed to . . ."

Pretend like it wasn't happening, I finished mentally for her as she broke off, grimacing.

"More coffee?" she asked.

"No. Sally, please think." She'd convinced me she wasn't secretly canoodling with Bailey Lyman. But what had happened?

"He had to get your number from someone. Who might've given it to him? And why would that be, do you suppose?"

A fresh wave of anxiety over my grandson made me feel dizzy and almost weightless, suddenly, as if I were poised at the edge of an impossibly high cliff.

"Damn it, Sally," I said when I could speak again, "little boys don't just vanish out of their beds, okay?"

I sucked in a shaky breath. "So if it's not a coincidence that your husband and my grandson are both missing, if you think that someone might, say, be trying to distract me and Ellie from looking into Paul's disappearance—"

Besides Ephraim's safety, it was my worst, most nightmarish fear: that I had unknowingly brought this calamity down upon an innocent little boy.

"—then you'd better tell me right now." I got up and faced her. The kids had heard my raised voice and were looking over their shoulders at us worriedly.

"There's no one," I demanded, "who you think is opposed to your finding out what really happened to Paul? Who might even do something terrible, just to knock me and Ellie off the track?"

She spread her hands helplessly at me. "I'd tell you if I knew something. Really, I would."

One of the children toddled into the kitchen, whining, and grabbed the side of Sally's gray sweatpants. She leaned down to press her head to the side of her mother's thigh, then looked up again.

"You know what, though?" she said. "I'll bet it was Paul who gave Bailey the phone number. Sure, he'd do that."

Her laugh sounded brittle. "It got so he acted like Bailey bothering me was a hoot. Like, a joke among family."

She put a bitter twist on the final word. "Or if he wanted something from Bailey," she added.

It made me want to push Paul Coates off a boat, myself. But at this point I'd gotten all I could from Sally, apparently, even though it wasn't much.

"I'd help if I could," she repeated when I'd thanked her for the coffee and apologized for getting hot under the collar.

"Sally," I said, pausing in the doorway. "About Bailey."

"What?" She looked around distractedly. The toddler yanking now on her pants leg moaned insistently while inside, the other two were getting into a squabble.

I looked around again, too, only now spying the rat's nest of cables, wires, plugs, connectors, and other electronic stuff on the buffet in the kitchen's far corner.

"Sally, forgive me, but you do know Bailey's dead, right?" Someone would have called her by now, maybe even the cops.

But when she straightened, her face was unreadable. A stray

hank of straight, wheat-blond hair flopped down over her eyes; she shoved it back impatiently.

"No. I didn't know. I was over at my mom's . . ."

Right, with the phone whose number no one had except the guy who shouldn't have had it.

"But how? How did it happen?"

The kid yanking her pants whined fretfully.

I supplied the short version: death by fireplace poker, not self-inflicted, obviously. "Someone killed him," I finished. "Maybe while they were looking for the coin."

Behind her, the children's bickering progressed to punches and shrieking. She ignored them and the whining yanker, instead staring at me with those pale-blue eyes, the color of thin ice.

"You're saying that someone went out there and beat him to death?" she said.

"That," I agreed, "is about the size of it."

I was about to add that I was very sorry for her loss, such as it was, but she spoke before I could.

"Good," she said.

After seeing Sally, I stopped in at the Moose, where Ellie was elbows-deep in dough. Already-measured-out melted butter, cream, chocolate sprinkling sugar (the fancy, glittery kind), and a box of ruby-red dried cranberries from Mingo's farm on the mainland stood at one end of the butcher-block worktable.

"Hey," she greeted me with her voice full of concern. A thin coating of flour dusted the table's other end, where she was rolling out a batch of dough.

She put down the rolling pin. "Have they found him yet?"

I shook my head, sank onto a stool opposite her. "No. Everyone's on it, the state police, county and local, the Amber Alert people."

I said it like repeating a prayer. "Lizzie's a real pro, seems like. Got everything organized. She's even dragged Dylan Hudson on board."

I tried chuckling at this last part, wound up bursting into tears, instead. "Ellie, I'm so scared."

She frowned, then went to assemble a cold, wet washcloth, wrung out nearly dry and wrapped around a cup of ice chips.

"Press this to your forehead," she said, so I did, and it shut off the tears; then I put it over my eyes.

Meanwhile I told her about my visits with Julio and Sally. "Ellie, she didn't even know Bailey Lyman was dead until I told her."

Unless she had known, and was a better liar than I'd given her credit for. I explained that, too. "But I think for now we should let her go on thinking we trust her completely."

Which I at least did not, and she wasn't our only question mark, either. Our captain on the voyage to find the guy in the lagoon, Carl McFaul, had inexplicably put us ashore in a less-than-ideal spot, and the strange, grouchy, nearly murdered witch of Walk Island was no picture of normalcy, either.

Even Peter Waldron, the shark guy with the big, expensive research boat, didn't exactly ring my *he's okay* bells. Bottom line, we still had no idea what had happened to Paul Coates and we still hadn't found his coin.

Only his empty shoes and—maybe—his life vest. I took the cold washcloth off my head and regarded it approvingly. Not having overheated brains was making them work better, it seemed.

"But, Ellie, listen to this." I went on to describe Sally Coates's kitchen, with special attention to the taken-out-of-service dog dishes and the heap of wires and electronics stuff.

"She got rid of the dog and disconnected all the security monitoring," I said.

Ellie cut another pie-shaped wedge from the round, rolled-flat scone dough and laid it on a baking sheet. In the cut edge I could see crimson cranberries and the unmistakable shapes of chocolate chips.

The last bastion of the unimaginative, Ellie calls them. Personally, I like to eat them right out of my hand, but in a Chocolate Moose product, she's right.

"So just tell me this," I said, "if George"—Ellie's husband, George Valentine, I meant—"set up a security system and even bought a watchdog—"

I now knew, or thought I probably did, where Barney the German shepherd had come from. He was the watchdog Paul Coates had bought, and Sally must've unloaded the dog onto Bailey.

"—and then George suddenly disappeared for some reason," I went on.

Ellie slid the pan of scones into the oven and set the timer. "For some reason that I do not know?" she clarified. "A mysterious or suspicious reason?"

"Correct. So if it happened, would you promptly dismantle the security and get rid of the dog?"

"Nope." While the first batch of scones baked, she mixed up the next: milk, melted butter, baking powder, flour, salt.

"I'd get another dog and some motion-sensing sprinklers." She turned the fresh scone dough out onto the floured end of the worktable. "A dozen sprinklers, maybe."

When a motion-sensing sprinkler senses you, it squirts you—hard. A dozen of them firing out of the darkness might not put off a trained assassin, but it would discourage anyone else.

"Yeah, well, that's not what Sally did." I described the heaped wires inside and the loose-hanging ones outside.

"I'd have asked about it, but I didn't want her to know I'd noticed," I finished.

Ellie pulled the baked scones out of the oven, then slid them from the baking sheet to a wire rack, swiftly painted them with cream, and shook sparkling sugar over them.

"Maybe without Paul, she can't afford wired security." And suddenly here we were in I-should've-thought-of-that territory.

"You think she might've arranged all this just to get rid of Paul Coates?" Ellie went on. "Seems complicated, and then why ask us to snoop into the whole thing?"

"To get the coin back. Maybe somehow that part of her plan didn't work out, and she needs us to find and retrieve it."

I poured some water from the pitcher in the fridge, drank half the glass despite the ice-cream headache it triggered; in the heat, just driving around felt equivalent to shoving myself into the oven along with the scones.

"And you think the man we found dead in the lagoon was part of this plot of hers, too?" Ellie took a scone from the rack and bit into a corner of it.

"Nah," I replied carelessly, "I'm sure that was merely a coincidence. It's been raining dead guys around here lately and we just happened to find a couple of them, is all."

Ellie nodded patiently at my sarcasm but she got my point: Of course the lagoon guy was involved. One may be happenstance and two could be coincidence, but we had three, if you counted Paul Coates, himself.

Ellie looked at the scone she'd bitten into. "Such high hopes I had for you," she sighed at it.

"No, huh?" I took it from her and bit into it, too; she watched my face.

"Yeah, not quite," I agreed. It was fine. It was good, even. But: "It needs . . . something."

There was always our famous chocolate sauce, which was a good idea for almost anything. It would give the fresh berry garnish that Ellie planned something to stick to.

I reminded her of this, but it didn't satisfy her, and meanwhile Ephraim was still missing.

"I keep imagining him in some water-filled hole somewhere," I told Ellie. "Walking into it, maybe, sound asleep."

Unless someone really had taken him to distract me, an idea so unpleasant that just peeking at it again made me want to (1) slam the lid down on my brain, and (2) throw up.

"I've got to go," I said. Outside the shop's front window a pickup truck went by, its bed crowded with forestry students in cargo shorts and T-shirts. More searchers, I realized, and felt a surge of gratitude wash over me, followed by a wave of fright.

Ellie came to the door. "I'm so sorry to leave you with all this," I said. "The shop, those scones . . ."

Another pickup went by. I recognized the crew from Sam's landscaping company, solemn-faced young men and a few women in orange vests.

"I should be out there with them," I said. It was like a bad dream; I wanted to wake up, but time kept on passing and passing and still I didn't.

"No, you shouldn't be," said Ellie firmly. "Half the county is out looking for Ephraim. And will be, until they find him."

Gratitude flooded me again, this time for the reassurance. "Okay." I steadied myself. "You won't get overwhelmed, here?"

"Lee's agreed to help." Excellent news; Ellie's daughter was nearly as good as Mika at the Moose.

"I told her I'd pay her," Ellie went on, "and since she seems to be in an earning-and-saving phase, somehow—"

Ellie glanced appreciatively at me; I'd quietly educated the girl on the wonders of compound interest, and now at fourteen she was planning to major in economics when she got to college.

So at least something was going right around here. "Great," I said. "Just don't let her restructure us into a corporation while I'm gone."

Outside, the heat was like a smothering hand. I'd gotten into the Fiat and was sitting there debating whether it was worth it to put the car's top up when Dylan Hudson appeared on the sidewalk beside me. Two minutes later he'd hauled the car's black canvas top up over my head and latched it tight.

The sudden shade made me sigh with relief. But then he got into the car beside me. "Man, this day is just going down ass-over-teakettle, isn't it?"

"Yeah. It is." No solid leads from Julio, very few straight answers from Sally . . . I backed out and turned left between the big granite post office building and city hall.

"I thought you were manning the phone," I said finally as the Fiat growled uphill past the art center, the nursing home, and Spinneys Garage. Heat shimmered off the blacktop ahead, and in the rearview mirror the sun glittered mercilessly on the bay.

"Lizzie's there. She's made herself a little headquarters in your kitchen," he replied.

He found the seat's forward/back lever; it gained him a few inches' leg room. "So, where we going?"

I glanced sideways at him: dark hair, high cheekbones, a generous mouth, and a dangerously stubborn-looking chin with a dimple in the middle of it. It was that smile of his that did it, though: *whammo.*

Okay, Lizzie, I get it, I thought at her. "Lubec," I said. "The town you can see from Eastport looking south down the bay."

We sped out Route 190 toward the causeway. "But why are you with me, that's what I want to know."

"Couple reasons." He was wearing a white polo shirt and a pair of slacks that belonged on a jungle expedition, light khaki with numerous zippered pockets.

"First, about the lagoon," he said as we turned onto Route 1 and I floored it; the Fiat leapt forward with a snarl of joy.

Hudson leaned back, unfazed as evergreens and fields flew by. "You were looking for what, again? Coates's body?"

He knew that's what we'd been looking for. Lizzie would've filled him in on the whole trip, I felt certain.

"I thought if we found Coates's body, we'd find the missing coin, which his widow, Sally, needs to support the family."

He'd have known that already, too.

"That's all she wanted?" he persisted. "She wasn't still hoping he was alive somewhere?"

"I don't think so." I thought back to Sally's practical comments about trying to find the coin despite what people might think of her.

"She's a realist." *Not that she had much choice*, I added silently.

By now we'd blazed through the crossroads towns of Perry, Pembroke, and Dennysville, and were zipping around the turns along the river past the sawmill and the Whiting general store.

I turned at the intersection onto a narrow, winding road and the Fiat lit into it: *vroom*.

"Nice car," Hudson observed. Then: "Listen," he said, his tone changing suddenly. He turned to me as well as he could with his seat belt fastened.

So he was smart, too. Nothing in the vintage Fiat reminded anyone to buckle up; no buzzers, no printed stickers on the sun visor. The car even had an ashtray.

"Did she really say that about me?" Hudson wanted to know, and despite my state of mind I nearly laughed, the question was so unexpected.

"What, that you're a low-grade Lothario?" We swung into the first of a truly lovely series of S-turns that the engineers had banked perfectly when they rebuilt the road five years earlier.

"No," I said as the Fiat gobbled the turns. "I made that up. I was mad at you and my mouth gets ahead of me sometimes."

I expected annoyance, got a look of boyish relief instead. "Yeah, people say I've got the same problem."

He sank back in his seat again. He'd been worrying about this, I realized suddenly. To break the silence I snapped on the Fiat's radio; something bubble-gummy blared out of it.

Hudson reached out and snapped it off, producing instead a cassette player barely bigger than the teensy-weensy cassette he slipped into it.

Moments later a jazz tune I didn't recognize floated out into the Fiat's passenger compartment. Hudson saw me glancing down curiously at the extremely small player.

"Cop gear," he explained. "I wasn't supposed to keep it signed out, but now with all the new technology no one else uses it. So I sort of confiscated it."

That smile again. Damn, I hadn't wanted to like this guy. "So," he said, sitting up straighter. "What's in Lubec?"

He answered his own question: "Peter Waldron. The shark guy. From, among other places, the Florida coast. Where Bailey Lyman was once stationed."

I hadn't known that, but it would have been an easy thing for Hudson to check. "Nice," I said.

We emerged from the S-turns onto a gently downward-sloping section of road winding between more fenced fields, hardwood forest, and small, widely spaced houses with woodpiles already in their dooryards because yeah, it was hot now.

But not for long. "Lizzie asked you to keep an eye on me, didn't she?" I said, slowing for the 25 MPH sign at the edge of town. Next came Willard's Drive-In, its gravel parking lot full of cars, and after that the KAT-TAIL MOTEL: KLEAN, KOMFY, AND NATURALLY AIR-KONDITIONED!

"Yeah," he answered me, but that was all. We'd entered a district of two-hundred-year-old houses with porches, bay windows, and multiple gables pulled up close to brick-paved streets; you could practically see the horse-drawn carriages waiting under gaslights, when the houses were in their heyday.

We headed downhill toward the water. "So let me just see if I've got this straight," Hudson said. "You want to ask Waldron if he knows anything about Bailey Lyman. If maybe the two of them collaborated somehow on killing Paul Coates and taking his gold piece."

I glanced again. He wasn't smiling anymore. "Something like that. I figured—" And then I realized. "Oh."

Small laugh from Hudson. "Yeah, coming over here is what Lizzie wanted me to ask you to do. Along with," he added, "me."

I glanced over at him but he was looking straight ahead at the cars and pickups, many of them with boat trailers attached, glittering in the marina's parking lot. Even the old-timers on Lubec's new dock wore hats; behind them, racing waves glinted metallically in the sun.

We parked and got out of the car. Peter Waldron's big, white science boat, bristling with antennae and satellite dishes and who knew what other gear, floated at the dock's far end. From the deck Waldron spotted us making our way out there and waved.

"Permission to come aboard, sir?" I called. Might as well keep things friendly as long as I could, I thought. I just hoped Hudson had the same idea.

Thirteen

"Welcome aboard." Peter Waldron waved us up the *Consuelo*'s companionway into a bright, spacious saloon furnished with low tables, rattan carpet, and comfortable-looking armchairs with clean lines and good upholstery.

Toward the bow, the helm looked like the dashboard of a commercial airliner, all screens, gauges, and slider switches; there were a lot of knobs, too, some that got twisted and some that got slid back and forth, or up and down.

It all looked wildly expensive. "Have a seat," Waldron invited cheerily, "and I'll be right back."

The chairs he'd waved us toward were bolted to the floor, I supposed in case of rough seas. Also, and I could hardly believe it, the whole enclosed common area was air-conditioned, chilling my sweat-damp shirt and hair.

Taking in more of the *Consuelo*'s luxury brass fittings, polished teak, a map table built of some exotic black wood, I sat back and enjoyed the coolest, driest air I'd breathed in over a week.

But Hudson scowled. "Now really I don't trust him," he muttered. "Nobody in Maine wants unexpected summer company, even I know that. They just pretend they do, like this guy."

I was about to reply when the guy in question hurried back into the room carrying a tray of wheatmeal biscuits, a wedge of Brie, and a pitcher of lemonade.

"There's coffee, also," Waldron said, gesturing at a carafe and cups on a nearby credenza.

He wore tan shorts, a navy-blue T-shirt, and sneakers. "So to what do I owe, et cetera?"

I'd meant to start out by asking him whether, when Coates was crewing for him, Coates had ever mentioned a valuable gold piece. We'd see where we got to from there.

But Hudson had other ideas. "You kill him? Bailey Lyman, Coates's half brother, used to be a Navy diver down around your old stomping grounds. You by any chance bash him in the head?"

That, Waldron's face said, was a fine way to talk to a person who's feeding you lemonade and wheatmeal biscuits.

"Well?" Hudson prodded. "It's a simple question."

By then I was practically spraining my face trying to get Dylan Hudson to shut up, to no avail.

"No," Waldron replied, drawing back with a grimace. "I did not kill Bailey Lyman. You see, I don't even know who that is, so I'd have no reason to—"

I turned to Hudson. "Zip it, dammit." Surprise made him snap his yap shut. Then to Waldron:

"My grandson's missing."

Waldron stared. I went on. "Did Paul Coates ever mention anyone he thought might harm him? Or his family?"

From the amount of dismantled security gear I'd seen at his place this morning, I thought everything but the refrigerator door must've had an alarm on it until Sally took it all apart.

"Yes," Waldron said. "Wouldn't say who. He'd had a couple of—"

He tipped back an imaginary cocktail glass. "Mumbled stuff

about how this guy he knew wanted something he hadn't earned."

Waldron looked puzzledly at me again. "But what would your missing grandchild have to do with that?"

I hadn't known before. But I did now. Maybe it was the air conditioning, waking me up, or maybe it was that phrase: *wanted something he hadn't earned.*

There were only a few ways to get those things, and one of them might be taking something you *didn't* want. Like a little boy, for instance, so you could trade him for something you *did*.

Which would mean . . . *We already have it*, I thought in the moment before all my lights went out.

When I came to, I was flat on the pleasantly smooth rattan-carpeted floor of the *Consuelo*'s luxurious lounge area.

"Get her feet up in the air," I heard someone say, "let the blood rush back to her head."

I opened my eyes. Dylan Hudson peered down at me. His lips moved silently. *Play this my way.*

I blinked once to signal that I understood. He nodded, then spoke to Waldron.

"Heat exhaustion," he said, sounding certain, although I was sure, now, that it wasn't that at all. I felt drugged.

I closed my eyes, moaned faintly, and went limp again. Who knew what substances Waldron might keep on this vessel; things to knock out white sharks with, no doubt.

Whatever it was, I can report on good authority that it was tasteless in the lemonade that Waldron had served us. Through squinched eyelids, I noticed Hudson's untouched glass; then I felt myself being lifted up off the floor.

"I'd better get her back to the car," Hudson said as he hurried down the half dozen steps to the *Consuelo*'s main deck with me in his arms. Out here the sun was so bright that I could see a red glow through my closed eyelids.

"Uggh," I fake-groaned, and then, once we were on land, again, "put me down, dammit."

"Okay." Hudson set my feet down on the parking-lot gravel and kept walking. He didn't seem a bit tired from carrying me a hundred yards or so, much of it on a floating dock.

Noticing this, I sank to my knees, then sat down hard. Hudson came back and crouched beside me.

"He's watching us, in a minute he'll be here insisting we go back to the *Consuelo*. You're so ill, you can rest in the air-conditioning, et cetera."

Damn, first a knockout potion gets me off the boat, now not being able to stand upright without passing out was going to get me onto it again.

"Sorry." Just breathing in and out made my head spin, and the shards of sunlight bouncing off the water stabbed my eyes.

"Yeah, me too," he said, "but we're getting out of here."

In the next instant I got flung up and over his shoulder like a sack of flour, with my feet hanging down his front, my arms hanging down his back, and my mouth wide open in a yell they could probably hear in Canada.

But everyone on the dock and the parking lot could hear it, too, and from their faces it was clear they thought I was being (1) murdered, or (2) kidnapped so I could be murdered later.

Near the Fiat, Hudson set me down again and I clung to his arm, managing to stay upright. People were still staring but at least nobody had a phone out, yet.

"Okay," I muttered, and then I began to scold him loudly, using words like *stunt*, *show-off*, and my personal favorite, *complete jackass*.

All of this Hudson absorbed very contritely until we got to the Fiat, and got in. "Did they buy it?" he asked from behind the wheel; no way could I drive.

I glanced back; everyone seemed to have lost interest in us. "Yup." I handed him the key. "You drive a stick?"

He looked at me, then started the Fiat like he'd been doing it all his life and peeled us out of there at a speed that had the dock folks staring again.

"Yeah, I guess you can," I conceded. When we got to the open road, he drove even faster than I had.

"So what do you think?" he asked when we were zipping down the twisty two-lane.

"I think we just barely got out of there. I had no idea he would be—"

"What, lying in wait? Drugged drinks ready in advance for whoever shows up asking questions?" It seemed so improbable.

Nevertheless, my insides all shifted uncomfortably as Hudson swung through the S-turns. "He knew you and Ellie are nosing around about Coates?"

I nodded; the movement only made my gut lurch twice, so I figured I was improving. But just then Hudson glanced at me and what he saw made him pull the car to the side of the road.

Ten minutes later, bent over a grassy ditch, I was pretty sure I'd just upchucked everything I'd ever eaten in my life.

Hudson handed me a half-empty water bottle he'd found under one of the car seats; I rinsed and spat.

"Look," I said when I'd straightened, "I started out this morning thinking that somebody took my grandson for some reason connected to Paul Coates and his [expletive deleted] gold coin."

I got back in the car and we took off again. "And now I think it's maybe to trade him for the Coates's gold piece."

Hudson's lips pursed. "One problem. Well, two, actually."

I was already nodding. "Yeah. How'd they get him out of the house? We have two big dogs and neither of them let out a peep."

I might not have heard them, but Bella would have. If, I mean, Ephraim hadn't simply gotten out of bed, wandered outside in his sleep as he already had a history of doing, and run into any number of possible hazards.

Water, for instance: Around here if you go far enough in any direction you'll hit it, sometimes by walking straight into it, other times by tumbling off a cliff.

But you'll get there. "Let's just assume someone did get in and out of your house unnoticed, though," said Hudson.

He drove easily and well. "Right. That brings us to problem number two," I said.

He downshifted for the exit lane off Route 1, braked at the yield sign, and gunned it heading east on 191 to Pleasant Point, where we slowed for the speed limit. Then:

"But we don't have the coin," he pointed out.

We accelerated onto the causeway. "Precisely," I replied.

At Carrying Place Cove, a blue heron was lowering itself on wings spread massively out like a parasail, its sticklike legs reaching down for the sand and small stones at the water's edge.

"Unless," I said slowly, the taste of lemonade filling my mouth again as I remembered, "we do."

Hudson shook his head. "I don't know, Jake." His sunglasses were the mirrored kind, so when you looked at him you only saw yourself.

"You're pretty far into the speculation department with that idea." Also, it was the first time he'd called me that.

I changed the subject. "Why do you think Waldron tried to drug us? What would've been the point? And are you going to let him get away with it?"

At even the hint of feeling worse than I already did, I'd have asked Hudson to aim us straight at the Calais Hospital emergency room. But instead the driving and fresh air seemed to be clearing my head, and I wasn't about to sideline myself from the search for Ephraim unless I had to.

Entering Eastport, we zipped between the airport and the RV campgrounds; to our right, a small,white Cessna was taking off into the blue sky.

"For now," Hudson said, "I'm not going to do anything,

and neither are you." He glanced at me. "It's better if Waldron goes on believing people trust him."

I couldn't disagree; it echoed what I'd thought about Sally Coates. Still, "Waldron's got an alibi for the night Coates went missing," I said. "He was in Julio's all evening."

"Yeah, well, nobody said anybody did this whatever it is without help," Hudson replied. "And people don't go around dosing people's lemonade for no reason. If he did, that is."

Rounding the last long curve into town past the Mobil station and the hair salon, I felt my anxiety over Ephraim come roaring back.

Hudson sensed the change. "We're going to find him," he said, turning into my driveway.

Ellie was with Sam on the back porch. Mika sat on the step below. I practically flew out of the car, dodging a wheelbarrow full of mixed concrete and the shovels leaning against it.

The builders were at work again, the sound of hammers and circular saws filling the air. I didn't care.

"What's happened?" I gasped. "Is Ephraim—?"

Ellie shook her head. Mika wept silently into her hands.

"Sam?" Behind me, Hudson was crossing the driveway toward us. "Sam, what's going on?"

My son's face looked the way it had on the day long ago when I took him out of the city: confused, angry, frightened. He shoved an envelope at me and went on to sit with Mika.

In the envelope was a color photograph. In it, a worried-looking Ephraim sat on a bench of some kind, holding up the front page of Eastport's newspaper, the *Quoddy Tides*, which had just come out the day before.

Ephraim didn't look hurt or in distress. He was not in a hole full of water or at the bottom of a cliff. So I felt better on that account, anyway.

About knowing for sure, though, that someone had taken him? Yeah, not so much.

* * *

An hour later, after the state cops and the sheriff's deputies had seen the photograph and asked a lot of questions and gone away again, Ellie and I went back to the Moose. Ellie went straight to the test batches of scones she'd been working on and sent Lee home, not forgetting to pay her.

"It worked out pretty well that we told them we're amateur sleuths," Ellie said of the police when the girl had gone.

She was trying to talk me down from my state of red-alert anxiety, not to mention flat-out terror.

"Once someone's sure you're a silly little woman—"

The cops hadn't said that in so many words, but we'd both caught the drift.

"—they're probably not going to bug you much more," she finished.

I wasn't so sure. They'd had a lot of questions, many of which we hadn't been able to answer. But it was true that we didn't need official scrutiny while we were doing things like breaking into houses and finding murder victims in them.

Or searching for Ephraim in places they'd probably not approve of our going, like sinking barges. Ellie picked up the mixing spoon.

"And if I could figure out how to get some pizzazz into these scones, I could think about what we should do next," she said.

I had no doubt that she was already thinking about it. Deep in her brain, wheels were turning; they always were.

And that was a good thing because I was fresh out of ideas. So I was sitting there still feeling hungover from that glass of doped lemonade I'd drunk, when the bell over the door jingled and the owner of the candy store next door to our own shop came in.

"Hello, girls," said Janetta Cline. "Any biscotti today?"

Janetta was tall, blond, and slender, dressed in a white smock and black slacks with a silver pinstripe in them. And we did have biscotti—chocolate, with ginger bits—so Ellie went to wait on her while I took over the scone dough.

"Okay," said Ellie when she returned, "so maybe Waldron killed Coates to get the coin, but it turned out Coates didn't have it? So now for some reason Waldron thinks we have it?"

I'd told her about my visit with Hudson to Lubec and the *Consuelo* on our way down here.

"Maybe Coates told Waldron about the coin because he knew Waldron had been shark-hunting in Florida, in the area where the coin was found?" I floated the notion.

"Bailey Lyman was a diver in Florida," I pointed out. "Why not ask him instead of some guy Coates just met recently?"

"That's why," Ellie replied promptly. "Coates knew his half brother was a bad actor. He didn't know anything about Waldron except that Waldron was smart and talked a good game."

"Which he does," Ellie agreed, sliding the bowl of scone dough into the refrigerator. "Cheery little guy, too."

Right, even when he's serving you some spiked lemonade, and why would he do that, anyway?

I still couldn't figure it out. "So he kills Coates," I went on thinking aloud, "after Coates has revealed the clever place where he hides the coin: in the sole of his shoe."

"But when he looked in the shoe after killing Coates, the coin wasn't there," Ellie said. "So now he's looking for it?"

"No. Not since Sally visited us and then took all her husband's security equipment down and even got rid of the dog."

"And she did that because . . ." Ellie still looked puzzled.

"To send a message," I said. "Nothing here to safeguard. No treasure on the premises. No need for security measures." I took a breath. "Or maybe you're right and she just couldn't afford it. But I'll bet Waldron thinks Sally had the coin all along and gave it to us for safekeeping."

It explained why he might try to trade my grandson for it.

Ephraim might even have been on the *Consuelo*; I'd seen no sign of him, but it was a big boat.

"Waldron does seem like the kind of guy who a fellow like Coates might ask for advice," Ellie conceded. "About the coin, valuing it and selling it and so on. Meanwhile"—she dragged her hand across her forehead—"it's way too hot in here, and we haven't had a customer except for Janetta in two hours."

She was putting away ingredients as she spoke; I got the mixing bowls, measuring cups, and baking sheets into the sink.

"We need an awning," she said, "to keep the afternoon sun from baking the customers. I think maybe word has gotten around that it's not comfortable."

"And we need an air conditioner that actually blows cool air," I said. The one we had still wheezed in the kitchen window, but it had ceased all meaningful cooling operations.

"Fine," said Ellie. "But for now we should go home. It's almost closing time, anyway."

I stopped in the act of stowing the flour sifter back into its cabinet. For Ellie to suggest closing early was unheard of; the previous autumn she'd come to work in the nor'easter that blew the old Lubec dock right out into the ocean, never to be seen again.

"You want to leave?" I asked. "To do what?"

No answer from Ellie, but a faint smile played around her lips. She went on looking thoughtful while she turned to the rest of the dishes. I went out front to close the cash register, bag the cash, and turn off the card reader, the radio, the fan, and the lights, preparatory to our departure.

"But what about the scones?" I asked as we hurried to the Fiat parked just outside. I wasn't about to let her walk home in this heat, and for once she didn't argue.

"They've moved the conference back," Ellie said. "Something about flights being delayed? Or canceled, I forget which."

It hardly mattered which, I thought as relief rushed through me, if it gave us more time.

"Anyway, I need to think some more about them." She sighed as we got into the Fiat. I backed out onto Water Street, heading for Ellie's house at the north end of the island.

As we drove, another surge of panic welled up in me, along with the impulse to weep. But I shoved it all back down again; as usual, neither of those things were going to do me any good whatsoever.

I pulled the car over to the side of the road with a vacant lot on one side and a view all the way across the water to New Brunswick, Canada, on the other. Ellie had been silent since we began driving.

"Speak," I said, and she shook off whatever calculations she'd been doing in her head.

"Okay," she began, holding up an index finger. "First Sally wants us to find out what happened to Paul *and* get a coin back for her."

Deep breath, second finger. "Now Peter Waldron has somehow gotten the idea that we have the coin."

"Maybe," I emphasized. "We don't know that for sure."

It would leave a lot of explaining to do in the drugged-lemonade department, but maybe he was a regular user of whatever he'd given me, and had meant the doped glass for himself.

Hey, stranger things had happened. "But we do know for sure that *we* don't have it, so—wait."

Another thought occurred to me. "How do we know Bailey Lyman didn't have it? Because otherwise, why—?"

"You think somebody killed him and then left the coin in his house instead of taking it?" Ellie looked skeptical.

"Hmm. Well, they might've. If they couldn't find it."

"But then why kill him at all?" she shot back. "If he's the only one who knows where the thing is . . ."

Yeah, on second thought bashing the poor guy's brains out before discovering what they contained did seem shortsighted.

"Anyway," she said, "if someone had searched it, the house would've been a lot more trashed when we got there."

Drat, right again. "So you think somebody just got mad and clobbered him, basically?"

Ellie gazed out at the view from the car: a grassy field baked yellow in the late-afternoon light, the blue water calm and hazy with gathering mist under a deepening sky, hills in the far distance.

"Oh, no," she said mildly, watching the schooner *Martha*'s red sails bellying gently toward home port.

"No, I think he was in on all of this, somehow, and that's why they killed him," she said. "So he couldn't tell anyone else what was going on."

Out on the water, the *Martha*'s red sails fluttered and dropped as she got into the shelter of the island where the breeze dropped off; they'd be motoring to the dock.

"Well, that's just great," I said. "So now all we can do is keep bumbling around while we wait for a call asking for a—"

A ransom, basically. We've got what they want, they want what we've got, easy-peasy.

Only we didn't have it. But Ellie seemed unfazed. "Jake, never mind Waldron for a minute. Just tell me this: If you were a piece of pirate gold, where would you be?"

"On a pirate ship," I answered promptly, not even having to think about it. Ephraim loved pirates and everything about them, even the hooks and eye-patches.

Then I saw what she was getting at, and that it had nothing to do with Ephraim—except, I mean, for his probable location and that of the coin Paul Coates got killed for, too.

"A *sunken* pirate ship," I breathed as we got to the end of Water Street and turned onto her driveway. I stopped outside the small fenced pasture area where the goats grazed.

Ellie was looking something up on her phone. "High tide's right now," she reported, which was not good news.

To do what we both were thinking, we needed to be able to get close to a tiny point of rock sticking up out of the bay. On it was perched the tiniest, ricketiest, least comfy waterside villa in the world, home to the unlikeliest of witches.

So we needed high water, and after right now we wouldn't have any again for another twelve hours.

"Tell me again why this is a good idea?" I said as I backed out of the driveway and aimed us toward downtown and the harbor.

Ahead, a pickup truck with a trailer on it backed down the boat ramp behind Rosie's Hot Dog Stand. By the time I'd parked the Fiat, the truck's driver had backed the trailer down the ramp into the water and was quick-stepping out one of the finger piers to his boat, a sweet little vintage Chris-Craft runabout with red leatherette seats and more teak than a sauna.

When we got to the Bayliner, he was driving the Chris-Craft unerringly from the water right up onto the trailer. I watched a little enviously—it's not doing it that scares me, it's doing it for the first time. I went down to the cabin to sort through our equipment and supplies while Ellie got ready to cast off.

As I popped my head up out of the cabin, the pickup truck was pulling away into the golden late afternoon. Around us, men shouldered duffel bags, climbed off fishing boats, and headed for home.

Suddenly a stab of fear shot through me. *We ought to be cooking hot dogs outside on the grill right now*, I thought. *And Ephraim ought to be with us. But he's not . . .*

I looked up; Ellie was watching me. "Look," she said quietly, "there's enough volunteers out there to search this whole island ten times over, inch by inch."

The radio spat static; she turned the squelch knob. "And that's what they'll do. And there are enough cops of all different kinds to be sure all the possibilities get covered."

I bit my lip, which had begun trembling. "Maybe I'm wrong, maybe Waldron didn't try to drug me. Maybe it was a mistake."

The electric motor that lowered the outboard engine into the water made a low whine that sounded loud in the boat basin's watery hush. But when Ellie turned the key, all I heard was a low burble. I'd been expecting a roar, forgetting how quiet the new engine was.

She hopped off the boat, cast off the lines, and hopped back on. Then, in the shade between the mooring dolphin and the fish pier, we motored out into the bay.

By now it was nearly dusk, and lights were going on over the outdoor dining areas of the restaurants and drinking establishments overlooking the bay. Tourists strolled, kids raced on bikes, an accordion-and-ukelele band played to a small crowd in the park between the wine bar and the pet store.

To the west, mounded clouds turned from yellow to pink with the approaching sunset; it was a perfect summer-evening scene, with just one fly in the ointment.

Or oinkment, as Ephraim would have put it. I swallowed a sob—I would *not* weep, I would *not*—just as a breeze sprang up to riffle the champagne-pink water.

Speaking of which: "Go look in the fridge," Ellie said, and glanced over wisely from the helm where she was aiming us toward Walk Island.

So I did, and in the boat's built-in refrigerator I found two wrapped chicken sandwiches, a sleeve of Oreos, and a split of champagne. And—hallelujah!—a coffee thermos.

"What's all this?" I carried the stuff up on deck. There was even a pair of glasses to drink from. "When did you put all this here? And . . . champagne?"

Eyeing the glowing GPS screen, she adjusted our course slightly and looked satisfied before turning to me.

"Jake, if you're going to get anything done out here, you need to feel better."

She pointed at the elegant picnic she'd prepared. "So eat that, and drink that," she instructed, "and while you do it, we're going to have a talk."

"Well, if you put it that way," I sniffed, but soon her delightful chicken sandwiches beat my absence of appetite into submission, and the champagne didn't hurt me, either.

I held the bottle out to her but she refused: "I'm the designated driver tonight. Unless—?"

She stepped aside as if to offer me her spot at the helm; I brushed away her generosity. "No, thanks, you're doing fine."

By now we were halfway across the bay and a light chop had developed, the wave-tops like sharp, silvery-blue teeth.

"Anyway, here's the thing," she said. "Let's assume for a minute that Bailey *didn't* have the coin, and—here's the important part—whoever killed him knew it."

"Okay." I gazed back at Eastport's twinkling waterfront, now rapidly receding. Fright still felt like a pit I was being sucked down into, but now the fresh air and the slap of cold spray in my face—and, I suppose, that champagne—made things seem more possible, somehow.

Ellie's theory, for instance: "Because look, would you let someone beat you to death with a fireplace poker instead of just giving it up?"

The coin, she meant. Now the heavily treed shoreline of Campobello Island loomed; we eased in slowly under the branches overhanging the dark water.

"And if Sally had the coin, I'm guessing she'd never have asked us to go hunting for Paul," Ellie went on.

The branches made a green, high-ceilinged tunnel lit from below by our running lights; the tunnel smelled like pine sap, green algae, seawater, and wet sand.

"Or if she got it later, she'd have called us off the job," Ellie said as we emerged from beneath the branches into the blue light of evening.

"Because it was all she really wanted?" Now that I knew more, it made sense: She might not want her emotionally cruel and physically violent husband to return.

"But she hasn't," I added. "Called us off, that is."

Ellie finished scanning the water from the relative cover of the tree-lined shore, then took us back into deeper waters. The last thing we wanted now was company.

Speaking of which: "You didn't call Lizzie," I said.

Ellie must've had this trip planned all day; she'd had the refreshments made and stowed when we got here. So she'd been thinking about where pirate gold might be since this morning, but hadn't alerted our new police chief about the possibility of a boat trip.

"Couldn't risk it," she said, squinting again at the GPS before turning to port. "She might not tell those other cops, but—"

But then again, she might: County and state cops, the major crimes unit, and if this went on there'd be the federal folks— she'd have had to brief them all if only to keep her credibility with them.

"Besides, I'm not so sure she'd be comfortable with our methods," Ellie added.

Which made me laugh, since our methods usually consisted mostly of charging at whatever was in our way while yelling and, if necessary, punching.

"And I'm not sure I want Dylan Hudson along," she finished, and I knew from her voice that this was the real reason.

"How come?" We rounded the northern tip of Campobello and headed on out toward wider water.

"He just strikes me as kind of a take-charge type of guy," she said, steering us into a patch of what she'd have called hectic water and I called nerve-shredding turbulence.

Grabbing the rail, I hung on for dear life, and have I mentioned how distant the shore looks from a boat at night?

"And I don't want him taking charge," she finished, and then her face changed.

"Jake, what's that?" she asked, pointing at something in the water a hundred yards off our port side.

She didn't sound scared. She just sounded curious. Me, too, especially when I realized (a) how big the thing was and (b) how fast it was coming at us.

In addition, I couldn't help noticing how tall, leathery-shiny and sort of triangular it was, like . . .

The truth hit me, and *then* I was scared. "Ellie? Do you have an oar on board? Or something else big, like maybe a—"

Rocket launcher. Because that was most definitely a shark fin now zipping through the water at us, and unless I missed my guess there was a shark firmly attached to it.

"Jake," Ellie said quietly. "Sit down and hang on, I'm going to—"

Suddenly she shoved the throttle forward so hard that I thought the whole boat might just leap out of the water and fly, which was certainly what I felt like doing.

After a few minutes of good, old-fashioned running away, she dropped the throttle back. We scanned the water as best we could but saw only wave tops racing, and of course there was no shark lurking under them.

Of course not. "Ellie? Do you really think we should . . . ?" *Keep going?* I was about to say, but instead heard my own voice trailing off.

"Jake." Ellie spoke from the helm, where she stood outlined in the soft glow of the instrument lights. "Jake, we're going to find him, okay? If not where we're going now, then in the next place we look. Or the next. I mean it, now, so buck up. You need to be alert and well-oriented."

It was a challenge; hearing it, I sat up straighter, dug in my pants pocket for a tissue and gave it a long blow. Behind us, the Cherry Island beacon swung a saber of bright white light across the water.

"Can you see Walk Island, yet?" I asked, crossing the deck to the cabin hatchway and descending.

The Bayliner's cabin felt snug with its neat, small galley and cushioned berths well-furnished with blankets and pillows. I got a sweatshirt from a pile of them and went back up on deck, pulling it over my head.

"There," said Ellie, steering toward a tiny speck of light in the distance. "Right where it should be."

I peered over her shoulder at the GPS screen's radium-green display. Yep, that was an island, all right. And the light must be emanating from the rickety, tip-of-the-tiny-island shack we'd visited earlier.

Then the pinprick of light vanished suddenly and we were in darkness.

I mean *complete* darkness.

Fourteen

"What just happened?" I blinked, suddenly blind. Not only had the small flicker on the watery horizon vanished; all the lights had.

"I don't know." Ellie's voice came from the darkness. "GPS and radio are gone, too. And it's not just us."

In all directions, the land was as dark as the water. Our deck lamps, cabin overheads, and running lights were out, too, and worst of all, our engine had quit.

"How's our pal, the shark?" Ellie asked distractedly as she turned the ignition key, again without success. "Any sign?"

It hadn't occurred to me that the creature might follow us this far, and now in the darkness I couldn't tell if—

Well, yes I could, actually. I'd just grabbed a flashlight and was aiming it at the water when a rubbery-looking gray nose broke the surface right behind us and bumped into the engine. Then the thing swerved away, its eye rolling whitely up into its head as it went.

I didn't quite pass out. "Um, Ellie? Maybe we should just turn around right now and . . ."

"How?" she inquired. "We have no engine, no navigation, and no way to get any help unless one of our phones works out here."

As she spoke, a memory pinged my brain; all at once I knew why we were in the dark.

"The solar flare," I said. "A big one, there's supposed to be an aurora from it later tonight."

"Yeah, but it's dark, now," Ellie objected from somewhere near the helm. "Shouldn't the sun at least be out for this to happen?"

"I don't think it works that way," I replied, my eyes still on the water. The flare meant possible electrical disruptions, Sam had said, but I hadn't thought of it in practical terms.

"Damn," Ellie said in the sweetly reasonable tone that means she has had it with whatever is going on. Then:

"Okay, get out of my way, please," she said, and a few minutes later by the light of her battery lantern she had the backup engine cranked down into the water.

I'd always thought of the little engine as more preventive than practical. If you had one you wouldn't need one, et cetera. But it seemed now to be our only hope of getting home.

I held my breath as she leaned out over it, tinkering with something, in case the shark resurfaced and I had to snatch her from its jaws. But it didn't, and by the time she was done, I was feeling pretty good: a spare engine! What a concept!

Then I saw that unlike the Bayliner's engine, the backup steered with a tiller and started with a rope, like an old-fashioned lawnmower. So Ellie still had to stand and pull the rope until it started, meanwhile looking way too snack-like.

After a couple of pulls, the Evinrude started. "Great," I breathed; the little engine's ungodly roar sounded as pretty as birdsong to me.

"Now we can get home," I said, hoping Ellie agreed. I'd have drowned for Ephraim, no problem whatsoever, but drowning without retrieving him was not on my to-do list tonight.

Ellie sat down on the engine well's low ledge, gripped the tiller, and gave the engine some gas. Still alert for the shark that was out there, somewhere, I felt our vessel lurch forward.

"These old engines don't have computers in them," she said, explaining why the solar flare hadn't fried this one.

And why we shouldn't go back, yet. "Fine," I said, "but in case you haven't noticed, we're on a biggish boat with a small engine, all alone out on the water in the dark."

I took a breath. "With," I added, "a shark."

Ellie looked up, her face stubborn in the lantern's murky glow. But she didn't get to answer because just then the huge, dead-white belly of an enormous fish surged up out of the water behind us and crashed down onto the boat's transom.

The tooth-studded mouth gnashed and snapped as the massive head thrashed angrily. Worse, the animal was far enough into the boat that I doubted we'd be able to lift it out again.

Complicating the problem, of course, was that if you got close enough to push on it, it would eat you. Worst of all, though, Ellie was trapped between the blindly biting head and the water behind her, which now, just to mess things up further, was still being churned by the little engine's propeller.

So you would not want to fall—or jump—into the water back there, which meant she was stuck where she was with the boat still moving forward; we just didn't know toward where.

Luckily, the shark didn't seem to know that she was trapped with it practically in her lap, a few feet from incisors that looked like a set of steak knives.

"Jake." She sounded surprisingly okay with this. "Go below and look in the toolbox. There should be a compass."

I didn't see how I would hold off a shark with a compass, but I found the thing all right.

"You know how to use it?" she asked when I returned.

I nodded, still puzzled. Meanwhile she was fending off the big carnivore's interest with a long-handled brush intended for cleaning the seaweed from propeller blades.

"Okay," she said, "go sit in the pilot's chair."

So I did that, too, but I didn't like it, and I liked even less what she said next.

"Take the wheel. Find east and steer us that way. I was just about to make the course change myself, but . . ."

"But . . ." I held the compass-face under my flashlight. "But the Bayliner's engine isn't running," I said doubtfully.

So how could I steer, I meant, but when Ellie just looked at me in reply I (duh) got it: the Bayliner's rudder would still turn just fine. Ellie could turn the backup engine to match it.

Big Mister-I'll-Bite-Your-Ankle-Off lay draped over the transom, his head on the deck and his tail bouncing along behind us. But he wasn't dead, proving it when he lunged for my kneecap as I went by; gasping, I just missed getting nailed.

"Ellie, I can find north with this thing," I confessed when I reached her with the compass, "but . . ."

But then what? I'd have asked, there on the water in the dark with a dead boat and a shark that wanted to eat me. But fear and frustration hit me again, instead; this was all my fault, someone had taken Ephraim because of me, and now Ellie and I were about to be munched.

And much more along those lines. Luckily, Ellie had heard the tears in my voice, and as always, she knew what to say:

"Just give me the damned compass, for Pete's sake."

She thrust out her hand, whereupon the shark's head swung upward, its maw lurched fast toward her, and it bit down hard.

Just not accurately; at the time, though, it about scared the bejesus out of her and me, too, and next time the monster might manage to improve its chomping aim.

That, plus the fact that my grandson was still missing and the shark was in my way—anyway, I was mad and it was probably very stupid of me, but I snapped and dove head-first at the beast, plunging one arm underneath and the other one around the cool, sandpapery-feeling body.

But by now, with its teeth sunk deeply into the boat cushion it was savaging instead of Ellie, the shark had realized its mistake. It flung the shredded cushion aside and cast about for something tastier, and the organism clinging desperately to its body apparently qualified.

The jaws snapped together like castanets, inches from my face, and despite the thing's rough skin—it was rubbing the insides of my arms raw—it was somehow also very slippery.

"Ellie," I managed. "Give me a hand, here?"

The shark was about to take mine, starting at the shoulder. All I could hear besides the outboard engine was *snappity-snap-snap!* right next to my ear.

Ellie turned the throttle on the backup engine, braced the tiller, and got to her feet.

"I hope I don't have to drop anchor again for this," she said as she went by. Then from one of the bins in the deck she pulled the very thing I'd wanted from her earlier: a wooden oar.

Earlier, but not right now. "Don't you think that with me in such close proximity, there might be a better method for . . ."

The oar was a stout, sturdy one, I saw in the moment before she raised it high over the shark's head. When she brought it down I turned away, and that's how I happened to see the other boat materializing out of the darkness behind her.

You really haven't lived until you've had a big shark die in your arms, is my position on the matter. By the time I'd squirmed from beneath its corpse, Lizzie Snow and Dylan Hudson had already climbed over onto the Bayliner's deck.

Lizzie took a long look at the situation—dark boat, backup engine, dead shark, empty champagne bottle—then sat in the chair at the helm and leaned over the back of it toward us.

"So, what's shakin'?" she asked, but her eyes didn't smile and her tone didn't match her jaunty query.

"Oh, not much," I replied, still catching my breath after my up-close-and-personal shark experience.

Ellie returned to the transom and unclamped the tiller on the backup engine. Lizzie turned alertly to her.

"Yeah, no," she said. "Dylan, find some line and lash our boat to this one, will you please?"

That got my attention. She meant to tow us home, which under other circumstances would've been great. But:

"Are you taking us into custody? Because for one thing, I'm pretty sure we're outside your jurisdiction..." Heck, I was pretty sure we were outside our whole country.

"Nope," said Lizzie, still sounding way too cop-like for my taste. "I'd just rather a pair of my favorite Eastport citizens didn't go off half-cocked and end up drowning, or worse."

She let out a sigh. "Anyway, I saw that the Bayliner wasn't in the boat basin so I figured you two were out here somewhere."

Done with lashing the boats together, Hudson returned to the Bayliner where this time he saw the dead shark on the deck and nudged it with his foot. It flopped reflexively, but to his credit he did not let out a shriek.

It was a low, appreciative whistle, instead, and it made me think again that the guy wasn't too bad in small doses. Just not right here, right now, and I could tell Ellie felt the same.

"Now what?" she asked from her perch by the engines; she didn't want to go home and neither did I.

Around us, the bay lay dark and silent except for the small waves slapping our hull. The shorelines were all still dark, too, although I imagined that by now there were candles lit and flashlights turned on everywhere.

"I'm hoping to persuade you to come back with us," Lizzie answered Ellie. "This isn't safe. Of course you're right that I can't make you come, but—"

"Okay, here's the situation," I interrupted, because not only did we not want to be towed home, but if we were going to get to Walk Island tonight, we'd need Lizzie and Dylan's boat to get there on.

So I laid out all we'd done and learned in the couple of days since Sally Coates came to us asking for help: the sunken barge with a rumored-to-be witch trapped in it, the life vest and the empty shoe, the taken-down security system and re-homed dog, and the things that Julio had told me.

Also: "He says Bailey Lyman was basically a creep, and Paul Coates went from annoyed bitching about it to practically encouraging it for some reason," I said.

"Don't forget the hidden phone number," Ellie put in, so I told Lizzie about that, too. By now she was listening intently and so was Hudson.

"So the thing is this," I finished. "Every cop in the world, and every volunteer, too, is out looking for Ephraim. And they don't want to hear about pirate gold or missing fishermen."

I took a breath. "They probably know by now, most of them, that someone took him for their own reasons. But they don't know who, or why."

Hudson's lean face in the battery-lantern's sallow glow had gone still as he listened.

"So where's the harm in following up on other angles?" I went on. "It's not like the police need us on shore, and the things I've been telling you are . . . curious. Right?"

Lizzie and Dylan looked at each other: *right.* "But your boat's crippled," he said, "you've got no electronics, and—"

"Neither do you," Ellie pointed out. "Or any lights. And you must have an old engine without any of the modern electronic components, or it wouldn't run, either."

I'd been wondering about that.

"But what I'd like to know is how you found us," she added in the reasonable tones that she generally uses just before she hits you over the head with some unwelcome—but absolutely correct—logical conclusion. "Seeing," she added, "as we don't have running lights, or anything else you could've picked out just by looking."

Suddenly I realized what she was getting at. There was only one way they could have found us.

"So, Dylan," I spoke up, "how come the solar flare didn't fry whatever tracking gadget you put on Ellie's boat?"

Another shrug: *caught.* "More cop gear," he admitted as I re-called the ridiculously tiny tape player he'd had. "And it did fritz out. But we'd located you by then."

"Hmm," remarked Ellie, not sounding pleased, and I wasn't, either. Back in the bad old days, my ex-husband used to track me in case I was dallying with any boyfriends (I wasn't). This was pretty funny—or anyway it was funny later—since my ex was so non-monogamous, he was practically a legend to those who knew him.

"Anyway," said Lizzie, "why not just come back to East-port on our boat and when the power comes back on, we'll—"

"No," said Ellie, and we all turned to look at her. With her strawberry-blond curls turned reddish-purple by the lantern light, and the shark in a crimson pool at her feet, she still gripped the oar's handle firmly in both red-streaked hands.

"We're going to Walk Island to find Ephraim, if he's there. We're going now, and we're going in your boat."

Turning to Lizzie, she smiled in the half dark. "Unless you want to explain to the city council why the new police chief's boyfriend is stalking women with a stolen tracking device?"

I nearly laughed. *Checkmate,* Dylan's look said clearly, and Lizzie's answering glance agreed.

And then—*poof!*—the distant shoreline lit up all at once, like a magic trick. The Bayliner's gauges and instruments glowed greenly to life, the radio spat static, and our running lights winked on all at once.

While the rest of us were still looking around in silent won-der, Ellie jumped up, crossed the deck in three strides, and reached past Lizzie to turn the ignition key. And—

Vroom. We were back in business.

So we didn't need Lizzie and Hudson's boat after all, and minutes later after unlashing the two vessels, we were again on the open water in the Bayliner with the lights of Grand Manan Island gleaming ahead of us.

"This is just a needle in a haystack," Dylan complained, but then Ellie spotted the tiny rock we were looking for once more; tiny at high tide, that is, which it still nearly was now.

"Ellie," I said quietly as she stood at the wheel, "what if we don't get there until the tide's gone out too much?"

We needed to fetch up as close to the cabin as we could, and for that we needed deep water.

"We'll think of something," Ellie answered, her eyes on the helm's gauges. She could've locked our course in and walked away for a little while; we had twenty minutes or so yet to go.

But she wouldn't, because after the solar flare she didn't trust the electronics, and that's how she happened to be there when the oil light flashed on.

"Jake?" I'd sat down on the deck with my back against the rail. At her voice, I lifted my chin muzzily up off my chest.

"Wha—?" Beneath me the boat thudded along, bump-bump-bump.

"Jake," Ellie repeated. The flat lack of urgency in her voice told me something was up.

"Go pull the cowl off the engine," she said, to which of course I did not reply, *What are you, crazy?*

Instead, feeling a mixture of determination and impending doom, I stepped cautiously past the inert shark body—we'd tried, but even with the four of us he was too heavy and slip-pery to shove overboard—to stand by the engine. Luckily the shark wasn't quite big enough to sink the boat's stern; I braced my feet and bent over the cowling, which is the engine's cover; big, heavy, and fiendishly unwieldy.

My searching fingers found the latches that held the cover down; naturally the latches were stiff, but I only sprained two fingers prying them up, and next came lifting the cowl itself.

I'd seen Ellie do it, so I knew it was possible. Bending my knees and wrapping my arms around the cowl the way she had—and may I remind us all here that the engine was still running, so if I fell in, I'd be mincemeat?—and *lifted*.

The cowl didn't budge. Dylan climbed to his feet. "Give you a hand, there, little lady?" he asked with a grin that was about as subtle as a poke in the ribs.

But I did need someone's help, so I watched him—and after that, Lizzie—try and fail, too. Finally, Ellie put me at the helm while she lifted the cowl easily and set it on the deck; I guess you just had to know how.

"Hudson, hold this." She handed a flashlight to Hudson and by its light opened a small tank mounted on the engine's side.

"Darn," she said, then waited until the dark fluid in the tank rose up to the brim and snapped the top back down fast.

"Have to check it when we get home," she said, unperturbed, and I figured that next she'd jump out and take a few steps on the water. But instead the warning light on the console went out and we were back to normal again.

Well, sort of normal. "How much farther?" Lizzie asked.

"Not far. We should see it, soon." Ellie consulted the GPS once more. "We saw a light earlier, but—"

But not now. To our east, the moon rose blood orange. In a few minutes Ellie spoke again, just one syllable.

"Huh." She frowned in the glow of the GPS, then suddenly dropped our engine into neutral, followed by reverse.

The boat started backing up. "What?" said Lizzie, getting up off the deck. Hudson stepped out onto the bow, peering around, and that's when I saw the pointy tops of the jagged granite ledges we'd somehow blundered into a cluster of.

Then Walk Island appeared, its rough shale beach half-exposed; as I'd feared, the tide had gone out considerably. It had taken us longer to get here than we'd thought it would.

"Drat. Now we've got to climb that beach," I said. Also there was the little matter of getting to it at all. I squinted unhappily at the remaining distance between us and land.

Ellie had gone below to haul something big from the storage area under the foredeck. It looked familiar, but I couldn't quite place it; then from the cabin came a hissing sound.

I couldn't place that, either, although I'd heard it somewhere before. "You figure there's any more sharks out here?" Hudson asked as he eyeballed the situation.

"You figure there's anybody in that shack?" Lizzie asked, coming up behind him.

"I don't know, but I'm going to find out," I said, still not understanding what Ellie was doing or why the thing she'd hauled out onto the deck seemed to be growing.

Nor did I care, turning my gaze to the island where all was still dark. Nothing moved, and I spotted no sign of the barge that had sunk near it, either, although the dinghy tied up to the precarious shack still floated.

The moon had risen all the way up over the horizon, casting the many-angled dwelling into a jagged black silhouette of jutting stovepipe, slanting roof, and a rusty glint of reflected moonglow like a long, red blade in one of the dark windows.

Ellie climbed out onto the Bayliner's bow to drop anchor; we couldn't get closer without impaling the boat on one of the ledges. We heard the clanking of heavy chain and the anchor's splash, then the rest of the chain rattling up out of the chain locker.

Finally she returned, dusting her hands together, and the next thing I knew I was climbing over the engine and transom, hoping to land in—I kid you not—that damned rubber raft that Sam and the kids were so fond of. That's what Ellie had been dragging up from the cabin and inflating.

Now she looked back from the helm at me. "Bet you're glad I brought it, though, aren't you?"

I rolled my eyes at her; just because Ephraim was worth it didn't mean I had to like it. Still, it was better than landing into the water, I thought as I jumped.

Then my feet hit the bouncy, rubbery rim of the raft. I felt like a trick seal balancing on a beach ball, then slipped off the rim and landed on my butt.

Inside the raft, fortunately. Hudson came next, and after that Lizzie landed lightly and settled herself; Ellie got in last. The thing bounced and wobbled alarmingly and any instant I expected a dunking, but the waves were cooperative in washing us closer to the rocky shore.

And then I got the dunking; Lizzie slid easily and fast off the raft's balloon-like rim where I'd found, I thought, a secure perch. But as her side lowered nearer the water, the other side rose suddenly, flipping me backwards into the cold shallows.

I staggered and spluttered, then sprawled. But somebody grabbed my collar and someone else seized my sleeve, and then I was scrabbling uphill over wet, sharp stones.

"Nobody's here," Hudson muttered in a voice that suggested his patience was dwindling rapidly.

"Ssh." A dark figure I thought must be Lizzie put a hand up. We were nearly to the shack; I could see through the stumpy wooden pilings beneath it to the moonlit water beyond.

The hand went down again. "I just thought I might've seen something move," a familiar voice murmured.

It was her; I let my breath out. Lizzie scrambled past me up the exposed rocks at the top of the beach, and from there scampered nimbly onto the shack's narrow wooden porch.

"This isn't a building, it's a heap of driftwood," Hudson

grumbled, then followed Lizzie's example. But Ellie stayed back on the beach with me.

"What's wrong?" She bent to me but I turned away, not wanting her to see my face.

"Hudson's right," I said bleakly. "Ephraim's not here. This is a fool's errand."

She stood up straight. "We don't know that," she insisted, and grabbed my shoulders until I had to look at her.

"We don't know that at all," she repeated, urging me along until the others could take my hands and haul me up beside them.

But now that we were here, I knew I'd fallen for wishful thinking, no real evidence at all, and the truth was that I was afraid to go in and have that terrible truth proven to me.

But the shack's open door beckoned darkly to me, and when I balked, Ellie muscled me toward it.

"We came to find out, and we're going to," she said. The smell of damp ashes in a cold woodstove drifted from inside, the smell of nobody home.

Ellie's flashlight beam bounced around the tiny, cluttered interior, picking out a teacup here, a broken lobster trap there. On the floor a small object, not sun-bleached or sand-smoothed.

I picked it up. "Ellie?" It was a kazoo. A *familiar* kazoo.

She peered at the thing in my hand. It was Ephraim's toy musical instrument.

So he was here, I thought, buoyed for a moment by sudden, wild hope. But . . .

But where is he now? A cold feeling squirmed in my gut and curled a tentacle around my spine and squeezed.

A shout cut the shack's ominous stillness; we rushed out to the porch where Hudson pointed at the water.

"What the hell is that?"

I looked, but by now I was nearly weeping again with misery and self-blame. I'd been so sure of myself, but—

"Hey." The tears shut off suddenly as my mouth fell open and the word dropped out of it. The tide had receded more since we'd arrived, and now where only flat water had been something big and dark stuck up from beneath the water's surface.

Lizzie pointed her flashlight at the thing. "What the . . . ?"

Ellie stared, too, but she knew what it was, I could tell by the look on her face. Maybe she'd even expected this.

"It's the barge," she said, and as the tide receded even more it was clear that she was right. The rusty old hulk emerged slowly but surely as the water receded: first the wheelhouse, then the sagging rail, finally the deck.

The sound of the water draining from the vessel froze my heart; if Ephraim was here anywhere, it had to be in there. The barge had been submerged . . .

But I'd been in it only the day before, and I knew that the raddled old tub still had some watertight compartments.

In fact, I'd been in one of them.

Fifteen

"This is ridiculous," Hudson groused as we all waded back through cold salt water to that infernal rubber raft. Getting into it meant getting wet again; it took me three tries to hoist my uncooperative backside up over the raft's rim and then swing my legs in.

"You want to swim out there instead?" Lizzie asked as she steadied herself once more on the raft's wobbly rim.

She'd thought that she and Hudson could check the barge out all by themselves until I informed them that if they went alone, I would swim there, dammit, and Ellie said so, too.

So we all got in and Lizzie started paddling with the big oar that Ellie had clobbered the shark with. Ahead, the barge's wheelhouse windows looked like the black, multiple eye of some strange drowned insect.

Lizzie wielded the paddle determinedly. I could see the ladder leading up the side of the barge's rusting hull, now, because . . .

"Hey," I said, "that's reflecting tape." Inch-wide, bright-red strips of the stuff. It hadn't been there last time I'd seen the *Carrie*. "*New* reflective tape."

"Huh," said Ellie thoughtfully, and Hudson and Lizzie seemed to catch on right away, too.

Someone had been here. Maybe, if I was right about parts of the barge still being watertight, they still were.

Lizzie paddled the raft up close to the ladder. Then: "Any of you have a belt? Shoelace, anything?"

But my sneakers were pull-on, Ellie's, too, and Lizzie and Hudson's athletic shoes had Velcro fastenings. So—to Hudson's disgust, but we outvoted him—we all quickly rock-paper-scissored who'd stay with the raft, and Ellie lost.

Or maybe she won, I thought once Lizzie and Hudson had gone ahead, because now it was my turn, and getting onto the barge's ladder—the raft's squishy rim had all the stable solidity of your average beanbag chair—was a challenge.

Then at each step the ladder's rungs sagged warningly, and from all around me came a soft grinding and grating as of metal rivets slowly loosening from the crumbling hull.

Also, a sort of unhappy groaning was coming from somewhere deep in the ruined vessel; no doubt I'd find out later what that was, and at the worst possible moment, too. But for now I hurried to follow a flashlight beam bouncing toward the darkly looming wheelhouse structure.

"Hey, wait up," I called, and as if in reply, the light vanished.

Annoyed, I stalked after it and at once tripped face first into a snarled mess of wires and cables, where I promptly became entangled. My dropped flashlight rolled away into the darkness; then, flailing around, my hand landed on something small and metallic.

It was *another* flashlight, not mine. Instead it was a tiny one that someone must've lost here very recently; using it, I found a handhold to pull myself up out of the wires, then crept forward once more.

Someone had marked the barge so it would be visible in the dark, then lost a bit of equipment. Whoever it was might even still be aboard.

And *Ephraim* might be aboard . . . Thinking this, I slid into a crouch and hunkered along in deep shadows, looking for the hatch leading down to the area below the deck.

The paling yellow moon cast my shadow onto a paint-peeling bulkhead where someone a long time ago had stenciled DOWN →. Encouraged, I reached out for the door just as a second shadow popped up beside my own.

A hand seized my shoulder, another gripped a fistful of my hair, and together they shoved me toward the hatchway.

"Eep," I said. Then, "You don't have to shove me." I was, after all, going just where I'd wanted to go.

"Quiet. I'm sorry about this," said a familiar voice.

I spun in surprise, knocking the hands away. "Oh, Julio," I said sadly, recognizing the spaniel-eyed saloonkeeper even in the gloom.

Julio pulled a gun from the hip pocket of the khaki cargo shorts he was wearing. "I'm sorry," he repeated.

His gun hand shook, not hard enough for me to try anything.

Hudson appeared suddenly out of the shadows behind Julio and in one swift motion flung an arm around Julio's throat while slamming the other arm down fast and hard onto Julio's wrist.

With a cry of pain, Julio dropped the gun. It slid away down the slanting deck.

"Don't. Freaking. Move," Hudson said in tones I thought I wouldn't like hearing in my own ear.

Julio sagged in Hudson's grip. I followed his hopeless glance over the rail and caught sight of the small, open boat he must've used to get out here. For a trip like that in a boat that small, he must have had a very good reason.

"Where's Ephraim?" I demanded, but his only reply was to look even more miserable and ashamed.

Lizzie appeared, striding toward us on the moonlit deck. "Dylan?" she said urgently, then stopped when she saw Julio.

"Oh, man." She frowned in thought for a moment. "So, we've got a problem. How do you suggest we handle taking this guy into custody?"

Because just as I'd suggested to Lizzie earlier, the two of them had massive jurisdiction problems here; we weren't in Eastport now.

"We don't," Hudson said. He gave Julio's sagging form a shake. "Too much trouble. Let's just ask him questions, and if he doesn't tell us what we want to hear, throw him overboard."

Julio's pale face went so much whiter that I could see its color fade even by moonlight. Speaking of which . . .

A bad thought hit me. "Um, guys? What time is it?"

We'd been out here longer than I'd expected. Lizzie checked her watch. "Four thirty."

In the morning, she meant. So on top of everything, Ellie and I had been out all night, no one knew where we were, and we couldn't call because—I checked again—the power was back on but my phone was still fritzed.

And so were the others' phones, too, even Julio's, which he handed over reluctantly. But there was nothing I could do about it, now. I lifted my chin toward Julio, jerked my head toward the hatchway leading below.

"He's here, isn't he?" I demanded of Julio. He'd dropped a plastic bag he'd been carrying; I snatched it up and opened it.

A sandwich. Some apple slices. Two cookies and a half pint of chocolate milk.

I flung myself at Julio. "You son of a—"

Lizzie pulled me back. "We're wasting time," she snapped, then added three words that chilled me more than anything else so far.

"Tide's coming in," she said.

The hatchway led down a rusty gangway to a large open area under the wheelhouse. It was a different section from the one

Ellie and I had been in before, but like the rest of the boat, everything here that had been metal was flaking away to rust.

"Where is he, dammit?" I snarled at Julio, whose arm Hudson gripped tightly as he marched the distraught tavern owner ahead of us in the gloom.

Lizzie's flashlight shone eerie yellow around the space, which was damp and cold and smelled the way an old penny tastes.

"I . . . I don't know," Julio gasped. "They told me to listen for music. I'm . . . *sorry!*" he gasped through his rising sobs. "But they made me come, they said if I didn't . . ."

He turned to me in teary appeal. "Jake, you know I have family in Florida, okay? Easy to find, easy to hurt, too. And these guys . . ."

"Who? Who threatened your family?" Lizzie asked, but before Julio could answer Hudson shoved him again.

"It doesn't matter. We'll find out later. Right now . . ." He gave Julio a look that should have incinerated him on the spot.

"Right now," Hudson grated out ominously, "we're going to listen for music. And you," he added, giving Julio's arm a yank, "had better hope we hear some."

Water dripped steadily all around us as we moved cautiously forward, and the agonized creaking and groaning I'd heard up on deck was louder here, too, as I picked my way cringingly among anonymous patches of seaweed and mold on the hideously squidgy-feeling floor.

Each repulsive step made my legs want to squinch themselves up into my shirt. But then I heard someone singing:

"*. . . on that farm he had a cow, ee-i-ee-i—*" Music; not the kind I'd been expecting, but—

"Over here," Hudson said grimly, crouched by a far bulkhead with the unfortunate Julio still firmly in hand.

Suddenly I didn't care if the floor was carpeted in bloodsucking leeches; at Hudson's words I just about flew across it.

"What? Where?" I babbled, shoving past him to peer at yet another hatchway door and then hurl myself at it.

If Old MacDonald hadn't been having a cow and then a pig on the other side, I'd have said it probably opened onto a gear storage bin, or some other uninteresting sort of nautical cubbyhole.

But a shiny new padlock held it shut, and while I was peering around for something heavy to try breaking the lock with, a bomb went off behind me.

The lock hit the floor with a muffled *thunk*. Hudson stood there, weapon in hand. The gun's report rang in my ears; through it, I heard the singing stop.

Somebody was crying; not Julio. "Ephraim," I heard myself whisper, yanking the door open.

Inside was a windowless chamber about twelve feet square, musty and stale-smelling. Someone tried to come in behind me.

"No." I stomped my foot, noting how springy the floor felt. "I have to find him, I have to find him and make sure he's—"

Shelves, sagging or broken, lined the walls. Large and small metal boxes had fallen from the shelves; each box had a small brass lock set into the lid.

The floor where they lay was dry; *the mail*, I thought. The *Carrie* could've hauled mail between islands or some other watery place, and they'd stored the mail here.

So it was watertight, or at least more so than the rest of this tub.

"Ephraim?" I tried calling for him as I made my way through bigger lockboxes, a damp-ruined ledger, the wrecked carcass of a vintage adding machine . . .

A sniffling sound came from behind a mold-furred chair. A pile of rags back there shifted and fell.

"Grammy?" a little voice piped frightenedly. His deep brown eyes, huge and terrified, appeared and found me; then he leapt at me and I fell back laughing and weeping, my arms full of boy.

"You found me," he wept into my neck, and, "I did, I did find you," I wept back, until Hudson must've figured that it was safe and came ducking through the hatchway.

"Hey, pardner," he said softly, chucking Ephraim under the chin, and then to me, "So, can we go, now?"

I looked at the pile of rags again. "In a minute," I said. "You go on back out, okay?"

He didn't like it, but he did it, and once he was gone I carried Ephraim to the rag-pile. "Glenna," I said.

No answer from the rag pile. "That was a nice song you were singing," I said. "It was good of you to do it. Thank you for taking care of him."

Now that Ephraim had been found by his grammy, he'd dropped off to sleep, a sweet weight against my chest. But we weren't out of this yet; the old barge's sad creaks and groans ramped up to rending and tearing noises, due, I supposed, to the incoming tide now rising high enough to shift the hull.

It happened at each change of tide, I imagined, but one of these times would be the last; the pressure against the boat would cave it in catastrophically, and I didn't feel at all like sticking around to find out if this time would be the one.

Still no answer from the pile of rags. "His mom might like to thank you," I said.

The rags shifted to show a pale blue eye balefully glaring. Then Glenna LaFarge, the so-called witch of Walk Island, sat up.

"Those sons of *bitches*," she pronounced venomously. "He out there? That worthless little worm, Julio?"

I knelt by her. "Yeah, he's there. Don't worry, the cops've got him."

Her lips stretched in a grin that said *she* wasn't worried, it was *Julio* who should be worried. "Too bad. I'd like a crack at him."

"Yeah, well, first let's get out of here," I said, taking her arm just as from outside the small room came a sound like somebody opening a metal barrel with a chainsaw.

Then the floor dropped sharply under our feet: *yeeks.* The witch of Walk Island and I hurried out of the room she'd been locked in, me lugging a frightened toddler. I'd have stopped to luxuriate in the sweet warmth and weight of him, but the barge was sinking.

"Come on," Hudson said urgently when we'd emerged. In the few minutes I'd been away, everything out here had flooded knee-deep and the water was still coming up fast. Pulling Glenna by her arm, I stumbled toward Hudson, who was urging Lizzie ahead of him while gripping a sullen Julio's elbow with one hand.

Lizzie made her way up into the gray dawn light. Behind her, I forced my legs through the cold murky fluid rising around me; it was up to my hips now, trying to float me off my feet.

"Grammy," Ephraim whimpered, clutching onto me. Then Hudson turned, hauling Julio along with him as he waded back toward me to help.

Which put Julio *behind* him just long enough for Julio to snatch a section of pipe dangling overhead, wrench it free, and swing it up over Hudson's head.

"No!" I yelled, but the length of pipe was already on its way down—and then it wasn't. Instead there was a *bang!* from outside; the pipe flew end over end before splashing into the fast-deepening water behind me while Julio just stood there, his mouth sagging open in astonishment.

Correction: it was the absence of astonishment that I saw on Julio's face. When the unlucky barkeeper toppled, I saw that a sizable chunk of his cranium was gone.

He hit the water and vanished beneath it as Lizzie appeared in the open hatchway above, holding a gun.

"Home," Ephraim moaned, wiggling fretfully as I stared at the spot where Julio had gone under. *But he was our friend*, my mind protested plaintively.

But he hadn't been, or not at the end, anyway.

Ephraim moaned again. He was hot, I realized with sudden anxiety, and damp with a feverish sweat.

"Go," Hudson uttered, half leading and half carrying me to the hatchway and bulldozing me up it. Behind us, something broke and water began gushing in earnest.

"He's burning up," I told Lizzie as I emerged into light and fresh air with the child of my child in my arms.

The water around us spread blue and pearl pink, the waves reflecting the first light of day. In the far distance a row of lobster boats headed out, seagulls clustering behind them.

"Guy was a real numbskull," Lizzie remarked.

She meant Julio, I supposed, and the lack of emotion in her voice made me shiver. But then I understood the reason for it as she gestured at something behind me, and when I turned, what I saw chilled my blood.

"Boat's breaking up," she said.

In the growing dawn I could see, now, that the break in the *Carrie*'s hull ran across the whole deck just behind where the wheelhouse structure rose up from it. The opening in the deck was about a foot wide already, and who knew how deep.

Hudson stared for a moment, then spoke. "Okay, we're at the heavy end of this tub and that's what'll go down first."

When the barge broke in two and each separate end slid down off the ledge the vessel was perched on; he'd seen what that big crack meant. Quickly he strode to the twisted rail and shouted over it to Ellie, still down on the raft, and waved his arms like a traffic cop. "Move! Around the side, get ready for us to jump!"

And back off fast if half a barge starts sliding down at you,

I'd have added. But by then Hudson was herding us all—Lizzie, Glenna, and me with Ephraim still clinging on like a feverish little clam—one by one along the deck and across the widening crack in it.

A seagull flapped by, angling his beady eye at us. I put a foot out, then made the mistake of glancing down at the crevasse whose dark opening was now visibly widening beneath me.

Behind me, Lizzie spoke. "What about Julio?" She glanced back troubledly.

Hudson touched her shoulder. "Yeah. Go on, though. We don't have time."

"Oh, never mind about him," Glenna advised darkly as I made it over the gap in the deck, "he'll float."

A screech of tearing metal interrupted, then trailed off into a groan, the barge's two halves sagging sharply away from one another. When they broke apart entirely, they'd sink fast.

"And then he'll wash up somewhere," Glenna cackled. "They do, you know, they always do. Serves him right."

She leaned out over the rail beside me. "Or a shark'll eat 'im," she said, not sounding as if she minded this idea, either.

I did, though, especially when I followed her gaze and at once knew why sharks had occurred to her just then: A black fin circled lazily down there, its shadow a dark patch on the water.

Ellie looked up from the raft; she'd had to paddle briskly to get here so fast, and now she looked exhausted.

"Uh, you guys? Listen, I see something swimming around down here, and not to worry anyone, but I'm pretty sure it's a—"

Yeah: *boat breaking, shark circling* pretty much summed up our current situation, and while boat trips for me were always a matter of fright punctuated by terror, this was ridiculous.

"Go," Lizzie told Hudson grimly. "You jump down, give Ellie a hand. I'll help these two."

I glanced back at the deck, now two halves—forward and rear—each slanting down toward the water and about to slide into it, one of them with us still on it. Meanwhile, right now the raft floated below me; Ellie held it there, clinging onto a piece of the barge's exterior bracing.

Which soon would be underwater. So I had to move fast; if I didn't, I'd be too scared to move at all. And in that situation, there's just one thing to do:

"Stand aside," I told Hudson, and then—I have no idea how—I climbed onto the *Carrie*'s shaky rail with a sweat-drenched Ephraim clutched tightly under one arm, and jumped.

Well, it seemed like a good idea at the time. Raft straight down, gravity still working—yeah, was it ever, I thought as we fell. Then I thought about the raft's position below me not necessarily being a done deal, because that's when the stern half of the barge started plunging in earnest, yanking the piece of bracing that Ellie had been holding from her grasp.

So now I was falling toward where the raft had been, and in its place was a black fin, cruising patiently. The good news was that we didn't quite fall into the carnivore's mouth.

But the bad news was really bad: When we hit the water, the impact squirted Ephraim out of my arms and away in the current, now surging as the tide rose. One instant he was there, the next . . .

Gone. He could swim, after all those lessons I knew he could definitely swim, but this wasn't a pool and there weren't any lifeguards . . .

And that shark was here somewhere. Coughing and weeping, I scanned around desperately but saw no sign of Ephraim. Above, Lizzie was shouting and pointing; Ellie paddled toward me as fast as she could, but against the current she made slow headway and then I saw the fin slicing through the water at me.

An ear-splitting symphony of agonized thuds, shrieks, and massive cracking sounds drowned Lizzie's voice as the barge broke fully apart. A wave smacked me in the face, then another, and all at once I couldn't breathe; from below I sensed the dark chill of a watery grave beckoning to me and started to panic.

Then Hudson, who'd made it to the raft somehow while I was busy not-drowning, dove into the water. At the splash, the shark veered toward him; then Lizzie hit the water beside me and came up fast, already cocking a clenched fist.

"On your back, dammit," she gasped, and I obeyed her since otherwise she'd have punched me out cold. And that's how I got floated to the raft in a genuine, no-kidding lifesaving carry, my chin in the crook of Lizzie's elbow and my eyes flooded with tears, gazing up at the pitiless sky.

"He's gone," I sobbed as she shoved me up over the raft's rim. "I couldn't hold on, he's drowned, or the shark—"

A spasm of coughing seized me; I lay on the raft's rubbery-smelling floor bringing up salt water, seaweed bits, and what felt like most of my left lung. From somewhere in the distance I could hear Lizzie calling for Hudson but not getting an answer.

Ellie paddled us toward them as I sprawled in the raft. Then Lizzie hoisted herself hastily up over the side, her eyes wide. A ripple in the water behind her, the brief, dead glare of an onyx-black eye, and finally the fearsomely toothy jaws gaping before silently submerging again said she'd made it by inches.

She didn't seem fazed, though. "Gimme," she said, grabbing the paddle from Ellie, and jumped back into the water again.

"Are you nuts?" I shoved myself up on one arm to yell at her, but she was already yards away. The fin followed, arrowing through the water. When Hudson's head surfaced only a few yards from her, I heard her curse in surprised relief.

Then he dragged a squirming Ephraim up alongside him, and seeing this I may have uttered a few relieved bad words, myself.

But the three of them still had to make it to the raft, a project that looked iffy in the extreme. Also, half the barge still loomed over us, groaning ominously, getting ready to fall, and if we were here when it did, it would swamp our raft.

Then without warning the Bayliner emerged from the far side of the barge carcass, bobbing on whatever rogue current had torn her from her anchorage. The boat floated past our raft with her anchor chain stretched taut alongside; below, I realized, that anchor sailed freely along like the tail on a kite.

And that gave me an idea, one that might even work. Too bad I'd have to go swimming with the sharks to find out.

Sixteen

"Not you," I told Ellie, who was exhausted from battling the waves with nothing but a wooden paddle. I turned to Glenna.

"You come and help me, though, will you, please?"

Once she'd gotten into the raft safely, the white-haired old witch hadn't seemed to care much about anything, and why should she? She'd been this close to meeting a terrible end, not to mention whatever else that fake friend, Julio, had put her through.

But now she stirred grudgingly, shifting sideways across the raft's rubbery bottom. It was only a couple of feet—the raft wasn't huge—but she made it seem like a heroic task.

"Give me your hand," I said as she reached me, then steadied myself with it and stepped yet again up onto the raft's plump, bobbling rim.

I'd have sat on the raft's edge and slid in feet-first but the thought of a shark latching onto one of my favorite toes stopped me; if any of my parts were going into the water, my fists had to be among them right off the bat.

A punch in the nose seemed a feeble defense against all those pearly-whites, but it was better than nothing; meanwhile, no shark fins poked up from the water at the moment, and the Bayliner hadn't floated too far away . . . yet.

"Jake, don't," Ellie breathed in dismay when she saw what I was doing, but I was too busy ignoring my own fears to reply. We had one chance, but only right now, not after I'd thought about it for a while.

Besides, if I thought about it, I'd never do it, so once again I just jumped, steeling myself for the cold water and very aware of not wanting to get shark-nipped. Then, once I'd splashed and resurfaced uneaten, it hit me how much farther away the Bayliner appeared from the water than it had from the raft.

Swim, said the voice in my brain that's in charge of making sure I don't drown. *Swim fast*, it said as the big boat moved rapidly away and my brain went on showing me full-color images of bloody shark attacks.

Meanwhile, have I mentioned how poorly I did in that swim class? The Bayliner was farther away now than when I'd started, and the raft was somehow equally distant. Then a breeze kicked up, hurling salty waves at me.

My eyes burned. My lungs burned. My arms and legs burned, too, from more exercise than they'd had in a month, but there was no help for it; no one was coming to our rescue. So I kicked once, then again, and swam a little more, mostly just to see if I could.

And then the most amazing thing happened. Remember that anchor, the one I said was sailing like a kite-tail underwater, towed by its anchor-chain behind the drifting Bayliner?

Well, just then a large object surged up at me from below and in my fear and exhaustion, once I saw that it wasn't the shark, I somehow believed that it might be a life ring and grabbed blindly for it.

And caught it, managing not to let it take out my appendix and not to let go, even though it was moving along very swiftly. It was the Bayliner's anchor; the current's force must've pulled it loose very abruptly, and the taut, suddenly-released anchor-chain had recoiled forcefully, yanking the anchor toward the boat.

But not for long. The anchor slowed and began sinking again, now pulling the Bayliner nearer to me as it went down. Once I reached it, I seized the chain desperately and hauled myself up it as quick as a little monkey, a feat I managed only because I knew sharks liked eating monkeys.

But I only got halfway up before I realized that I'd never make it; a natural vine-swinger I ain't. Instead I needed the swim ladder at the Bayliner's stern. So I had to swim again, then climb the ladder and heave myself over the transom.

And then, not quite believing it myself, I was aboard; half-drowned, falling-down exhausted, and sharing the deck with a shark's corpse. Not until I'd stumbled to the helm and found the key in the ignition, though, did I remember:

That anchor. It had to come up, and you raised it with a crank, and the crank was on the bow. To get there I'd have to get out *onto* the bow, inching my way along a narrow walkway with a sharp drop to the water on one side, and nothing to hang on to on the other.

Or that's how I'd done it before, but now the hell with it; I strode halfway out there, froze in panic, then gave myself a good hard kick in the mental backside and went the rest of the way. The anchor was heavy and so was the chain, but the crank worked smoothly; trembling with exhaustion, I guided the chain into its locker and secured the anchor with the bungee cords I found looped around the capstan.

And *then* I went back, started the engine, put it in gear, and . . . nothing. The engine ran fine but the boat just sat where it was, emphasis on the word *sat*. We were stuck on something, I strongly suspected, probably on another one of those granite ledges that Ellie had picked our way through so carefully, earlier.

"No, no, *no* . . ." Angrily I slammed the shift lever forward;

nothing. Back: nothing again. The Bayliner shivered and tried to move each time I revved the engine, but . . .

"Oh!" The word burst from me as, with a great deal of loud grinding and crunching, the boat lurched. A few times more of backing-and-forthing and—

The Bayliner slid backwards off the keel-trapping ledge into deeper water, bobbing freely until I hit the throttle again and promptly ran into yet another chunk of underwater granite.

Chastened, I backed off, then consulted the GPS. Glowing green numerals showed a way through the ledges, but before I tried, I thought I'd better get out the life rings.

I'd be throwing them to Hudson and Lizzie in a few minutes, I reasoned; they'd better be handy. So after putting the boat in neutral I stepped over the dead shark's body to get to them.

That's when the shark either came back to life or had never really been dead at all. Suddenly the sweetly marine-scented air was full of teeth, gnashing and slashing; startled, I hardly knew whether to jump overboard or out of my skin.

In the end I just leapt back toward the bow, and the animal quieted. Reflex, I told myself, that primitive brain is just having a last spasm. But as I thought this, the long, fishy body sort of sproinged itself into the air again, its jaws snapping.

Unfortunately, it didn't sproing itself right off the boat. So I did the only thing I could think of; I grabbed the life rings and vaulted over the shark's body while he made another fast grab for me.

And missed. Pushing the throttle, I began picking my way through more of the underwater granite ledges. Every cell in my body screamed *hurry*: The shark on the deck was getting his wind back, and the one still in the water could be attacking someone right this minute.

At last the numbers on the depth finder climbed, indicating deeper water; I was safely past the ledges. But as I hit the gas to charge toward the raft, I spotted another boat approaching.

Sure, now *you show up,* I thought. Then as it drew alongside I saw who it was: Peter Waldron, on the deck of the *Consuelo.* And he was pointing a gun at me.

Meanwhile, now only a few yards from the Bayliner, Lizzie smacked the wooden paddle's flat side down hard onto the water. Nearby, Hudson swam one-handed, clutching a sobbing Ephraim in his other arm and struggling to reach the raft.

Waldron's bullhorn-amplified voice rang out. "All aboard," it said, and for emphasis he fired his weapon.

The bullet hit the silvery propeller atop the wind-gauge on the Bayliner and sent it whizzing around. *Consuelo* moved stern-first toward where Lizzie was looking up at it in surprise.

When the boat's rear deck ladder neared her, she grabbed for it and hoisted herself up. Next, Waldron angled the boat around so Ellie could grab the ladder, too; she helped Glenna onto it, then climbed it herself.

Finally Hudson went up, still carrying Ephraim. And since I wasn't going anywhere without him, and besides, Waldron would shoot me if I tried, I dropped anchor again, and climbed up onto the *Consuelo* with the rest of them.

Once we were all on the *Consuelo,* we got relieved of our phones, which didn't work anyway. Waldron aimed his own weapon at Ephraim while Lizzie and Dylan slid their weapons across the deck to him. The guns probably didn't work, either, after their bath in salt water, but I still hated to see them go.

Then we were shepherded together in the same comfortably appointed room that Hudson and I had seen: rattan carpets, up-holstered furnishings, big windows, and a very large TV screen that hadn't been there before, mounted on the aft bulkhead.

The man liked his luxuries. A rare coin would buy a lot of them, I guessed. I didn't know if Julio's death would change his plans, but I did know that we were all prisoners here on his big research vessel, where he still held a gun on us.

"The hell," Hudson uttered in disgust. Still dripping salt

water, he squidged across the rattan to the room's well-stocked wet bar, grabbed a bottle of brandy, and swigged.

Then he passed the bottle around while Waldron just stood there and watched us, weapon at the ready. I took my swallow, shuddered and took another, then turned to Waldron.

"The little boy is sick," I said. Limp in Ellie's arms, Ephraim coughed alarmingly as if to confirm this. "I need warm water, blankets . . . do you have any Tylenol?"

He'd probably have ignored me, but I was standing two feet from him, staring into his tanned, boyish face. He was the one with the weapon, but he blinked first, I saw with satisfaction.

Yeah, screw your gun, I thought, *and screw you, too.*

"Oh, come on." I got right up in his face and snarled at him, "I know you've probably got a whole sick bay on this tub, just let me into it."

Thinking *scalpels, needles . . . anything sharp and/or weapon-like . . .* But Waldron was no dummy, unfortunately.

"Yeah, no. I'll get you the pills." He waved toward a door at one end of the room we were in.

"Bath, kitchenette, full laundry, towels, blankets."

So it was to be a luxurious imprisonment. He turned and left us, and the door that he pulled closed behind him locked audibly.

"Well," said Glenna, who was already on her fourth swig of brandy, "*this* is a fine kettle of fish."

Hudson turned to her. "Listen, we need to think, so how about if you don't have anything to contribute, you shut up?"

Then he turned away, heading for the bath area; she stuck her tongue out at him as he went.

"Dylan's right, though," Lizzie said quietly. "We need to figure out something."

But then he came back. "It's okay in there, good towels and all. Better take the boy and get him warmed up."

You could've knocked me over with a feather; I'd been sure he'd meant to grab first dibs on getting warm and dry.

But he hadn't. Lizzie's gaze turned slowly to me, her dark eyes communicative: *See?*

Yeah. He was a prince, all right, even if a bit of a mixed blessing, in the day-to-day. But could he leap tall buildings or stop locomotives?

Because a comic-book superhero was exactly what we needed now, as Ellie agreed while we sat a listless Ephraim in the bathtub's warm water, sponging him down before wrapping him in warm towels.

"What I don't understand is how he's managed it all," said Ellie, meaning Waldron. "So much has happened, he couldn't have done it all himself, and what's Julio got to do with it, anyway?"

"I don't know. Maybe Waldron did threaten his family?" I said, remembering Julio's soulful dark eyes and spaniel face.

"Or maybe he just said that to try getting himself off the hook," I added. "To me, none of this is making sense."

The distant *whap-whapping* of a helicopter's blades came from outside. "They're out looking for us," I said. "George and Wade."

Of course they were, we'd been out all night; by now, Wade would've enlisted the port authority's helicopter. Soon they'd find Ellie's boat and the raft, and probably the wooden paddle, too, still floating around out there.

"They're probably fit to be tied," said Ellie, and that was an understatement. But there was nothing we could do about it now, and while we were drying Ephraim's hair—his eyes stared glassily, his cheeks pink with fever, and Waldron still hadn't returned—Lizzie came in.

"I found some honey in the kitchenette, along with some Tylenol." She held out a pill bottle and a jar with a spoon in it. "The honey might make giving the Tylenol easier."

I didn't kiss her feet but it was close. Crushed into the honey, the Tylenol went down okay, Ephraim took a few sips of some ginger ale we found, and when we put him down on a couch in the lounge area and covered him, he slept.

"You're right, though, Waldron must've had help," I went on to Ellie half an hour later when we'd had hot showers. A closet held clothing in various sizes, perhaps left by previous guests.

Luckily, I didn't mind the luxury brand-names, although I do know I'll never fit again into what high-end designers think is a size eight. When we were dressed, we went back out into the common area for coffee.

"Who else? Sally Coates?" I recalled the small, crowded house and her story. "I don't care how much she tries to defend her missing man, she couldn't have been that sorry to be done with getting yelled at and clobbered."

I got up and poured more coffee at the credenza near the door. The fancy contraption that brewed it looked complicated enough to refine uranium in.

"So maybe Sally and the shark scientist meet cute while he's got her husband working for him?" Ellie theorized when I returned. "And what, cook something up together?"

"It would be a good team," allowed Lizzie, sitting nearby. "Her on the home front, playing the poor widow, keeping Waldron informed of any important developments . . ."

"And Waldron doing the dirty work," I finished for her. "My next question, though, would be why in the world Sally got Ellie and me involved? And what happened to the"—I broke off as a low vibration began humming in the floor as the *Consuelo*'s engines started—"gold coin?" I finished.

"That's more than one question," Waldron said from behind me; he'd slipped in silently.

"Hudson's in the shower," I said inanely. While we talked, the rest of us were taking advantage of the fruit and pastries on the buffet, except for Glenna, who'd found another bottle of brandy and was sipping steadily from it.

The booze didn't keep her from watching Waldron alertly, I

noted; from beneath her damp fringe of thick, still-damp white hair, her eyes remained fixed on him.

"I want you all to know that I'm really very sorry about this," he began, pouring himself a glass of club soda at the bar and dropping a slice of lime into it.

The *Consuelo* lurched backwards suddenly, startling and then puzzling me. "Who the heck is driving?" I demanded.

He smiled condescendingly. "Jake, I know how you like to be in control of everything . . ."

Control this, I thought angrily at him.

". . . but from here on, you don't have to do a thing," he went on. "Everything's being handled."

Hudson exited the bath area with damp hair, a fresh shave, and a stony expression, wearing a set of excessively fashionable men's clothes that he must've pulled out of the castoffs closet.

"What's going on?" He looked around at all of us, then at Waldron again. "And what the hell do you think you're—"

Waldron stepped back, then turned quickly and fired his little handgun at one of the lounge windows, which exploded.

"Okay, so have I got your attention now?" he demanded.

But by then I was long past feeling menaced by a weapon; I'd been menaced by a sinking barge, Julio's treachery, and more sharks than I could shake a stick at, all just that morning.

I was all menaced out. "I want," I repeated, "to know who is driving this boat. We have a right to—"

Waldron fired the gun again, whereupon naturally I wondered how many rounds it held, and whether I could get him to fire the rest of them without hitting any of us.

But just then the boat's motion halted; moments later the door Waldron had come through opened again and a man I'd never seen before came through it.

"Folks," said Waldron, raising his hand like some jolly game-show host, "say hello to the not-even-murdered-a-little-bit Mister Paul Coates."

I looked at Ellie and she looked at me: *Of course.* Coates was a big, bulky fellow with a broad, sun-leathered face, dark, untrimmed hair and whiskers, and a general air of being in way over his head.

His dull gaze meandered around the room. "Why do I think none of this was his idea?" I whispered to Lizzie.

"Because first he'd have to have ideas?" she responded venomously; investigating murder cases whose victims were only fake-dead was not her favorite activity.

Waldron was talking again. "If you all could've minded your own business, none of this would've—"

"Sally's my friend," Ellie cut in hotly. "People who aren't monsters help friends, okay? So don't try blaming this on—"

The calming motions Waldron made with his hands caused me to want mine wrapped tightly around his throat. Coates came back from the fridge with a beer and one of those frozen meat-pastry gadgets that you heat up in the microwave.

He took a large, unselfconscious bite of the unwarmed food item, chewed energetically, and washed it down with beer.

"Just tell me how it worked, will you?" Lizzie said quietly as Waldron prepared to go on with whatever goofy little lecture he thought he was delivering.

"Why?" he asked. "I mean, it's not like you'll ever be able to do anything about—"

He stopped, seeming to realize what he'd very nearly said: that we weren't going to live long enough.

Ellie turned pointedly away and addressed Coates. "So you just left them? Sally and your kids, you took the coin and ran off and let them think you're dead?"

Coates's eyes closed tiredly as if he'd already read himself this particular riot act many times.

Poor baby, I thought meanly. But then another thought hit me. "So let me guess," I said to the very-not-dead fisherman. "You told Waldron about the coin while you two were out shark hunting together? You running the *Consuelo*, him doing . . . whatever the hell it is he was doing?"

Heck, maybe he really was a shark scientist . . . emphasis on the *was*, if I had anything to do with it.

But that remained to be seen. "You told him because he'd studied sharks off the coast of Florida," I said, "so you must have thought he knew all about the place."

Coates listened sulkily. "And he encouraged that belief," I went on. "He said he knew people there, that he could sell the coin for you, get big money and just take a commission."

I took a breath. "But it could only be you two, not the wife and the kids. Did he paint you a pretty picture of life as a rich guy? A *single* rich guy?"

I turned to Waldron, who was leaning casually against the wet bar with his seltzer, looking bored.

"I suppose it's handy, having another boat guy aboard," I said to him. "So you'll probably wait until you get to Florida to kill Coates, too, right?"

Coates looked outraged.

"Oh, come on," I told him, "why would he need you? Once he's got the coin . . . you haven't given it to him yet, have you?"

A furrow appeared in Paul Coates's forehead, quickly replaced by what he probably thought was a look of sly cunning.

"Don't worry about me," he said. "I've still got it. Pete's gonna help me sell it, is all, I'm not giving it to him."

Correct, I thought. *He'll just take it.*

Back in the bad old days, my bosses thought nothing of patting some guy on the back, then wrapping a bicycle chain around his neck and pulling hard on it; that's how I knew. But Coates still didn't believe me, Waldron still had the gun, and I stood there between them.

If I made a move, one of them could grab me, a fact Glenna noticed and seemed to think was entertaining as she swigged from the brandy bottle, then regarded it with sudden interest as if some new thought had occurred to her.

But now while I had the chance, I'd try one more question:

"Paul, did you give your half brother, Bailey Lyman, your

wife's private phone number, just to sweeten the pot a little? Let him keep harassing her so he'd help you?"

Coates nodded reluctantly, looked down at his feet. Having all this laid out for him was making it look different to him, I gathered from his expression; different, and worse.

Lizzie spoke to Waldron. "You killed the lagoon guy, too, didn't you? Little guy," she added to Coates's look of troubled surprise. "Red hair, red hat?"

"Howie Fairbrother?" Coates looked at Waldron, dismayed. "I mean, I get it about Bailey. Once he'd put it where we needed him to put it, he had to go. Guy talked too much. Worthless bastard, anyway," he added. "Always was. I mean, running people over in parking lots? Come on."

The way he said it made me think he was parroting something that Waldron had told him; that by killing Bailey Lyman, Waldron hadn't only been protecting their scheme. He'd been performing a public service.

"But Howie was a decent guy. He didn't really see anything important out there, why did you have to—?"

"Shut up." Waldron put his glass down sharply. "We've talked about this. I decide stuff, remember?"

He moved toward the door. "So, Paulie, you stay here, keep an eye on these folks. I'll run the boat for a while, okay?"

"That's right, Paulie, you'd better remember who the real boss is around here," Hudson put in sarcastically.

Which only made Paul Coates madder, just as Hudson had intended. Waldron reached out for the doorknob, not seeing Coates angrily stepping toward him with something in his hand.

A Swiss Army knife; the one Sally had mentioned to us, I supposed. I'd forgotten all about it until now.

"You bastard," Coates uttered, and I don't know what he'd have done next but in fact it turned out to be nothing; instead, Glenna was on her feet very suddenly, raising the brandy bottle she held and bringing it down onto the back of Coates's skull.

A look of surprise crossed his heavy features as his hands dropped. The knife fell and then he did, collapsing to his knees before toppling forward onto his face.

Waldron had his gun out but Hudson lunged and knocked him sideways before he could fire; the gun tumbled through the now-open doorway and Waldron followed it, slamming the door.

Or trying; Lizzie caught it before it shut completely and raced after Waldron, and then Hudson ran after Lizzie.

"He's got another gun, watch it!" Hudson shouted. A gun-shot, followed by the *ker-whang!* of a ricochet, confirmed this.

I started off behind Hudson, but Ellie stopped me. "You'd better look at Ephraim."

Fright pierced me; in all the ruckus he'd been quiet and, I'd thought, still sleeping. But back in the lounge where we'd tucked him in, I found him even hotter than before, with beads of sweat glistening on his forehead.

"I tried my phone again," said Ellie. "Still nothing."

"He's burning up, the Tylenol didn't help. We've got to get him to a doctor."

Across the room, Coates was beginning to struggle up off the rattan carpet. Ellie stood at the window.

"Jake, look down there."

I did. "Oh," I breathed, thinking *Oh, let it be true.* "Is that what it looks like?"

About fifteen feet long, maybe eight feet wide, the large, unwieldy-looking shape was lashed to the *Consuelo's* rail with a tautly strung rectangle of canvas tied down over it.

"It is," Ellie confirmed as behind us the not-dead Paul Coates finally struggled to his feet. "It's just what you think it is," she said happily.

It was a lifeboat. Now all we had to do was get down there, get the thing into the water, and get ourselves all into the vessel without drowning any of us, all while praying that the engine had a key in its ignition and the lifeboat didn't leak.

Sure, it would be easy.

Not.

I carried Ephraim and Ellie helped a somewhat sozzled Glenna put one foot in front of the other down the passageway, with the somewhat-recovered Coates leading the way.

He had, I gathered, reversed his opinion of Peter Waldron; now when I'd told him what we intended to do, he nodded grimly and he led us to a door that opened onto the main deck.

Ellie peeked out, then stepped out and waved for us to come, too. The deck thrummed faintly under my feet as somewhere below us, the boat's engine started; Waldron must've noticed the search helicopter.

By now the sun was halfway up into the brutally blue sky; around us, the water was as flat as a mirror.

"Watch for another search helicopter," I said, shielding my eyes. "If you see one, wave like your life depended on it."

Because there was still a good chance that it did. "If they spot the *Consuelo*, though, they'll just ask Waldron if he's seen us and he'll say he hasn't, end of story," Ellie pointed out.

"Yeah. That's why we need to get on that lifeboat."

We crept along the *Consuelo*'s rail to the aft deck, where the little emergency craft was stowed. Ellie untied the lines holding the tarp down; meanwhile I expected Peter Waldron to show up and shoot us, but he didn't; maybe Lizzie and Hudson were keeping him busy, I thought hopefully.

But speak of the devil: "Gotcha," said the shark hunter, popping out of the same hatchway we'd come through. Stupid face, sunglasses, gun . . .

Oh, nuts to this, I thought and was on the point of rushing him when Coates did it for me.

The burly fisherman lowered his head and charged like a

bull, driving his noggin into Waldron's midsection. Waldron's feet lifted up off the deck, his midsection flew back, and his arms swung out, his right hand losing its grip on the weapon.

It flew, landed hard, and fired with a concussive *pow!* that woke Ephraim from a fretful half dream. Then it spun across the deck at me and I snatched it up.

Behind me, Coates lay still, a red pool spreading beneath him. Waldron stood over Coates, poised to run, but hesitating.

Eyes resting covetously on his gun. He wanted it badly, of course; if he didn't have it, it was just him alone against us.

"Come and get it," I taunted him. "Come on, you want it or not?"

I crooked my trigger finger at him; the one, I mean, that wasn't already on the actual trigger. Oh, I wanted so much for him to give me an excuse. But he didn't move and then Hudson and Lizzie were there, him bending over Coates's motionless form while she got zip-ties around Waldron's wrists and yanked him to his feet.

"Okay, buddy," she said as she moved him back in through the hatchway door, "let's get you where I can keep an eye on you until the state cops get here and take your sorry ass away."

Which meant she could call them; I pulled out my phone as Hudson glanced up, nodding.

"Yeah, phones're back. We called in already, gave our location."

The jagged metal clamp came off my heart for the first time in days; just not all the way. Ephraim coughed fretfully, his eyes glazed with fever, and now I spied Glenna LaFarge slumped on a deck chair nearby; the brandy had finally gotten to her.

I heard the helicopter before I saw it, the LifeFlight 'copter with the big red cross on the door. The copilot waved and pointed, indicating a rooster-tail of white, foamy engine wake on the watery horizon to the northwest.

I recognized the Coast Guard's big orange-and-gray rubber Zodiac boat, and then everything went by in a rush. The 'copter swerved away and we all got loaded very kindly and efficiently into the Zodiac. I kept thinking I was forgetting something but I didn't have time even to wonder what, much less go back.

Soon we were speeding across the water in the hot sun, on our way home. Still shivering with fever, Ephraim lay in my lap; his hot, miserable little body was the only thing that felt real to me just then, as if all the rest was a bad dream. *Come on,* I urged the Zodiac forward.

Ephraim opened his eyes, looked steadily up at me, and smiled. "Grammy," he said clearly.

Well, I just about melted through the boat's thick rubber floor; then, as if that smile had been a hint, I turned my face into the sun and salty spray that I was being zoomed through.

And for a moment it was glorious: calm water with seagulls overhead, a fresh breeze smelling of salt, tar, and seaweed, and out past the Zodiac's tall, white rooster-tail wake, a black fin trailing us . . .

Wait a minute. "Ellie." I nudged her and pointed.

Her eyes got big. Hudson and Lizzie hadn't seen it; they had Waldron between them and were occupied with making sure he didn't throw, as Sam liked to say, a wrench in the monkey-works.

And Glenna was asleep. Ellie got up and poked the guy at the Zodiac's helm, then gestured behind us. The Coastie glanced over his shoulder, then reached hastily for his radio.

"Mayday, mayday," he said into it. Hearing this, Waldron looked up and followed the Coastie's alarmed gaze back to where the shark cruised.

"Must go faster," I heard myself say, and the Coastie must have had the same thought, because he did. But the fin didn't drop back, or even better, go away. Instead the beast seemed to accept our challenge by shooting unnervingly right up alongside our little vessel, which may I remind us all was made of rubber.

Heavy-duty rubber, but still. To a shark, it probably looked like a teething ring. "What, you couldn't find a paper sailboat?" I asked the Coastie, gesturing around at this laughably inadequate rescue vehicle.

He shot me a look. "Ma'am, it was the only boat that wasn't already out looking for you, and all of them are pretty far from here."

"Oh," I said, chastened. Then Waldron sat up straight, his eyes narrowing as the shark fell back to make a run at us, then chomped us when he caught up. His teeth made a rubbery squeak that put my own on edge.

But no harm done, or so I thought until the Coastie at the helm shoved the throttle forward all the way and told his guys to get out some position flares.

"Mayday," he repeated into the radio, now sputtering with traffic triggered by the earlier distress call. Then suddenly the helicopter's *whap-whapping* was loud, the aircraft was right overhead, and the barrel of what I sincerely hoped was a bazooka poked out the copilot's open door.

But it wasn't a bazooka, I saw as they hovered, it was only a high-powered rifle. Besides, the shark was too close to the Zodiac for anyone to shoot at it safely; the 'copter backed off.

Then more good news: the shark's teeth had punctured something; from the sound of air hissing, I guessed it was one of the air cells—the things that kept us afloat. Now, the vessel had many of these, plenty for us to float just fine on despite the damaged ones.

But this particular one was in the stern, I realized when I narrowed down the sound, very near the engines. As the air cell deflated, the Zodiac's massive twin 300s dropped heavily down, lowering themselves into the water a foot or so. As the cell went on deflating, the lowering and listing to port would continue; this, sadly, meant that at least one and probably both engines would eventually get swamped.

Ephraim woke suddenly, gasping; the gasp fractured into a cough that tailed off wheezily, then began again. He was pale, now, his lips turning faintly dusky.

I was afraid to hold him any tighter than I already was. Then Glenna spoke up again. She'd gotten back some gumption and now she sat with her arms on the Zodiac's padded rail.

"Isn't anybody going to do anything about this?" she asked, and when no one answered her—to be fair, by that point I think we were all too busy saying our prayers—she clambered up.

Sighing heavily—this should be somebody else's job, her face said clearly—she grabbed one of the metal oars clipped into place under the Zodiac's rail, then climbed with it up onto the Zodiac's bouncing, now somewhat deflated rim.

"Come, fishy," she uttered darkly, and for a moment there, I really believed in what people called magic; the black fin appeared right away and sped toward her as if she'd called it.

And then the shark hit us, not glancingly like before but full on, ramming straight into us. The watercraft's gray rubber side flew up, Glenna toppled backwards, and the shark's head lunged up over the rim in a thrashing, gnashing frenzy.

Glenna grabbed the oar and brought it down on the animal's nose, but the shark was undeterred. Meanwhile its weight sank the boat's rim very neatly into the shape of a pouring spout, so you can guess what the water all around us did then, can't you?

Correctamundo, as Sam would say; suddenly the Zodiac's floor was like a kiddie pool with a shark in it, and he smelled blood. Ephraim screamed as I clawed across the floor, trying to haul us toward the helm and away from the teeth madly snapping at us; I mean, the thing was *right there*.

But the raft's floor was slippery, cold water covered it, and every time I made a little headway the shark made some, too. He wasn't actually in the Zodiac with us, but he was trying. Then, just as I thought that in the next instant he'd succeed, Ellie was there, pushing me with one hand and dragging Glenna by her arm with the other.

"Hi," she gasped at me, and pushed me some more. But now Lizzie and Hudson were missing. Or . . . no, they weren't. They were farther astern, on the far side of where the shark had now slid back into the water.

But he was still right there in our wake, no doubt planning his next run at us. Meanwhile the water that had poured into the Zodiac was pooled in the stern, lowering it even more.

The Zodiac's crew had weapons, but the shark was so close that nobody could shoot the animal without blowing a hole through the Zodiac, too, and we had enough holes in it already.

Meanwhile Lizzie and Hudson were conferring hastily with Peter Waldron. He had, I saw with alarm, a gun in his hand. I couldn't imagine why he had it, but they looked unalarmed; one of them must have given it to him, I realized, and cut the zip-ties from his wrists.

"Jeeze," breathed Glenna as Waldron approached the Zodiac's stern with the shark's fin zooming behind just a few feet away, "the kid's got guts."

Or a death wish, maybe; his boyish face had a sort of wild glee on it, and the idea hit me that he didn't mean to survive the coming encounter, whatever it was. I still didn't know what he meant to do, but then I glimpsed the big syringe he gripped, as big as a turkey baster with a needle the size of a railroad spike at one end.

He'd tucked the gun away somewhere. He must mean to inject the big fish with something, I understood suddenly, the way forest rangers do when they have to tranquilize wild animals.

But why had he been carrying a massive syringe with what looked like half a pint of nighty-night juice in it at all? He must've already had it on him back on the *Consuelo*, when he introduced us to Paul Coates.

Then it hit me; he'd intended to use it on us. After all, he had to get rid of us somehow, and shooting people was messy. Thinking this, I watched him get as close as he could to the Zodiac's stern, until he was leaning out over the transom.

"Here, fishy-fishy," he crooned evilly, his menacing grin stretching into a grimace as he crooked his finger at the churning water. "Come on, you filthy son of a bitch—"

And I guess those must've been the magic words, because the shark surged up suddenly straight at Waldron. But he was ready for it, the syringe already raised high over his head as he hurled himself at the beast.

Maybe that was why instead of pausing at a safe distance, he let out a cry and flung himself on the huge fish, scrambling until he was astride the creature.

Meanwhile his leap had briefly lowered the stern enough for more water to pour in. The dual engines coughed intermittently as our sagging stern kept dunking them. Then, just as Waldron plunged the big needle towards the animal's flank, it gave a massive, sinuous twist and bucked him off, into the water.

What happened then took only a moment. The shark caught Waldron's foot in his teeth. Waldron tried yanking himself free, but no luck. Then the shark rolled lazily and disappeared under the water, dragging Waldron along with it.

And then they were gone. Twenty minutes later our wounded vessel limped in past the breakwater, rounded the mooring dolphin at the boat basin's entrance, and finally reached the dock.

No one had spoken since Waldron went overboard. Except for the crew members performing their duties, no one had one single, solitary thing to say. But now:

"Why'd he do that?" Hudson asked Lizzie puzzledly as the

Coast Guard guys got us off the Zodiac. We all headed for the gangway leading up onto the breakwater's deck.

"I don't know," she told him, sounding drained. "We'll talk about it, but not now, okay?"

At the gangway's top, everybody who'd been waiting there surged forward. George, Bella, senior officers out of the Coast Guard building . . . plus dozens of tourists and locals gathered to see what the sudden commotion on the water was all about.

Sam and Mika shoved toward us, both looking shredded with anxiety until I put Ephraim into Sam's arms.

"Thank you," Mika wept, nearly collapsing until Sam caught her. Once we'd embraced I urged them both toward the ambulance waiting nearby for Ephraim.

Behind them, Ellie's husband, George, looked as if he had a lot to say and would say it later, in the privacy of their home. But in his eyes, Ellie could do no wrong, I knew; by the time *later* arrived, he'd have gotten over his worry enough for them to kiss and make up without even fighting first.

Hudson and Lizzie tromped soggily off toward all the county sheriff and state cop cars and SUVs parked at the breakwater entrance. Glenna LaFarge made a beeline for Rosie's, where she walked calmly up to the window and placed an order.

Some cop or another would catch up with her eventually, I supposed. In any case she clearly didn't want any company and she seemed at least physically okay, so I let her go, meanwhile watching Ellie walk slowly off toward Water Street with George's arm already around her.

Then I squinted back out at the water where Waldron had gone, taking with him, I supposed, the location of the missing coin that had started all this. Unless . . .

"Lizzie!" I called. She looked over from where the state cops had her and Hudson cornered, asking questions and taking notes.

"Tell them to check Paul Coates's pockets," I called to her. "And his shoes!"

They'd want to go over the *Sally Ann* again, too, because he hadn't said he'd given the coin to anyone, had he? He'd said something about Bailey Lyman putting it somewhere, but not that it was still there.

So maybe he'd still had it, there on the *Consuelo*. Maybe Ellie and I could still get Sally some financial relief, at least, even though we had bad news about Paul Coates, himself.

The part I really didn't understand was Julio's role in the whole thing. But before I could think more about it, Wade pulled in, swerving his pickup truck narrowly around the cop cars blocking the breakwater and slamming to a stop. He jumped out of the cab and ran to me, looking all kinds of relieved.

And incandescent with fury. "Hi," he exhaled, seizing my shoulders, peering intently into my face. Then he pulled me to him and just about crushed me against his chest before holding me away again.

"You got Ephraim." I nodded hard, unable to speak.

"That's wonderful. I'm so relieved. And proud of you. But I'm also so mad at you, I hardly know which way to look."

I nodded again as a breeze off the water gave my sunburned arms goose bumps, chilling me in my wet clothes. He hadn't known where I was or what was happening since late the night before; in his place, I'd have been out of my mind with worry.

"I'm so sorry," I managed. "But the power, the phones . . ."

Behind the gates of the Coast Guard's white, red-roofed headquarters, Lizzie and Hudson were being escorted inside by several state police officers.

Wade nodded absently, watching them. "Yeah," he said. "The whole country was blacked out."

We climbed into his truck. From there I could see the Coast

Guard's wounded Zodiac in the boat basin. Nobody on it; all inside writing their reports, I supposed.

Thanking their stars they were alive to do it, probably. The cop cars began departing and things on the waterfront were getting back to normal—men fishing, kids running, cars idling and motorcycles rumbling.

So, I thought as Wade pulled out onto Water Street. *So now it's over. All over but the shouting.*

Although to be fair there ended up being a *lot* of shouting.

Seventeen

Early the next morning I stood on the breakwater watching the Coast Guard tow the *Consuelo* into the boat basin. Dawn spread pink across the bay's foamy chop; overhead, streaming fog turned pale gold as the sun came up behind it.

Paul Coates's body had already been recovered from the *Consuelo* and examined. He was not in fact part of the scientists' meeting here in Eastport; they had just been convenient cover for him. Also:

"No coin found on him," Lizzie reported, watching with me. The big white research boat slid halfway up onto a trailer behind an oversized pickup truck with state markings on it; the truck's winch whined, hauling the boat up the rest of the way.

"That's too bad." I was due at the Chocolate Moose, where Ellie and I had an early morning date to bake those raspberry-chocolate scones, come hell or high water.

Lizzie walked with me up the breakwater toward Water Street. "If Waldron had had it, he'd have been gone already," I said as we headed in the Moose's direction.

When we got there and went inside, the little silver bell over the door jingled brightly and the tantalizing aromas of coffee and chocolate filled the air.

Dylan Hudson sat at one of the café tables. "'Morning," he said evenly to both of us; in response, Lizzie looked as if she'd like nothing better than to swat him with the newspaper he was reading.

Apparently the previous evening had been about as calm and pleasant for them as it had been for me. After dinner, Wade and I had gotten into his pickup truck again so that we could express ourselves freely—also emphatically, and at top volume, too—without an audience.

And in the end, after apologies, explanations, and from me plenty of reporting on just exactly what had happened from start to finish—Wade and I had worked things out fine. Now I left Hudson and Lizzie eyeing one another the way you do when you've fought recently and are now feeling gun-shy about one another.

In the kitchen, Ellie was already cutting butter and flour together. The raspberries, raspberry jelly, and chocolate chips were set out, waiting to be added after the eggs and milk went in.

"What's he doing here?" I asked, taking over the butter-cutting so Ellie could start flouring the rolling pin.

"Don't know. He's being quiet. Just wanted coffee. How's Ephraim?" Ellie regarded me with concern. "And how are *you*?"

"Ephraim's good. I mean, he's still sick, but the hospital only kept him overnight as a precaution. He's had four doses of his antibiotics, and when I left the house he was already up and jumping on his bed, wanting his breakfast."

Ellie made a well of the crumbly mixture in her bowl and poured beaten-together eggs and milk into it, mixed the result until it was all just barely moistened, then dumped it out onto the floured butcher-block.

Then she reached for the fruit and chocolate chips, not looking happy about the latter. "These are fine, I guess, but they're so boring. I wish—"

"Aha." Hudson appeared in the kitchen doorway holding a white paper bag from the candy store next door.

"Those scones aren't in the oven yet, are they?" he asked, and when we said they weren't, he went on:

"I got distracted." He angled his head back to where Lizzie still sat. "Nearly left this too late."

He held out the paper bag. I took it and looked into it, then up at him.

"But these are . . ." They were chocolate candies. At his nod, I took one and bit down; a familiar fruity taste spread over my tongue.

"These are chocolate-covered raspberries," I managed around the morsel. I could already tell that the chocolate coating made the raspberry sturdy enough to survive getting folded into the scone batter. Ellie clearly agreed. She took the bag and went right back to work, calling thanks over her shoulder to Hudson.

Hudson had brought enough chocolate-covered raspberries to make all the scones; how he'd known we needed them, or that Ellie was still working on the scones, I had no idea.

"Oh, I hear things," he answered wisely when I asked, but without actually giving me an answer. "There's something else, too," he added.

He pulled a smallish object wrapped in a napkin from his jacket pocket and drew the napkin back. Lizzie got up, Ellie came back over to us, also, and I just stood there, staring.

The thing Hudson held out was an irregularly round disk, gleaming gold and stamped with crosses, a few Latin words, and Roman numerals.

I looked up questioningly at Hudson. "I went down to Rosie's Hot Dog Stand last night," he said. "Because," he added with a look at Lizzie, "no one else wanted to get dinner."

She rolled her eyes exasperatedly; he continued. "So I get

there, the teenaged girl at the counter wants to know if I'm really a cop. Someone told her I was, she said."

"And?" Ellie urged him on with a glance toward the kitchen; those scones still waited.

"And when I showed her my badge, she looked relieved and told me a strange old lady had given her a gift earlier, and wouldn't take no for an answer, but now she—the girl—didn't feel right about it."

He hefted the coin in the palm of his hand. "She thought maybe it was stolen."

Lizzie spoke up. "So she gave it to you? Why, for you to check on it and then give it back to her, or what?"

Hudson shook his head. "She doesn't want it. Said it gave her the creeps."

A long-ago shipwreck, a kidnapping, three murders, several attempted ones, and as the pièce de résistance, a suicide by shark . . . yeah, that coin had amassed some bad karma, all right.

I wouldn't want it, either. "It should be in a museum," I said. Let them deal with the karma. "But it really belongs to Sally and his kids, I guess."

Lizzie nodded. "For now it's evidence. But she'll get it eventually, I imagine."

"I'll bet that her kids will inherit whatever Bailey Lyman had, too," said Ellie. "He was their uncle, and I don't think he and Paul had any other family."

So Sally would end up all right. Lizzie moved toward the door. "All right, then, I guess if everybody's squared away for now I can—"

Hudson turned quickly, wrapping the coin again. "Hey, can we go up to your office and secure this thing? I don't want to be . . ."

He followed her out. I stuck my head out after them. "Hey, Dylan, thanks again for the raspberries!"

But the two of them, striding away side-by-side with their heads bent together, were already too far away to hear me.

That night we all got together for dinner at home. Wade had gotten over his entirely understandable upset, Bella and my dad were beyond ecstatic to have Ephraim back, and Mika and Sam wore the dazed, exhausted looks of parents whose kid has gone through something unthinkable and survived.

"What I don't get," Bella complained over a summer dinner of barbecued chicken, steamed green beans from the garden, and potato salad, "is how it all got started."

Hudson nodded, forking up some chicken. He and Lizzie were joining us tonight at Bella's insistence.

"I made some calls," he said, "and Peter Waldron was really a shark hunter with a grant from a Miami marine science outfit."

He looked around at us. "But he'd also been a well-known con man, down in the Keys. Buying and selling bits of so-called treasure that amateur divers brought up, fragments, mostly."

He drank some wine. "The guy I talked to in Key West said Waldron had a partner for a while, a local bartender who usually heard first when someone found something valuable."

And then the bartender—Julio—got into some trouble, moved here to Eastport, and started his own place, where Coates might've trusted him enough to tell him about the coin and ask for advice. Hudson said all this, although not in as few words.

"Then," he went on, "I'm thinking that Julio would've let Waldron know about the big score he was looking at."

After that, our recent shark sightings would give Waldron an excuse to show up, hire Coates, and gain his confidence.

Lizzie took up the tale. "But then Waldron killed Howie Fairbrother. He told me and Hudson so, and quite a few other things, right before he saved all our lives by stuffing himself into the mouth of a shark."

Bella frowned. "But why would he confess?" she wanted to know. "Little late to start trying to redeem himself, I'd say."

Waldron's seeming change of heart at the end had surprised me, too, although the part about stuffing himself into a shark's mouth was what I found most puzzling. I mean, why do that?

Lizzie shrugged, spreading her hands. "I think by then he was just trying to get a break any way he could."

"And," I said, "he thought he'd win."

They all looked at me. "He'd done it before. He had an accident in a shark cage, nearly got eaten. But he survived, to dive—and study sharks—again."

"Sounds right," said Lizzie. "He said they'd only meant to take the coin, once they were all on the *Consuelo* and on their way back to Florida. Then they'd put Coates ashore somewhere, sadder but wiser."

Her brow knit at the memory of Peter Waldron trying hard to extricate himself from the mess he and Julio had made. "But then Howie Fairbrother accidentally came upon the *Consuelo*," she went on, "just when Bailey Lyman happened to be diving alongside Walk Island. He was sticking a magnetic box to the outside of Glenna LaFarge's barge, below the waterline."

The light dawned. "Waldron didn't realize that at low tide, almost the whole barge would be out of the water," I said.

Wade nodded. "Tides in Florida hardly matter, in some places they're only a few inches. You get used to that, it'd be easy to forget that up here, the tide can drop twenty feet."

He drank some wine. "Glenna must've seen them out there. I'm guessing they dealt with her by putting her *in* the barge."

I looked at him, surprised. In the truck the night before, we'd gone over every detail of what I'd been doing and why, and what I'd learned—or thought I had—while it all went on.

He'd even told me, once he'd cooled off a little, that he'd gone out to look again at those belt-buckle marks on the *Sally Ann*'s freshly painted rail, and he'd figured them out.

"They're not buckle marks. They may look like they're from a buckle, but they're marks from the lines on his traps."

In the dashboard light, his wind-weathered face had been youthfully earnest. "It's why he'd painted, to keep water from getting into the wood, but of course you just go out and do it again, mark it up again right away," he said.

But I hadn't realized he'd been thinking so carefully about all the rest of it. "Because look," he said now, "what they did know was that the old barge was on the point of breaking up. So they stuck Glenna down there to drown when it happened, planning to retrieve the coin before the waves scattered the wreckage."

So far it made sense to me. They'd have had no idea exactly when the barge would break up, but it had to be fairly soon, and they must've thought the coin was worth waiting for.

And if it didn't break up, they'd just go get the coin anyway; by then, Glenna wouldn't be a problem for them anymore.

Now my dad, who'd been silent so far, spoke up.

"How come Coates didn't remind his buddies about the tides, that the box would get exposed? He'd have remembered."

A fisherman; sure, he would. But: "I could be wrong," I said slowly, "and I guess there's no way of knowing for sure."

I remembered again the dismay on Coates's face when he found out that Waldron had killed Howie Fairbrother.

Dismay, but not surprise. "But I wonder if even back then Coates was already having second thoughts," I said.

Hudson's eyebrows went up. "You think maybe he meant to go back alone and retrieve the coin, himself? Go home, even, maybe?"

It was exactly what I thought, that maybe Coates just got homesick. Missed his wife and kids, wished he'd never left them. Just wanted to go home.

"Yeah," I said, suddenly on the point of tears. "But he never got a chance."

Ellie saved me. "But after we rescued Glenna from the barge, she went back and retrieved the box, which was exposed at low tide. She didn't have to know where it was, all she had to do was look. So when the men went to get it from where they'd put it and it wasn't there, but she *was* there—"

They'd drawn the obvious conclusion.

"So Glenna got the coin," Sam said. "And she wouldn't tell them where it was?"

He'd been eating his dinner and washing it down with Moxie very industriously as if to make up for the calories he'd burned searching for his son.

Now he sat back as Lizzie replied. "Yep. So they put her down there again, and Ephraim, too, once Julio had nabbed him. You were right, by the way," she added, turning to me. "They grabbed Ephraim to get you two off their tail. They thought everyone, including the police, would be so distracted by a missing-kid case, they'd all concentrate on Ephraim and forget all about them. Why didn't you, anyway?"

"Guilt," I said simply, looking at Sam and Mika. "If I'd put him in danger, I had to get him out again, and just the suspicion that he might be in harm's way because of me meant that I had to know for sure. Know, and do something about it."

Of course, it hadn't hurt that Waldron & Co. were so unimaginative about hiding places; they could've kept Ephraim on the *Consuelo*, for instance.

But they hadn't. Lizzie was watching me. Our eyes met, and I thought once more of her long-lost niece. Then she was smiling again.

"Anyway, you'll have to ask Glenna LaFarge about standing up to those thugs," she said. "If you can, that is; I haven't seen her since we got to shore, yesterday."

"You mean they meant to let both of them drown?" Mika piped up faintly. She looked horrified.

"No," I said firmly, thinking *Yes, probably.* "I'm sure that Julio must've meant to retrieve Ephraim before—"

But Sam wasn't fooled. "I guess a degree in oceanography or

whatever doesn't make you a good guy, huh?" he commented, once more applying himself studiously to his potato salad.

I nodded hard at him. Last-minute confessions or no, anyone who stole a kid right out of his bed should learn oceanography from the bottom of one, was my opinion on the matter. However:

"It was Julio who actually took Ephraim," I said, because of course it was. The dogs lying now in their beds by the stove weren't guard dogs, not even Barney the German shepherd. A few rib-eyes from Julio's freezer had kept them quiet.

Julio had even known the house layout, and that the spare key was hidden in that worst of all places, under the doormat.

"So that's why I found bones buried in the couch cushions!" Bella said. "I *wondered* where they'd come from!"

She eyed the dogs like naughty children as Wade spoke again: "Seems like somebody must've done a lot of fast talking, though, to rope Coates into this scheme at all."

Hudson looked wise. "State cops've got the tape from the security cameras at Julio's. Seems our barkeeping pal spent a lot of time talking to Coates, when Coates was in there alone."

"Trying to talk Coates into something?" I asked.

Hudson nodded. "That's what it looked like. Scaring him a little, too. Maybe about how it wasn't safe to carry a valuable item around with you, or even leave it at home."

"Waldron mentioned that," Lizzie said. "Julio told Waldron that it was probably Coates's half brother, Bailey, who would try to take the coin. It's why Coates got the elaborate security system and the dog, and why he gave in when Waldron said Bailey had to go."

The security system that Sally had disconnected because she couldn't afford it, I realized, glancing at Ellie.

"Anyway, the story about Julio's family in Florida being menaced by some unspecified 'they' was completely fabricated. His family's in Ohio, not even in touch with him," said Hudson.

Julio had just hoped he could lay the whole thing off on Waldron, probably. But enough of this *maybe* and *possibly* stuff; I got up impatiently.

"The trouble is, we're mostly just theorizing," I said. "We don't know any of this for sure. Or not much of it, anyway."

"That's right," said Ellie resignedly. "I guess we're never really going to know exactly what happened."

But Lizzie shook her head, turning to pull something from the soft black-leather satchel that she'd slung over the back of the chair.

"Yes, we will. In fact, for the most part we already do."

She held up a small green leatherette-bound notebook. Suddenly Sally Coates's trembling voice was in my head: *He was always scribbling in it.*

My opinion of Paul Coates rose, as it should have back then. It hadn't occurred to me that a guy who by all accounts wasn't a big thinker might keep a diary. Day after day, year after year . . . it was like Sam said, that people were smart in different ways.

"It was lying on the deck by his body," Lizzie said, "and I snatched it up as I went by. Then in all the commotion I forgot about it. When I fished it out of my pants pocket this morning, I didn't even recognize it at first."

She took a breath. "But then I read it. Coates wrote it all down. You got most of it right, especially you, Wade. Good thinking."

Wade looked pleased, although by now all he really wanted was to go watch the ball game.

"Anyway," Lizzie said, "they were con men, and Coates was the mark. He just realized it too late."

Silence fell around the table. Then: "I saw Sally today," Ellie offered brightly.

"How is she?" I sipped icy Chablis, enjoying the crystal glasses that Bella had set out for the occasion, although after all we'd been through, I thought, we should be gulping it from the bottle.

"Sally's distraught, exhausted, angry . . . yeah, it was a lot to find out. She's taking the kids to her mom's for a while."

My dad, who'd been listening with interest, spoke again. "Sounds like a plan. But what about the other man, the dog's—"

"Dead human?" Hudson finished for him, and my dad, who positively adores having his sentences completed by younger people who think they know what he's going to say, looked stern.

"Yes," he replied in his best *Watch it, whippersnapper* voice. "Although *late owner* was probably the phrase I'd have chosen had I been allowed to complete my thought."

Hudson blinked, and after his first moment of surprise you could practically see his heart melting.

"Sir, I apologize," he said contritely, but also tenderly; as I've said before, my father was a very old man with a face like a carved walnut; long, stringy, gray hair tied back in a leather thong; and a ruby stud glinting in his earlobe.

Also he was smart and had an edge like a bright Sheffield blade; it was that part, I thought, that I'd just watched Dylan Hudson falling in love with.

"As for Bailey Lyman," Lizzie took over for Hudson, "it was just like with Howie Fairbrother. He knew too much, and they weren't about to cut him in to keep him quiet. Simple as that."

I looked at her. "Did he say why they stuck the coin to the barge in the first place? Seems they went to a lot of trouble to do it, so . . ."

Lizzie gestured with the diary. "Coates says it was to keep any of them from being able to get at it easily, then grabbing it, ditching the other two, and taking off alone. He was not," she added, "happy about it."

"Boo-hoo," said Mika, echoing my feelings.

"Okay, one last thing," I said. "That drugged lemonade on Waldron's boat. Why in the world would he do that?"

Hudson looked rueful. "The boat's already been gone through pretty thoroughly. No substances but booze on it."

Meeting my gaze, he added, "Maybe what we thought was an attempted drugging might've been heat and dehydration, instead?"

Whereupon I considered, realized that I probably had been hot and water-depleted, just too wired-up to know it, and nodded briefly at Hudson. Then I changed the subject; so much for my thinking I'd been poisoned, and now I felt silly for making such a fuss about it.

"I think Bella has a raspberry pie in the fridge," I said, not only for the diversion and later when the pie had been eaten and exclaimed over, the coffee drunk, and the dishes all washed and put away, Ellie and I stood on the porch watching fireflies flashing in the dusk.

"I feel bad about thinking that Carl McFaul might've had something to do with all this," I said after a while.

I should have known from that pair of great boys he had raised that McFaul wasn't a killer or a thief, I realized now.

"All he wanted was not to be on the far side of that island so the Canadians wouldn't spot him," I added.

I'd gone down to the WaCo Diner very early that morning and asked him about it, and now that he knew he wouldn't come under suspicion for Howie Fairbrother's murder, he'd been cooperative.

"He reported Fairbrother's body to the Canadians," I said. "Once he had some time to think about it, he figured the truth might serve him best."

After all, that's what he taught his boys, wasn't it? And wonder of wonders, the Canadian cops had said yeah, they knew. It turned out that by chance a couple of Canadians with metal-detectors had been on the island before we were, that morning, and found Howie before we did.

Luckily, the Canadian Coast Guard just hadn't yet gotten the message about it when they came upon McFaul and the *Frinch*.

"And Sally's phone number?" Ellie asked. "How'd Bailey Lyman get that, do you think? She still insists that if it wasn't Paul, she doesn't know."

Pale flickers of lightning in the northern sky said a cool front was coming in, likely bringing rain.

"It was just like she thought, Paul did give it to him," I said. I'd asked Lizzie back in the kitchen if Coates had written about this and he had, and she'd told me what.

"It was how he persuaded Bailey to do the diving job on the barge. That and a promise of payment, of course," I said.

The others were inside: Sam and Mika in the kids' usual bedtime routine, Wade and Lizzie in the living room with the ball game on, and my dad and Hudson bent over a chess game while Bella took her shower.

My father would win the chess game, but Hudson didn't know that, yet. Around us, the breeze grew chilly and the moisture in the air condensed in the hairs on my forearms.

"It was Fred Monk whose body they brought in, that first day when Lizzie arrived," Ellie said.

"Huh. Sally was right again. Poor Fred, I guess he made good on his threat to jump, finally."

We stood there silently for a while. The fireflies were abundant this year, darting and twinkling. "Did the shark folks like the chocolate raspberry scones okay?" I asked at last.

We'd delivered them on time to the convention room at the port authority building; Ellie had stayed, in hopes of drumming up future business.

I'd left her schmoozing pleasantly with the convention attendees. A few of them had heard of Peter Waldron, but not in a good way, I'd gathered from their expressions.

"They did like the scones!" she said happily now, her face brightening. "They all raved about them, the chocolate-covered raspberries, especially. They want twice as many of them for the regional meeting next week."

"Wonderful," I said, groaning silently as Ellie looked out over the dark yard. A thin mist began falling through cool air fragrant with the smell of the lavender in Bella's herb garden.

"What's happened to Glenna, d'you suppose?" I asked. Out past the maples, the mist made glowing orbs of the streetlamps.

"Don't know." Above, a sliver of moon slid behind mounded thunderheads. Raindrops pattered tentatively. Then:

"Who, me?" The voice came from the driveway. Its owner stood outlined in the streetlamp's yellow glow.

"Hello, girls," Glenna LaFarge said. She looked wonderful, her hair bright-white and her billowy white shirt and trousers elegant. A pale-green gemstone twinkled in each earlobe, sandals were on her feet, and I'd have sworn that a moment earlier she hadn't been there at all.

"I'm fine," she said. "Don't you worry, an old witch like me can take care of herself."

"So why didn't you?" I demanded. "For Pete's sake, what's the use of having powers if they don't do you any—"

"That's the trouble with what people call *powers*," she cut in. "You don't have them. They have you."

Her gaze held me. "And they're not," she said, a warning in her voice, "a wish-granting machine. You pay for what you get."

She paused, possibly recalling what she'd gotten and paid. Then: "Perhaps this time I just couldn't afford the price."

She looked much older, suddenly, and a chill like an icy-cold droplet trickled through me; coming from someone else, her words might have been unconvincing. From her, they weren't.

Speaking of prices, though, "Glenna," I asked, "one other thing. Who paid for your satellite internet connection?"

Because Starlink worked well if you could afford it, but to foot the bill, she'd have had to do more than beachcombing.

Her laugh interrupted my thought. "Oh, my dear. You think I'm a poor old lady, don't you? Do you know how much people will pay for the right color beach glass? Or a real, intact clay pipe from the nineteenth century? One that some anonymous fisherman must've smoked two hundred years ago?"

I didn't know. "A lot?" I guessed, and she laughed again. "Yes. In some cases, an enormous amount. But you have to keep at it, make it happen. Like a lot of things, hmm?"

I turned to look up at the sharp, dark angles of the half-built house addition. My father had begun joking darkly that we should build it in Hillside Cemetery, since that's where he'd be anyway by the time it was finished.

He could haunt it more conveniently there, he said, and recalling this I decided suddenly to switch contractors, get new work crews, change suppliers—start over again, really. Maybe we could be done by Christmas.

"Well, I'll be seeing you," Glenna said from behind me. Her laugh, strangely musical, hung in the air. But when I turned back to her, she wasn't there.

She'd walked away without my even noticing, I thought, so I went after her, meaning to offer a cup of tea, or better yet, a drink of the brandy that my dad and Dylan Hudson were polishing off over their chess game.

But when I got out to the street and looked both ways, Key Street lay empty, its black pavement gleaming wetly and the maple trees overhead moving uneasily with the rising breeze.

"She sure went somewhere quick," Ellie observed when I got back to the house.

"Yes, she did," I said wonderingly, still gazing toward the empty street.

Then we went inside to hear about how my dad beat Dylan Hudson two games out of three, but a rematch was scheduled and Dylan meant to study up for it. Finally Sam and Mika went tiredly upstairs with the bathed and pajama-clad children, Ellie went home, and my dad and Bella went up to bed.

"Thanks," Lizzie said at the door; Dylan was pulling the car up to the front so she didn't have to walk far in the rain.

"It was a nice evening," she said wistfully, looking around at the back hallway: tiny shoes, a pair of swim fins, leashes and collars, my dad's walking stick, and the pieces of a shotgun that Wade meant to take to his workshop, all cluttered the space.

"Yeah." I nodded, suddenly comforted by the mess. "Yeah, I'm a lucky duck." Then:

"Listen. I'm glad you were here, okay? For all this . . ." I spread my hands. "You're going to make a great police chief for Eastport, and you're welcome at our house anytime."

With or without Hudson, I'd have added, but when I looked at her face I decided not to mention him. That part of her life, like her search for her lost niece, was an ongoing story; we'd get to it in time.

Or not. Her choice. "See you soon," she said, meeting my gaze as she stepped outside, then went on down the front walk to the waiting car. Its taillights blurred red in the rain as they drove off, and they were gone.

And of course she was right. I did see her soon; the next morning for coffee at the Moose, in fact, a routine we repeated the next day, and on many days after that.

Glenna LaFarge was another story, though. Since the night she appeared looking magical in my driveway, no one's seen the witch of Walk Island again, in Eastport or anywhere else.

Yet.

Chocolate Raspberry Scones

Ingredients

For 8 scones:
 2 cups flour
 6 tablespoons cold butter
 1 tablespoon baking powder
 $\frac{1}{2}$ teaspoon salt (omit if you're using salted butter)
 $1\frac{1}{2}$ cups half-and-half
 1 teaspoon vanilla
 1 cup raspberries
 $\frac{3}{4}$ cup chocolate chips

Instructions

You'll need a rolling pin, a pastry cutter, and a cookie sheet to make these scones. You can use fresh or frozen raspberries, and for the half-and-half you can use whole milk (or if you're feeling decadent, heavy cream).

Mix the dry ingredients together in a large bowl. Cut the cold butter into chunks and put them into the bowl with the dry ingredients. Use the pastry cutter to cut the butter into the dry ingredients. This will seem hopeless at first but carry on bravely, cutting the butter and floury mixture together over and over until the bits are about the size of small corn kernels.

Now add the raspberries and $\frac{1}{2}$ cup of the chocolate chips. Stir it all together, add the cream and vanilla, and stir again until the ingredients are combined. The mixture will be shaggy and floury. Now move the mixture from the bowl to a lightly floured surface and squoosh it together with both hands five or six times until it holds together well.

Form the dough into a ball, put it on the floured surface, and use the rolling pin to roll it out into an eight-inch circle. Cut the circle into eight pie-wedged shapes. Lift each wedge carefully (I use the butter knife for this) and transfer it to the baking sheet.

Bake at 400 degrees Fahrenheit for 13-15 minutes; transfer to a rack to cool. When the scones are mostly cool, melt the rest of the chocolate chips (in the microwave, or in a double boiler) and stripe the scone tops with the melted chocolate.